Praise for C

Matters of the Heart

Matters of the Heart is a lesbian medical romance where a doctor and patient find love together. I don't know how Catherine Maiorisi did it. I hated Darcy at the beginning and didn't think anything could redeem her—so much so that I considered putting this book down. I'm glad I didn't, however, because Darcy has one HECK of an arc, and is a totally different person at the end, through the love and patience of Andrea and some of their friends. I recommend *Matters of the Heart* to anyone who's looking for a solid, traditional romance.

- *The Lesbian Review*

I'm a sucker for a slow-burning romance, and this one nicely hit that spot. As is made clear in the introduction, it's Maiorisi's first attempt at a full-length romance—previously she has been known for murder mysteries. If she wants to continue in this genre, she's off to a great start.

- *Rainbow Book Reviews*

A Matter of Blood

This is an excellent mystery and whodunit with well-developed characters, an interesting backstory and great potential. The action is fast-paced but nicely interspersed with moments of stillness and humanity. Corelli's Italian-American family play a prominent role in creating a loving backdrop for a publically unloved figure. The mystery is multi-layered and, just like a good Agatha Christie, we really don't know who actually did it until every layer is exposed. But the whole murder mystery is superseded by the threat to Corelli and her family which only a moral dilemma can resolve.

Well written, enjoyable reading. I literally can't wait for the next one to see where Ms. Maiorisi takes us with both the crime-fighting team and the prospective romance.

- Lesbian Reading Room

This book was a long time in the pipeline for Catherine Maiorisi, and it shows. The pacing is perfect, and there has clearly been a lot of work done over a long period on making sure that everything is just right. As a result, this is a really easy read that will hold your interest until the final page. The characters are well fleshed out and relatable, with terrific chemistry between the leads and a great story line. There is nothing in this book that doesn't need to be there, and it was a pleasure to read from start to finish. My only gripe is that number 2 in the series is not out yet!

- The Lesbian Review

The Blood Runs Cold

While I did not read the first book in Catherine Maiorisi's Chiara Corelli series, this did not prevent me from thoroughly enjoying *The Blood Runs Cold*. Maiorisi populates her story with some much-needed diversity, but never strays into exhortative territory: these characters feel like individuals rather than stereotypes intended to fill a role (or purpose). The mystery is suitably complex, sure to keep readers guessing until late in the game.

- The Bolo Books Review

In most cases, I will say readers can start with the current book and not miss anything. With Chiara ostracized by other members of the department, readers should start with *A Matter of Blood* to get the full effect and the background of Chiara and PJ working together. Both books are fast-paced thrillers, where every minute could be their last, with no one to trust and nowhere to hide. The Senator, reporters, public opinion—it seems everyone is against the pair. Allies are few and far between. Chiara's a little crazy, but then who wouldn't be?

Love page-turner thrillers? Pick these books up—then try to keep up with Chiara. It'll be a breathtaking ride.

- Kings River Life Magazine

An excellent police procedural with twists, turns and surprises. Looking forward to other mysteries featuring Chiara Corelli.

- Map Your Mystery

TAKING A
CHANCE ON
Love

Other Bella Books by Catherine Maiorisi

Matters of the Heart
No One But You
Ready for Love

A Chiara Corelli Mystery Series
A Matter of Blood
The Blood Runs Cold

About the Author

Catherine Maiorisi lives in New York City with her wife Sherry. She is a full-time writer. And writing is what she most loves to do. But she also reads voraciously, loves to cook, especially Italian, and enjoys spending time with her wife and close friends.

The first full-length novel Catherine wrote was *A Matter of Blood*, the first book in her NYPD Detective Chiara Corelli Mystery series. It was a 2019 Lambda Literary Award Finalist. The second in the series, *The Blood Runs Cold*, is a 2020 Lambda Literary Award Finalist.

While writing that first mystery, Catherine wrote a short story to develop the backstory for Brett Cummings, Corelli's love interest. To her surprise, the story turned out to be a romance, a genre she had never read and hadn't considered writing. "The Fan Club" was published in the *Best Lesbian Romance of 2014* edited by Radclyffe.

Catherine has since published four romances: *Matters of the Heart*, *No One But You*, *Ready for Love*, and *Taking a Chance on Love*.

Catherine has also published mystery and romance short stories. Go to www.catherinemaiorisi.com for a complete list and while you're there sign up for her mailing list.

Catherine is an active member of The Golden Crown Literary Society, Sisters in Crime and Mystery Writers of America.

TAKING A
CHANCE ON
Love

CATHERINE MAIORISI

BELLA
BOOKS

2020

Bella Books, Inc.
P.O. Box 10543
Tallahassee, FL 32302

First Bella Books Edition 2020

Editor: Medora MacDougall
Cover Designer: Judith Fellows

ISBN: 978-1-64247-161-8

Acknowledgments

Taking a Chance on Love has been a tough one. Not because of the story or the writing but because of what was going on in my life while I was trying to write, then edit it. But, happily, that is in the past. The book is done and I'm proud of it.

Taking a Chance on Love started out as a few chapters leading into a, what happens after the happily ever after story, a theme to which I seem drawn. Comments on the manuscript indicated the book didn't work. After analyzing the manuscript, I realized I had two partial books—the beginnings of a romance and a partial something that could be called general fiction or women's fiction or family drama. The book you are holding in your hands is a romance. The second book is ready and will likely be published in 2021.

As always, first thanks to my wife Sherry for her support and encouragement and her patience with my obsessive need to be writing and reading. As my first reader, she gets to see the dreck and her gentle critique always helps me see the error of my ways.

Thank you, also, to editor extraordinaire Medora MacDougall, for bearing with me during this dragged-out editing process, for her willingness to push, for her patience waiting for me to get the point, and for her gentle but constant pressure to dig deeper, think harder, and write better.

No acknowledgment would be complete without a shout out to Jess and Linda and the other women of Bella Books for their support and encouragement. I appreciate all you do. Thanks.

And, finally, to my readers. Thank you, thank you, thank you for buying my books, for reading them, and for letting me know how you feel about them. I love every email, every comment on Facebook and Twitter, and every review. Keep them coming.

Dedication

To first responders who bravely run toward danger
every day to save strangers

CHAPTER ONE

Having completed the paperwork required at the end of her shift, Officer J. Quincy Adams stepped out into the muffled quiet of the snowy night. She tilted her face toward the gray sky, enjoying the crisp air and the feel of the icy snow on her face after the stifling heat of the station house.

The storm had surprised everyone, especially the forecasters who had predicted typical early October weather, mild during the day and cooler in the evening. But the pleasant fall morning had turned rainy, windy, and colder as the day went on, and an hour into Quincy's four to twelve a.m. shift a wet, heavy snow started falling so fast it almost seemed as if it was being shoveled from above. She hadn't dressed for snow, but it didn't matter much during the early part of her shift because other than stopping to pick up coffee and dinner, she hadn't left the patrol car. But as the temperature dropped and the snow piled up she'd been in and out of the car dealing with multiple fender benders, stuck cars, and frazzled drivers. By the end of her shift at midnight her uniform was damp and she was cold. Now she was looking forward to a hot shower, a glass of brandy, and snuggling under her afghan with a book.

Judging by the mound of snow topping her Subaru, about a foot and a half had fallen during her shift and the storm showed no sign of letting up. The lanes between the rows of cars in the lot had been plowed, but at least four inches had fallen since and the wind was whipping it into drifts. She hunched her shoulders, stuffed her hands in her pockets, and moved to the rear of her car. The trunk opened in response to the unlock button on the fob, but the weight of the snow kept it from rising more than a couple of inches. Using her arm, she brushed off the snow and pushed it higher. She happily pulled on the pair of gloves she hadn't remembered leaving in the trunk, then grabbed the shovel and the snow brush/ice scraper combination. An icy gust of wind blew snow in her face and on her unprotected neck. She shivered. Damn, she couldn't wait to get home and warm up.

Quincy cleared the windows and the roof, then shoveled enough snow from the front and sides of the car to ensure an easy exit from the parking space. Stamping her feet, she slid behind the wheel and turned the heater on high to warm up the car and herself. Since it was early October she hadn't gotten around to stowing a down jacket, a scarf, a hat, and snow boots in the trunk as she usually did in the winter. And given today's weather prediction she'd gone with silk thermals, her cotton uniform shirt, woolen uniform pants and jacket and her normal work shoes. She grimaced. *Note to self: keep a warm jacket, a woolen hat, a scarf, and boots in the car even in fall.* Now her feet were soaked and she was shivering.

A plow went by. She hoped they were keeping up with clearing the streets since she hadn't gotten around to putting her snow tires on yet. It would be slow going, but a lot easier if the plow had done its job. At least the Subaru had all-wheel drive.

It was twelve thirty on a Friday night but, thankfully, there weren't many cars on the road. As she drove slowly toward her apartment, the police scanner crackled, jerking her from thoughts of the shot of brandy and hot shower waiting for her at home. "Pileup at the Hudson Street exit of Route 80 West. All available cars needed immediately." The dispatcher repeated the message several times.

Quincy debated with herself. She was off duty, but she was less than ten minutes away from the accident, and a night like tonight always meant lots of emergencies requiring police assistance. She sighed. At Essex Street she turned left toward Hudson Street instead of right to go to her apartment. If they didn't need her at the scene, she'd go home.

Abandoned cars made it slow going on Hudson. At the scene, there was no place to park so she pulled over at the mouth of the exit lane. It was eerie. No lights. No police or fire emergency vehicles. Could she be the first responder on the scene? Through the blowing snow she caught glimpses of what looked like a jumble of vehicles, so she grabbed two emergency flares from the trunk, lit them and dropped them behind her car to ensure a driver blinded by the snow didn't attempt to turn into the lane.

If she grabbed the first aid kit in the back of the SUV, she might be able to help a few, but if she didn't light more flares to warn approaching traffic, additional people might die. Including her.

Wishing she was as compulsive about keeping the proper clothing in her car as she was about keeping a box of flares in case of an accident, Quincy pulled on her gloves, lifted out the box with the remaining flares, tossed the first aid kit in, and closed the trunk. Slipping, sliding, and flopping twice, she trudged along the exit lane toward the highway. She cursed. Now even the seat of her pants was soaked. She was not dressed for this weather. She'd leave as soon as reinforcements arrived.

Most of the cars she passed as she made her way toward the highway were jammed into each other, but they and their passengers didn't seem badly damaged. She let them know that help was on the way and told them to stay put.

Route 80, like most highways in this area wasn't elevated. Exit lanes were mostly level, but the slight incline on this one was making the going slow. Finally nearing the highway, she looked up. Was that the flicker of flames, or was the gusting wind playing tricks on her eyes? She sniffed. Smoke. Definitely flames.

Breathing hard and sweating from the exertion, she made it the last few yards. And gasped. She'd stepped into hell. Cars. Trucks. Twenty? Thirty? Hard to count. Stacked on each other across three lanes. The flickering flames, the snow blowing in her face, the smoke and the steam made it difficult to see more than a few feet ahead. Her eyes watered, her nostrils flared, and her throat burned from the acrid black smoke and the smell of gasoline.

The wind shifted and cars and trucks piled in random stacks facing all directions, some smoking, some in flames, came into focus. It was clear some vehicles had been hit multiple times at high speeds. Bodies were strewn over snow turned red by blood; some draped over shattered windshields, hanging half in and half out. Others still inside cars were suspended upside down or plastered against their seats by air bags.

Depending on the direction of the fierce winds, the scene alternated between an eerie world silenced by the heavily falling snow and the world of the accident—the hip-hop music blaring from a car whose driver was slumped over the windshield, the agonized screams of the injured, and the panicked pleas for help all around her.

Quincy swiveled her head toward the screams, not knowing where in the piles of metal they were coming from, not knowing who to help first. After a moment of panic, her training kicked in. She took a breath, performed a mental triage. First place the warning flares, then get people out of the burning vehicles before they exploded, and if help hadn't arrived by then, use the first aid kit to tend to the injured. She couldn't do anything about the spilled gas except hope that the snow would keep it from spreading and bursting into flames.

As quickly as she could, she trudged through the deep snow to the last cars, placed lit flares behind them and along the lane next to the accident to keep cars from adding to the pileup. Then she ran to the burning cars, dropped the box with the remaining flares and the first aid kid, and started pulling people out. The extractions from the first four cars in flames went smoothly. She was tall and she worked out, so she was able to carry or drag people far enough away from the fires to be safe, reassure those who were conscious that help was on the way, and leave them in the snow.

Sweating and breathing heavily she approached the last of the burning cars, a large SUV. A quick evaluation of the situation told her the driver, a woman, trapped behind the wheel wasn't getting out. The woman knew it too. Her eyes flicked to the rearview mirror and the flames licking at the back of her SUV, then bounced back to Quincy leaning in through the shattered window in her smashed-in door. She grabbed Quincy's arm and struggled to speak through her sobs. "Please get my children and my husband away from the car before it explodes."

Husband? Children? She'd noticed the empty passenger seat and when she'd glanced at the rear of the vehicle it appeared empty as well so she'd assumed the woman was alone. Was the woman hallucinating? Or had Quincy been misled by the tinted windows and the black smoke filling the car?

She tried the rear door on the driver side, but it had been crushed; she couldn't open it. She ran around to the passenger side of the vehicle and pulled that door open. In the smoke-filled interior she could make out two car seats with children and a man slumped behind the driver, presumably the husband. The smoke was getting thicker, more acrid by the second. She had to get them out of there immediately.

She quickly unhooked the outside car seat and placed it in the snow toward the front of the car. The child was breathing. Then she leaned in. She couldn't see where the rear-facing car seat was attached. She crawled in and felt around until she found the latch and was able to unhook it. She backed out, pulling the car seat with her. Outside in the fresh air she put her ear to the baby's mouth. It was breathing. She carried the car seat to the front of the car and returned for the man. She crawled across the bench seat and unhooked his seat belt. As she began to pull him out, coughing from the third row of seats got her attention.

She blinked and squinted into the thick smoke. Damn! She'd almost missed two children strapped into booster seats.

She did another quick triage. The children were in immediate danger from the deadly smoke. She left their father, took a minute to figure out how to move the second row seat to get access to the rear, and pulled the closest child out and laid him on the ground near the other two. She reached into the car again, eyes burning, throat raw, and freed the second, a girl. Out in the fresh air, the girl gasped and coughed. Quincy leaned her against her brother so she was semi-sitting to ensure she could breathe easily.

She stopped to take a breath, then stuck her head back in to be sure she'd gotten all the children. She crawled in again and glanced at the rearview mirror. The driver was watching, tears streaming down her face. Quincy thought the husband might be dead, but when she touched his carotid she felt a pulse. She gave the woman a thumbs-up, wrapped her arms around the man's shoulders, and pulled him across the seat, grunting when his foot caught on the seat belt. She crawled over him to free it.

It seemed to take hours, but finally she had him on the ground outside the car. She held her face to the snow, trying to clear the smoke from her eyes and nose and throat, then, one by one, she carried the children to the area where she'd moved the people from the other cars, far enough from the burning vehicles to be safe if they exploded. After she dragged the man to his children and checked the children, she ran back to the woman and gripped her hand. "They're all breathing." They both turned toward the whoosh as a nearby vehicle went up in flames but didn't explode.

"Thank you." The woman's eyes were wide with fear. "Make sure my husband gets this if he lives. Otherwise, give it to my parents for the children." Her shaking hands were filled with earrings, a necklace, a bracelet, and several rings, all diamonds it looked like, and a wallet. "And," a sob escaped, "tell them I love them."

Quincy hesitated, then removed her gloves and shoved the jewelry and the wallet into the pockets of her pants.

The woman touched her face. "Go or you'll—"

"I'm Quincy. What's your name?" Her gaze went to the flames shooting up the back of the car. Weakened by the terror in the woman's eyes but fueled by her own terror at the thought of leaving her to burn alive, she knew she had to try to save her.

"Er...Grace." The woman's teeth were chattering. "Run, Quincy, run."

"No, I...wait, maybe I can..." She smiled at the woman. "Don't go anywhere without me."

"You're crazy," the woman screamed. "Save yourself, Quincy."

Quincy dashed to the rear of the car and started frantically flinging snow on the fire with her hands, digging like a dog in the dirt in time to the rap music still blasting from one of the vehicles. She looked up and met Grace's panic-filled eyes in the rearview mirror. She nodded, then focused again on the snow. The intense heat of the flames was somewhat tempered by the snow blowing in her face, but the wind was also blowing the smoke in her eyes and the flames toward the gas tank. The smoke stung her eyes and tears blurred her vision. She stripped off her jacket so she could dig faster, then used her shirtsleeve to dry her eyes. She couldn't let Grace die. Despite her terror, her first thoughts were for the safety of her children and husband. Someone as brave as Grace deserved to live.

As soon as she'd cleared an area she moved to a fresh pile of snow. She lost track of time. Sweat stung her eyes. Her nose and throat were raw and burning. She was coughing and gasping for breath. Her nose was running. She couldn't feel her hands, but the sand was flying so she must be moving it. Saving Jen, throwing the sand on the flames was all she could think about. She heard her name from far away, but she couldn't stop; she had to save Jen. She swiped at the hand grasping her arm trying to pull her away. "Let me go. I have to save Jen."

"Quincy, Quincy." Louder. "Officer Quincy Adams, I order you to stop. Now."

She hesitated. Strong arms wrapped around her chest, pulled her to a standing position, then encircled her waist. Panting,

Quincy looked over her shoulder as Chief of Police Connie Trubeck dragged her away from the car.

She blinked, forced herself to focus. *Snow. Not sand. Not Afghanistan.* She started to shake. Her teeth were chattering. "G-G-Grace?" She tried to drag the chief toward the car, but she was depleted and the chief restrained her.

"The fire is out. The fire department is bringing the Jaws of Life up to extract her." Chief Trubeck spoke into her ear. "You saved this one, Quincy. Now let it go and breathe. Just breathe."

Quincy's eyes went to the rear of the car. No fire. She took a deep breath, then another. Her chest burned and she coughed. The chief held her. Suddenly, it was quiet. Someone had turned off the music.

Chief Trubeck tightened her hold on Quincy, trying to warm her. "I can't leave, but you're not exactly dressed for this weather. Let's get you checked out by the EMTs and unless they think you need to go to the hospital, I want you to go home, have a drink, and warm up."

Quincy glanced down, suddenly aware of the cold again. Her thermal underwear felt icy against her skin, and her pants and shirt were not only soaked but also streaked with blood and soot. Her gloves were stiff. Her hands and feet were frozen. Her eyes went back to Grace's car, now surrounded by emergency workers.

"They'll take care of her, Quince." Chief Trubeck took the jacket one of Quincy's fellow officers had retrieved from the snow. It was soaked, stiff. "You did an amazing job tonight, Quincy. You saved a lot of lives and what you did for that woman was beyond heroic." The chief waved an EMT over. "Get Quincy a blanket."

Quincy shivered. "Come with me." She led the chief to the area where she'd deposited the people she'd pulled from burning vehicles. "This is Grace's husband and four children. They need to stay together."

The chief was puzzled. "Who is Grace?"

Quincy accepted the blanket the EMT wrapped around her. "The woman in the car." She pointed to the car surrounded by emergency workers.

Chief Trubeck nodded. "I'll make sure they're taken care of and not separated, but you need to get checked." She looked around for help.

Quincy coughed and shivered again. "I'm just cold, Connie. The EMTs should focus on those who really need them."

"Then you need to go home. Come." The chief held her arm as they marched through the snow, stopped every few feet by police, fire, and EMS personnel as well as those accident victims who had stood back in fear while she fought desperately to save a woman in a vehicle they'd expected to explode momentarily. Quincy fell to her knees as they slogged through the knee-deep snow. "Sorry, Chief. I'm not sure I can make it. Maybe if I sit for a while."

"You're cold as it is." She looked around. "Hey, Jonas, get over here and give me a hand with Adams."

One on each side of her, they helped her stand, then, shouldering her weight, they moved slowly toward her car. Quincy was mortified, but there was no way she could hold herself erect, forget walking down the now-packed exit lane. At last they reached her car. Miraculously, it was only parked in by one ambulance. She'd left her door unlocked and her keys in the ignition, so the chief opened her door and helped her get in. Breathing as if she'd just run twenty miles, she closed her eyes and put her head back.

Chief Trubeck dismissed Jonas, hung Quincy's jacket over the passenger seat, then slid in. She turned the key and put the heater on high before helping Quincy remove her frozen gloves. She pulled some tissues out of the box on the backseat and dabbed at Quincy's face. "You'll need soap and water to get the soot and blood off your face, but at least it's dry." She dumped the damp tissues in the trash bag attached to the knob of the radio.

A police car pulled over and several officers started up the ramp. The chief leaned out. "Simpson." The officer turned. "Chief?"

The chief got out of the car. "I have to get back to direct the operation. Stay with Adams a few minutes until she warms up enough to drive home, then come up and help."

"Yes, ma'am." Tyra Simpson slid in beside Quincy. "Shit, Adams, are you all right?"

"Yeah, just…cold and exhausted. I was the first on the scene."

An EMT knocked on the passenger window. "She should probably use this for a few minutes. It will help her breathe. And here's another blanket. Use it to warm up her hands and feet."

Simpson helped Quincy tuck the blanket around her legs and feet, put the oxygen tank between them, and slipped the mask on her. "Give me your right hand and put your left in your armpit."

Quincy did as she was told. Simpson took Quincy's right hand between hers and held it under her jacket, then rubbed it. After a while Quincy flexed her fingers. "It's better. Work on the other hand a few minutes, then I want to go home."

Simpson did the same with Quincy's other hand. When she'd warmed both hands, Simpson pulled Quincy's jacket from behind her. "Jeez, this is too wet to put on. Keep the blanket around your shoulders, but get out of those wet pants as soon as you get home."

"Will do, 'Mom.'" Quincy removed the oxygen mask. She tossed the blanket that was around her legs into the backseat.

"Yeah, well, if you catch pneumonia, I'll have to do double shifts." Simpson took the mask and the tank and got out. "Take care." She shut the car door, waved, then handed the oxygen mask and tank to the EMT at the ambulance before going up to assist in the rescue operation.

Alone, Quincy observed, as if from a distance, the EMTs loading bleeding and broken bodies into an ambulance parked nearby. At one point the EMTs carried a stretcher with a woman close to her car and mimicked opening the window.

The woman's face had abrasions and was streaked with smoke and raw from the snow blasting around them. She removed the oxygen mask. Her voice was raspy. "Thank you, Officer Adams. I would sure as hell have died from the smoke in that car if you hadn't taken me out of it." She reached for Quincy, but grimaced.

The EMT put a gentle hand on the woman's chest. "Careful, hon, your shoulder might be broken."

The woman started to cry. "You saved me and my daughter and my granddaughter. I'll say a prayer for you every day."

Quincy swallowed the urge to join her sobs. "Thank you, Mrs...?"

"DiLeo. Maisie DiLeo." The woman fell back, obviously exhausted.

Quincy reached for the woman's good hand. "I hope you and your family members are not too badly injured." She nodded at the EMTs and watched them carry the stretcher to the ambulance blocking her car. A few minutes later lights flashing, siren blasting, the ambulance pulled away.

Her hands were still swollen and cold, but she thought she'd be okay driving. She shifted out of park and headed home. As she drove, images of a Humvee in flames seared her eyelids, the smell of burning flesh filled her nostrils, and familiar feelings of despair and hopelessness and loss filled her, making it difficult to breathe or drive or care about doing either.

She caught herself. No. She couldn't be alone tonight with the memories and the horrible pictures etched in her brain. She needed life and laughter. And she knew where to find it on a Friday night. She turned the car toward Maggie's Bar.

CHAPTER TWO

Though Lindy hadn't intended to go to the gathering of friends celebrating Babs' birthday, Babs was her best friend and she'd begged her to stop by at least for a little while. If they'd been at home, she probably would have chosen not to venture out in this surprise snowstorm. But she'd joined Babs and Dani for a celebratory birthday dinner beforehand, and the diner was just up the highway from Maggie's Bar. What the hell. She had her own car so she could leave whenever she felt like.

The snow had accumulated quickly while they were in the restaurant and though it was clear the plows had been through earlier, it didn't look like they'd hit this part of Route 4 in a while. Driving was tricky, but she drove slowly, patting herself on the back for purchasing the set of secondhand snow tires from Ed, a guy she and Babs worked with who was trading in his car for a newer, bigger model.

Once she parked in Maggie's lot, she spent a few minutes with her face to the sky, enjoying the feel of the snow. It had been eight years since she'd moved to New Jersey from Atlanta, and though she wasn't crazy about the cold winters, the sight of snow still thrilled her. She'd never told anyone, not even Babs, of her childish desire to roll in the snow, to build a snowman, and to have a snowball fight. She sighed. No fun doing those things alone. But she'd made her choice. She pushed the sadness away. She was there to celebrate Babs' birthday and standing in the parking lot feeling sorry for herself wasn't the way to do that. *Up and at 'em.* She walked into Maggie's.

While Babs was her only close friend, she knew all the women gathered to celebrate Babs' birthday. The ones who belonged to Babs' circle of close friends had become her friends, or what passed as friends for her, when she moved in with Babs. The others, who she considered acquaintances, were part of Babs' and Dani's extended circle. She'd been at Maggie's with all the women at one time or another so she received a warm welcome, especially from those whose partners didn't like to dance. Like the song said, she could dance all night. And she planned to. She danced with everyone who was willing, some two or three times. As these evenings go, she was having a great time.

Mainly she danced alone, though, with her eyes closed, just her and the music. As she swayed and twirled and swooped and dipped, her body became one with the music. She'd forgotten how much she enjoyed letting her body float free, how much she loved experiencing her sexuality on her terms, without anyone making demands. It was the only time she felt truly happy, truly joyful. She really should come to Maggie's more often.

Unfortunately, many women standing on the sidelines took her solo dancing as an invitation. They seemed to think she was dancing for them, to attract them. And that couldn't have been further from the truth. She really just wanted to exist in her own happy bubble. She tried to be gentle when she said no, but there were a few instances where the women got angry. Luckily, Maggie, the owner of the bar, wouldn't tolerate any roughness so the offenders were either ushered out or they apologized and left her alone.

She took a break to cool off and sat at the table sipping her seltzer. Someone said it was still snowing. That meant the roads would be worse than when she came and getting worse by the hour. It was almost one a.m. A few more dances and she would head home. Alone. Just the way she liked.

CHAPTER THREE

Exhausted and cold, Quincy rested her head on the steering wheel, questioning her decision to come to Maggie's. A sudden burst of laughter brought her head up. Four giggling women stood in the warm light streaming through the open door, singing along with the song that drifted after them. She watched them hug, break into couples, and tramp separately toward their cars. One couple stopped to kiss, then continued on laughing. Her need for that vitality, that energy had brought her here. And through the grayness of the wind-whipped snow, Maggie's beckoned.

She considered which would piss off Maggie more, her uniform jacket or a blanket draped over her shoulders. Since either would anger Maggie, she decided she would feel better in uniform. She got out of the car and struggled to get her arms into the soaking wet jacket, her teeth chattering in the bitter wind. Realizing she could freeze to death out here she gave up and draped the jacket over her shoulders before heading for the entrance. It looked a million miles away, but she pictured the warmth she'd seen when the women left and forced herself to move toward it.

Quincy luxuriated in the warmth of the lobby for a few moments, taking in the laughter and the music and soaking up the life force in the room bursting with happy lesbians. Just what she craved. Oblivious to the looks she received from the women she passed, she slid onto a stool at the far end of the bar.

Maggie glared at her. Wet and cold and dirty as she was and, she was sure, carrying the acrid smell of burning, she knew she must look like a street person who had somehow ended up sitting alone, hunched into herself, amid the exuberant Friday night crowd.

Quincy closed her eyes. Damn, she hoped Maggie wouldn't kick her out. Where else could she go to find what she needed tonight? She had friends. But what she needed was more than even her closest friend Amelia could give. She needed this, this vibrant, loving, very much alive, very much enjoying life, community of lesbians to remind her she too was alive. To remind her why she had to choose life over the alternative.

Maggie hurried down the bar, hissing as she approached. "You know I don't like you to come here in uniform." Quincy looked up. Maggie sucked in air. "You look like shit." Her fingers brushed Quincy's face, then pushed her dripping hair off her forehead. "And you stink. What the hell happened, Quince?" She didn't wait for an answer, just swiveled and poured a double of her top-shelf brandy. "Christ, Quince, your jacket is soaked. Drink this." Maggie put the glass in front of Quincy, then walked around the bar, removed the uniform jacket from her shoulders and draped it on the barstool to Quincy's left. She hugged her from behind. "Fuck. You're wet all the way through. Hang on, sweetie. The kitchen's closed, but I'm going to nuke some hot soup for you."

After putting the soup in the microwave, Maggie ran back with a coat and draped it over Quincy's shoulders. "It's my coat, small for you, but keep it over your shoulders until you warm up a little." She handed Quincy two bar towels, one damp, one dry. "Use these to clean your face." She rushed back to the kitchen, returning a moment later with a steaming bowl of French onion soup.

Quincy wrapped her hands around the warm bowl, brought it up to her face, enjoying the heat and the fragrance, then slowly ate the soup and sipped the brandy. Maggie checked on her whenever drink orders slowed. Not often. After about twenty minutes Quincy stopped shaking and her smoke-raw throat was less painful.

When Maggie appeared again, Quincy was able to offer an explanation. "There was a horrible accident and I stopped to help."

Maggie's eyes went to the TV playing silently near the bar. "That pileup?"

Quincy followed her gaze to the chaotic scene—EMTs tending to people on the ground, carrying people out on stretchers, police and firemen helping people out of cars, civilians huddled together crying. "Yeah." The breaking news banner flashed: At Least 21 Dead. She closed her eyes, wanting to block out the scene, not wanting to see the evidence of her failure. She should have done more. "Yeah."

Maggie patted her hand. "I have to get back to work. Do you need anything?"

"Thanks, Maggie, I'm good for now. Sorry—"

Maggie flushed. "I'm the one who's sorry, hon. I'm glad you came to me. Relax."

Quincy nodded. She watched Maggie move down the bar, chatting with customers, filling orders. Her instinct to come to Maggie, one of her oldest and most trusted lesbian friends, had been right. She sipped her drink and, for the first time since she'd arrived, lifted her eyes to the mirror behind the bar and focused on the reflection of lesbians laughing and talking and flirting on the dance floor and at the crowded tables.

Her eyes kept going back to one lively table of ten or twelve women, talking, laughing, and singing along with the DJ. They were beautiful, so full of life, so unaware of how quickly it could be taken. She couldn't stop watching them. Especially the willowy blonde prancing around the table, laughing, hugging, and joyfully pulling her friends up to dance. She was wearing close-fitting jeans and a shirt that showed some cleavage, nothing overly sexual, yet there was something about her, something magnetic. She moved gracefully, in sync with her partners, but when she chose to dance alone she seemed to float to some inner place and her body became an expression of the music. Quincy shifted her eyes from the blonde, taking in the women standing around the dance floor watching, and noted she wasn't the only one drawn to the sexy blonde with the blinding smile who glowed as if lit from within.

Maggie breezed by and topped off her brandy.

"Whoa, I have to drive home."

"Not tonight, sweetie. Relax. Lane would drive you, but you know she doesn't drive in snow. I'll find somebody or you can stay upstairs with me and Lane. But if you really want to go home, I'll drive you after closing. Think about it." She moved down the bar to take a drink order.

* * *

"What can I get you, Lindy?"

"Four beers, three gin and tonics, two merlots, a Coke, and two seltzers with lime."

As she filled the order, Maggie lifted her chin toward Quincy. "That's my friend Quincy. She had a shock tonight." She nodded toward the TV and the looping clips of the accident. "I've been feeding her brandy to warm her and now she's not fit to drive. If you're not the designated driver tonight, would you be willing to drive her home?" She rang up Lindy's tab.

Lindy gazed at the screen for a minute. "How awful. Was that her pulling someone from a burning car?"

"It's hard to see with the snow blowing and the smoke, but I'm pretty sure it was. That's her name on the breaking news banner."

Lindy's eyes went to the TV again. Maggie watched her read the captions scrolling by. "Officer Quincy Adams, the only responder on the scene for twenty minutes, is being hailed as a hero for pulling people from burning cars. She saved even more lives and avoided more injuries by setting flares on the highway that prevented additional cars and trucks from crashing into the pileup."

Lindy looked at Maggie. "Wow. Shouldn't she be doing a press conference or something?"

Maggie shrugged. "Does she look like she could do a press conference right now? She must have been desperate to show up here in uniform. She knows I don't like it because it intimidates some of my customers. She seems shattered, so I don't want her to drive home in this weather, especially after drinking. She doesn't live far. Essex Street in Hackensack. It's sort of on the way to Lodi isn't it?"

Lindy turned to the bedraggled figure at the end of the bar. "I noticed her because when I opened my eyes after dancing alone she was watching me in the mirror. Her intensity made me a little nervous." Quincy was staring into her drink now. "You know I'm not into picking up women. Would I be safe?"

"Quincy is a cop and a close friend of mine. I'll vouch for her." Maggie glanced down the bar. "Besides I doubt she could overpower a flea right now."

Lindy moved six drinks off the tray, placing them on the bar. "I'll be right back for these." She picked up the tray. "Do you think she'd let a stranger drive her?"

"Deliver your drinks and come back and talk to her. I think she needs some normal right now, and she seems focused on you and your friends."

After Lindy placed the drinks on the table, Babs grabbed her hand. "Have you noticed that cop at the bar staring at you?"

"It's okay. She's a friend of Maggie's." She tilted her head in the direction of the TV. "She saved a lot of people in that accident."

Babs nodded. "Just be careful, honey."

She chewed her lip. Maggie's request was way outside her comfort zone. So she was a hero. What did that have to do with her? The safe life she'd created for herself meant keeping to herself. She would tell Maggie she couldn't do it.

As she made her way back to the bar to pick up the rest of the drinks, her eyes met the cop's eyes in the mirror. The pain and the hopelessness and the loneliness she saw there were familiar. She'd been there. The cop had risked her life to save others. Why couldn't she be brave enough to take a few moments out of her own lonely life to comfort her?

Maybe she'd talk to the cop before deciding about driving her home.

* * *

Lindy leaned against the bar, next to her. "Hi. I'm Lindy. I noticed you staring at our table. Would you like to join us?"

Quincy hunched over her drink, elbows on the bar, hands gripping the glass. "Thanks, but I'm not feeling very sociable tonight. Maybe another time."

"So why are you staring?"

Quincy raised her eyes to the mirror and met the soft hazel eyes of the attractive blonde. "I just…I was enjoying watching you dance. You look so connected with the music, so alive, so happy."

"I love to dance. When I dance alone with my eyes closed, I feel…free to just be me."

"I'm sorry if I made you uncomfortable." Quincy gazed over Lindy's shoulder. "I was also staring because I like your group's energy. I could feel the joy from here."

Lindy grinned. "We're celebrating my best friend Babs' birthday. Babs is the chubby dark-haired woman dancing with the slender woman in dreads, her girlfriend Dani. Come celebrate with us. Really, we're very friendly."

Quincy shook her head. "I can't. I need…I need to feel the life, the energy, but I'm not fit for company. I don't have anything to give tonight. Besides I stink."

"Sorry. I didn't mean to pressure you. I was just being friendly." Not knowing what to do, Lindy looked down the bar. Maggie shook her head. No help there. "Maggie asked me to be your designated driver tonight." Lindy touched Quincy's leg.

"Shit, your pants are soaked. Do you want to go home so you can get into something warm?"

Quincy shook her head.

"Would you mind if I sit with you? We can talk or sit quietly if you want."

Quincy didn't respond so Lindy slid onto the stool next to her. She noticed the bar towels. "How about I use these towels to get the blood and soot off your face? You'll feel better."

Quincy looked at herself in the mirror. "I can—"

"No, let me." She picked up the damp towel.

Quincy closed her eyes and turned toward Lindy. Lindy gently wiped then patted her face dry. "That's a little better, but it needs soap and hot water."

"Thanks." Quincy blinked back tears. "You're very kind. Based on the number of women watching you dance, I'd say you're in great demand. Yet you're taking the time to talk to someone who looks and smells like she crawled out of a sewer. Why?" Her throat was still raw, and her voice was low and raspy. She wanted the woman to talk to her, didn't want her to go away, but she didn't want her pity. She lifted the bar towel. "I'm covered in blood and soot. For all you know I'm a serial killer."

Lindy clasped Quincy's arm. "I know Maggie is your friend. I know your name is Quincy. I see on the TV your last name is Adams and you're the police officer who pulled a bunch of women, men, and children out of burning cars."

Quincy lifted her eyes to the TV. "Typical hype. Making a big deal of nothing. Any officer would have done what I did. And it wasn't nearly enough. So many died."

The sadness and the desolation in Quincy's voice touched Lindy. She wanted to make this brave woman feel better. "Sitting here with you I can feel your pain. I would guess your thoughts are on those you couldn't save and you're feeling guilty and helpless and angry."

Quincy tensed. How could this stranger know—*oh, wait, she's talking about the accident tonight.*

Lindy rubbed Quincy's arm. "Don't punish yourself for what you couldn't do. Celebrate the lives you saved. Let yourself experience the joy of being alive as I'm sure the people you saved are doing tonight. Someone helped me once when I felt alone and lost. Call it payback. Let me help, sugah."

Lindy's husky voice was smooth as melted chocolate and its Southern lilt filled Quincy's head and, even in her numbed state, warmed her body. She relaxed.

Quincy raised her eyes to meet Lindy's again in the mirror. She saw admiration, not pity. "Do you believe in God, Lindy?" Her voice was an angry hiss, forcing Lindy to lean in again to hear it above the music and laughter and conversations.

Lindy brought her lips close to Quincy's ear to be heard. "Too many bad things are done in the name of God, sugah." She held Quincy's eyes in the mirror for a second, then tipped her head toward Quincy's ear again. "I don't believe in an all-powerful man sitting on a cloud in the sky or any religion or any church. But when I look at the beauty in nature or the goodness in people, people like you, or think about things like the perfect complication of the human body, I do believe there must be a higher power of some sort."

"How could any God let such awful things happen to people?"

"I know that's a rhetorical question Quincy, but pain and suffering seem to be part of the human condition. Who knows why? All we can do is lead the best life we can, being kind to others, doing what we can to make their lives better, loving, and enjoying the beauty of life. Holding on to the guilt and pain and the darkness deprives the world of the goodness you can do, of the love you can offer, of the joy you can bring to others. Letting go is hard, but it should be a no-brainer."

Quincy closed her eyes. What Lindy said could apply to… then…and to what happened tonight, but letting go was harder than it seemed. She took a deep breath, then put her hand over the hand Lindy had placed on her arm. "Thank you."

Lindy reddened. "I don't know where that came from, but you're welcome. We need people like you involved in life. If you want to talk, I'm ready to listen."

Quincy shivered.

"You really should go home and change. Come on, I'll drive you."

"What about your girlfriend?" Quincy tilted her head in the direction of the table with Lindy's friends.

"Don't worry. Some of those girls are my friends, but none of them is my girlfriend so you won't have to fight anybody for me." She smiled at Quincy in the mirror. "Shall we?"

Quincy stood and waved Maggie's coat to catch her eye. While Lindy was speaking to her friends, Maggie walked down the bar, took her coat from Quincy, and kissed Quincy's forehead. "You take care, sweetie."

As Lindy helped her into her jacket, Quincy turned to face the bar. She attributed the hostile looks on the faces of many of the women watching to her uniform. But when Lindy took her arm and started toward the door, she realized it was jealousy she was seeing, not trepidation.

A lot of broken hearts tonight. Even as wrecked as she was, Quincy knew they made a handsome couple.

CHAPTER FOUR

Battered by the glacial winds whipping snow at them, Quincy was shivering again by the time they reached the car. "G-g-good choice for tonight." She nodded approvingly at Lindy's Subaru. "I was afraid you'd have a compact."

Lindy had expected Quincy to insist on driving, but between the alcohol and the extreme stress, followed by the adrenaline drain, she appeared too wrung out to care. And her choice of car seemed to be a plus for Quincy. The Forester had a lot of miles on it when she bought it, but it was still going strong, so she had no complaints.

"Glad you approve, Officer Adams." Lindy opened the door for Quincy, then went around to the driver's side. She started the car and turned the heat on high. Seeing Quincy struggling with her seat belt, Lindy extended her hand. "Let me help, sugah."

Quincy tried again to lock the belt, sighed, and handed it over. She closed her eyes and put her head back, obviously exhausted and unable to stop the shivering. Lindy stretched over Quincy to pull the belt out. Her nostrils flared at the tang of sweat and smoke and gasoline and wet wool coming off Quincy. She clicked the belt into place, then reached into the backseat to retrieve the old blankets and towels she'd wrapped around a mirror she'd moved for a friend last week and tucked them around the shivering woman. It didn't seem to help.

Lindy got out of the car, brushed the snow from the windows and the roof and then got back in and turned on the wipers to clear the windshield. The car had warmed quickly and though the heat felt oppressive to Lindy and seemed to heighten the odors wafting from Quincy, Quincy hadn't stopped shaking so she left it on high. Maggie's plow guy had kept the lot pretty clear so she didn't have to dig the car out, but visibility was poor. She scanned the lot to find the exit onto Route 4.

"Where do you live, Quincy?"

Teeth chattering, Quincy stuttered out the answer. "Not too far. Essex Street, in Hackensack. Make a right out of the lot, take the right at the Bergen Town Center to Maywood Avenue."

Lindy drove out, taking shallow breaths, intent on getting her passenger home as soon as possible, for her sake and the sake of her olfactory glands.

The snow hadn't let up since Lindy's arrival at Maggie's and the roads were even more treacherous now. She hadn't learned to drive until she'd moved to northern Jersey where a car was a necessity, and she still wasn't comfortable driving in snow. Now, thankful for the all-wheel drive and her snow tires, she drove slowly with her full attention on the road. Except for directions, they were silent during the half hour it took to reach Essex Street. It was another couple of minutes before Quincy pointed to a series of low-rise buildings on the left.

"Turn in there. The sixth unit down is mine. It looks like they plowed recently so you can pull into the spot right in front."

Lindy turned into the road and swung into the spot Quincy indicated. She pulled the emergency brake up, then swiveled to face Quincy who appeared to be dozing. Lindy touched her knee and spoke softly to avoid startling her. "Hey there, you awake?"

Her eyes at half-mast, Quincy yawned and turned. "I think you should stay here tonight."

Lindy held Quincy's eyes. "Because of the roads or because you'd like my company?"

Quincy took a few seconds before answering. "The roads are treacherous and getting worse by the minute. It's dangerous driving by yourself." Quincy's smile was sad, but it was the first one Lindy had seen. "But the real reason is, I don't want to be alone." She tore her eyes from Lindy and stared straight ahead.

Lindy studied Quincy, noted her flush, her nervous picking at her wet pants, and the sound of her rapid breathing, and made a decision. She understood not wanting to be alone. She turned off the car. "Just so we're clear. I don't sleep with women I don't know. So sex is not included. And, uh, no personal questions allowed."

"Don't worry. Neither the mind nor the body could handle sex tonight. And I don't intend to interrogate you. What I want and need is what you've been giving me, human contact."

Lindy smiled. "So let's get you out of these stinky, wet clothes and into a hot shower."

Quincy's breathing slowed, her body relaxed, and she faced Lindy. "Thank you. I—"

"It's okay." Lindy put two fingers over Quincy's lips. "Come on, let's go." They exited the car and Lindy took Quincy's arm.

Quincy looked at her. "I'm not going to fall over."

Lindy grinned. "But I might, so hold on to me."

The recently shoveled path and the steps were a little slippery, but they clung to each other and didn't fall. When they reached her door, Quincy dug into her jacket pocket for her keys, but she couldn't grab them. "Damn, my fingers won't work."

"Let me do it, sugah." Lindy removed the keys and using the one Quincy indicated, unlocked the door. "I guess it's good I decided to stay or you might have frozen to death out here."

They entered a small foyer. Lindy removed her boots, then hung her jacket on the peg Quincy indicated. She tipped her head toward Quincy's jacket. "Should I?" Quincy nodded and stood with her arms out while Lindy unbuttoned and dragged the icy uniform jacket off her. "Where should I put this?"

"Just drop it on the floor in the corner. I'll deal with it tomorrow."

Lindy did as instructed. "What about your shoes?" Quincy looked down. "If you don't mind." Lindy untied Quincy's shoes and helped her remove them. "Should I take off your socks? They're soaked and your feet are blocks of ice."

"Thanks, I'll get them." Quincy led her into a living room and took a minute to orient her. "Kitchen, dining area to the right, my bedroom, a guest room and full bath down this hall. Make yourself comfortable."

"Did you check your hands for frostbite?"

"Yeah, at the scene." Quincy extended both hands. "Uh, I think they're okay. They're swollen and stiff, but they're itchy and tingly so feeling is coming back."

Lindy examined Quincy's hands. "They look fine. But your whole body is chilled. You should jump in the shower to warm up."

"Good idea." Quincy turned to leave.

Lindy put a hand out to stop her. "Should I make some tea or coffee?"

"Since it's two thirty in the morning, decaf coffee for me, if you don't mind. It's in the fridge. I'll only be a minute."

Lindy squeezed her arm. "We've already agreed I'm not going anywhere tonight. So don't rush. But be careful." She smiled. "I'm not sure whether it's true or not, but I read somewhere that after exposure to cold it's better to start with cool water and let your body adjust gradually before you make it hot."

As she was filling the pot with water for the Mr. Coffee, Quincy appeared in the doorway to the kitchen. She was red-faced. "Sorry. I, uh, I do need help with my buttons and my socks."

"Hmm, you want me to undress you? Is this some kind of seduction line?" Lindy looked serious.

"Remember these?" She held out her swollen fingers.

Lindy grinned. "Just playing, sugah." She pulled the kitchen chair away from the table. "Sit down and I'll take off your socks." With some effort she got the wet socks off. "Stand up." She unbuttoned Quincy's uniform shirt and eased it off, then unbuttoned her uniform pants.

Quincy backed away. "I can get the thermals and pants off myself, thanks." She dashed out of the room.

Lindy smiled. It was sweet that needing help embarrassed Quincy. She found the ground decaf coffee in the fridge. It looked dark and rich and smelled like it was mixed with hazelnut or chocolate. She counted out the right number of tablespoons, poured in the water, and turned the machine on. While Mr. Coffee did his job, she checked the cabinets for something sweet. Ooh, a box of Social Tea cookies. She'd never met anyone who shared her weakness for these cookies.

She wandered into the living room, looking for something alcoholic in case Quincy wanted to put it in her coffee. It was a comfortable room, decorated simply yet attractively in muted greens, tans, and browns with a large flat-screen TV, a music center setup for vinyl records and CDs, bookcases overflowing with books, a tan leather sofa that looked long enough for Quincy to stretch her nearly six feet on, and a matching easy chair. It felt homey and inviting. The nutty smell of the coffee drifted in, adding to the cozy feeling.

She peeked at the record on the turntable. *La Bohème.* Opera? Lindy thought people who liked opera were snooty, but Quincy didn't seem like that. She scanned the bookshelves. History, politics, psychology, and fiction, including a large collection of lesbian fiction in various genres. A reader. Like her.

She moved on to examining the framed pictures scattered on the bookshelves. A few of Quincy at different ages in the arms of or standing next to a tall woman with the same carriage and good looks. Her mother? It was possible, though Quincy's hair was almost black, her eyes a soulful deep brown, and her skin olive while the woman had dirty blond hair, blue eyes, and pale skin. One when she was probably six or seven standing between a shorter, more feminine version of her and a handsome young man. Her sister? A number featured Quincy with a petite, tan-skinned woman in various poses, starting as little girls, all the way up to present day. Their body language telegraphed that they were close friends. Others obviously taken when Quincy was in the service, some in fatigues in the desert, some in dress uniform looking proud. Most of the pictures in the desert included another soldier, a woman, almost as tall as Quincy with light brown hair and a sweet smile. From the looks on their faces and their body language, she surmised they were lovers. Was she still in Quincy's life? She moved on to a couple of Quincy in her police uniform. Shaking the hand of a woman officer, hugging the tall, now white-haired woman, and surrounded by a group of what Lindy assumed to be friends.

She went back into the kitchen and arranged the cups and cookies on a tray, then leaned against the counter and texted Babs. *Roads not good. Staying w/Officer Quincy Adams Essex St, Hack. All good. C U.*

It was hard not to contrast Quincy's friend- and family-filled life with hers a self-chosen loner with only Babs as a caring friend. Sometimes she fantasized about having a family—someone to love and children—but mostly she was okay with her life. She felt safe, and that was what she needed. It looked like Quincy had found love in the desert. Was she still involved with the pretty soldier? Or had it just been one of those situational relationships. Or—

Quincy emerged from the bedroom in sweats and thick warm socks, smelling a lot fresher. Her hair was damp, her face scrubbed clean, and she was holding her uniform trousers away from her body. "Would you mind emptying my pockets so I can pack up the pants and jacket to go the dry cleaners?"

"Sure." Lindy pulled a wallet from the back pocket and a couple of rings and what appeared to be diamond earrings and a bracelet out of the left pocket and placed them on the table. From the right pocket she pulled a necklace and placed it on the pile, then dug into both pockets again, pulling out a diamond pin and another wallet that she also added to the pile on the table. The jewelry looked expensive. And the wallets were suspicious.

She felt sick. Had Quincy stolen from the accident victims? She didn't know what to say. She handed the pants to Quincy.

"Thanks." Quincy grabbed a large plastic garbage bag, threw the trousers in, and carried it out to the foyer. When she returned, she gazed at Lindy. "What's wrong? You look funny."

Had she misjudged Quincy? Is it possible she stole from the people whose lives she'd saved? Or those she hadn't?

"Why do you have so much jewelry in your pockets? And two wallets?"

"A woman at the accident, Grace, thought she was going to die and asked me to give the jewelry and her wallet to her family. The smaller wallet is mine."

Lindy stared at Quincy. "Did she? Die?"

"No. She made it. But she was in pretty bad shape. They had to use the Jaws of Life to get her out of her car. And her husband was unconscious, so I figured I'd take it to her in the hospital."

"Glad to hear she made it." Relief flooded Lindy. "What do you want to do with it now?"

"Put it all in a large zip bag. Could you get one out of the top drawer to the right of the sink?"

Lindy carefully placed the jewelry and the wallet Quincy indicated in the bag, then handed it to Quincy.

"Thanks. In all the…frenzy at the accident I forgot she gave it to me or I'd have turned it in to the chief. I'll take it to the station tomorrow. That coffee smells wonderful. Is it ready?"

"Yes, ma'am. Let's sit in the living room."

Quincy placed the bag with Grace's jewelry on the desk in the corner of the living room, then sat on the sofa. Lindy followed with the tray and set it on the coffee table. She sat next to Quincy, and they each fixed a cup of coffee and took a cookie.

Lindy dunked her cookie. "Social Teas are my secret sweet indulgence. I've never met anyone who even knows what they are, forget having them in their kitchen cabinet."

Quincy laughed. "I confess. I'm addicted too."

"Your hands look like they need some attention." Lindy pointed with her chin as she spoke. "I have some lotion in my bag. It might soothe them. Would you like me to rub some on?"

Quincy examined her red, still-swollen hands. "If you think it would help."

She closed her eyes as Lindy gently rubbed the cream into her hand. "It's been a long time since I've felt so cared for, felt such a gentle touch not associated with sex."

"How long?"

Quincy took a minute to answer. "Five years next month to be exact." She opened her eyes. "I hear the South in your voice. Where are you from?"

"Remember, I said no personal questions." Lindy stopped massaging Quincy's hand. "What happened five years ago?"

Quincy pulled her hand away. "Sorry, I didn't mean to offend you."

Lindy could see she'd upset Quincy. The less Quincy or anyone knew about her, the better. She didn't mean to be secretive, but in the past information she'd shared had been used against her. She wouldn't let that happen again. Ever. But she'd never see Quincy again after tonight so she decided she would share a little. "I know. I'll answer just this one. I grew up in a very small town in Georgia about a hundred miles from Atlanta."

"How did you get from there to New Jersey?" Quincy gasped. "Ouch."

"Sorry, I forgot your hands are tender." Quincy was a cop. Lindy should have known she wouldn't be satisfied with the simple answer. She continued rubbing. She reminded herself that she'd trusted Quincy enough to come home with her and she wouldn't see her again so she'd trust her with a little more of her history. "When I was fourteen, I left home and took a bus to Atlanta."

"Alone? Atlanta must have been overwhelming."

Lindy ate another cookie before answering. "I was scared out of my mind, but staying at home was not an option." She smiled. "I was lucky. I met a woman in the bus station, and she helped me."

Quincy tensed. She looked alarmed. "Did she? Is that how you came out?"

Lindy was touched by Quincy's concern. And for some reason, she wanted to reassure her. "I know now that I got very lucky. I know now that if Sarah hadn't taken me under her wing I would have been in a drug-induced stupor, turning tricks for some pimp a couple of days after getting off the bus in Atlanta. But Sarah had me sit with her, showed me how to buy a ticket, and, having heard my story, took me in, gave me a place to stay and put me to work in her bookstore. She treats me the way I imagine a loving mother would treat a daughter."

"So how did you get to New Jersey from Atlanta?"

"No more questions." It came out harsher than she'd intended, but she'd revealed more than she meant to and it made her anxious.

Quincy looked uncomfortable. "Sorry. Occupational hazard. I don't mean to interrogate you. I'd like to know you better, but you're right. I'm not honoring your request."

Lindy reached for Quincy's other hand and massaged lotion into it. "How are your feet? Do they need lotion?"

Quincy looked embarrassed. "Probably, if you don't mind touching them."

Lindy laughed. "You just took a shower, so they shouldn't be too stinky. Right?"

Quincy blushed. "I hope so."

Lindy patted her lap and Quincy swiveled to put her feet there. She removed a sock and squeezed some cream onto Quincy's foot. She put the cap on the lotion and began to massage Quincy's foot.

Quincy sighed. "Keep that up and I'll be asleep in a minute."

"Don't worry, sugah. I won't let you sleep until I've gotten all *your* important information." Lindy tickled the bottom of Quincy's feet.

Quincy giggled and pulled her feet away. "That's not fair. Not sharing and tickling me."

"So what about you?"

"You won't share, but you want me to open up to you?"

"You owe me, sugah. Driving you home in a raging snowstorm, staying with you even though you're a stranger, *and* massaging your feet. I believe I deserve a full accounting of your history."

"A full accounting of my history?" Quincy pretended to think about it. "Well, I suppose I owe you something." She stared off into space for a moment. "I was raised by my grandmother."

"So the tall blonde with you in a lot of pictures is your grandmother?"

"Yes. There's one picture there with my mom and dad when I was six. My dad grew up Amish and was in California on his one-year Rumspringa—"

"Rums what?"

"That's a period of time Amish youth have to go out into the world before choosing whether to be baptized within the Amish church or to leave the community. My mom grew up in Hackensack and left home for college in California. They met and fell in love. He decided to leave the church and after one semester she dropped out of college to live on a commune with him and a bunch of other like-minded kids. When she got pregnant, they came home to Hackensack to stay with her mom while they waited for me to be born. Though they said my dad was a distant relative of John Quincy Adams and it made sense to them at the time, in reality, I believe they were stoned when they named me Johna Quincy Adams."

Lindy laughed. "Johna?"

"Hey, I did just say they were stoned. Even they call me Quincy. They were determined to see the world and intent on saving it, so when I was four months old they left me with my grandmother and took off for what was supposed to be a couple of months but turned into...forever. They visited from time to time while I was growing up, but they never stayed more than a week or two. My grandmother, Leigh Ann Summers, has always been Mama to me. She taught elementary school in Hackensack and later became the principal of the school." She sipped her tepid coffee.

Lindy looked toward the photographs.

"Mama loved kids and adored me. My grandfather died before I was born so it was just the two of us."

"Your mom and dad and grandmother all have light hair and skin. Did you get your dark coloring from your grandfather?"

"Yes. He was Italian. I don't know much more than that about him. Anyway, I had a great childhood here with Mama. But I guess I inherited some of my parents' desire to see the world because I joined the army after I graduated from high school. Needless to say, Mama was not amused. She'd expected me to go to college but, as always, she supported my decision. I was in the army for eight years, trained as an MP, and the only world I saw was the Middle East—one tour in Iraq, one in Afghanistan. After Iraq I joined the Hackensack police force and started Fairleigh Dickinson University nights and weekends to get a degree in political science. When my reserve unit got called up again, I did a tour in Afghanistan. After that, I left the army."

"Is your family still in Hackensack?"

"My mom and dad are still free spirits, still trying to change the world. They're in the Peace Corps now and last I heard they were headed to somewhere in South America. I get a letter or postcard from time to time."

She started coughing. Lindy got up and got her a glass of water. It took a few minutes for the coughing to pass. "Sorry. I inhaled a lot of smoke. My throat is raw." She took a breath, as deep as she could.

"After she retired Mama sold her house in Hackensack and moved to North Carolina with some friends. She spends a lot of time traveling and on cruises but visits me often." Quincy ran her fingers through her hair and smiled. "As I said, my dad grew up Amish in Missouri but chose to leave the community as a teenager. Members who leave are shunned and all ties are cut, so I've never met those grandparents or my two uncles and whatever family they have."

Lindy seemed lost in thought. "I have Sarah who I consider my adopted mom even though it's not anything legal, but I haven't seen or talked to my biological family since I was fourteen."

"I do have lots of chosen family still in Hackensack—my oldest friend Amelia, my friends Gina and Maggie and lots of other straight and gay friends. What about you? The group you were with tonight looked close."

"Those were mostly Babs' and Dani's friends. I consider some of them friends, but Babs is the only friend I consider chosen family." She threw the ball back to Quincy. "When did you come out? Does your grandmother know?"

Quincy thought a second. "Technically, I came out in high school, with my friend Gina. There was no spark but we were curious. Needless to say, the sex was a bust and we quickly decided to be friends without benefits. Gina, a sexy blonde, went on to seduce many of our classmates. I planned to enter the army and I didn't want to screw that up by getting labeled a lesbian, so I put sex on hold until after boot camp. My only real relationship was with Jen. The first time I brought her home, I came out to my grandmother. She didn't pretend to understand it, but she could see I was happy and that was enough for her. She took to Jen immediately. I...excuse me." Quincy left the room.

Quincy looked distraught when she left, but Lindy was a little unsettled herself. Her life was her choice, of course, but comparing it to Quincy's made her feel as if she was standing alone on an iceberg watching Quincy sail by in a cozy yacht surrounded by loving people.

She shook her head. This kind of thinking was nonproductive. She'd chosen and that was that. But what had upset Quincy? She didn't understand why she cared since, at best, they were casual acquaintances, but it was clear the subject was upsetting to Quincy and she wanted to know why. And, if she was honest with herself, she wanted to make Quincy feel better. So when Quincy came back a few minutes later, she asked a direct question. "Is Jen the woman in the pictures in the desert?" She pointed to the bookcase. "Are you still involved with her?"

Quincy considered for a moment, shook her head, then left the room again.

This time Lindy followed her and spoke to her back.

"Look who's being too inquisitive now. Sorry, Quincy, but I can see that you're really hurting. You can tell me to buzz off because I've pushed too much. Or you can cry on my shoulder. I'm not good at sharing, but I'm a very good listener. And remember, you'll never have to see me again. I'll be in the living room whenever you're ready."

She put both hands on Quincy's shoulders, squeezed, then returned to the sofa. Had she gone too far? She was pushing Quincy to open her heart and talk about her lover, or her ex, when she'd refused to share anything more than the basics about her own life. Was she merely curious or did she really think she could help?

Damn—she was channeling her therapist.

About ten minutes later, Quincy came into the living room, sat at the end of the sofa, and swung her feet into Lindy's lap again. She put her head back and closed her eyes as Lindy began to massage her foot.

"Jen and I met and fell in love in the reserves. We were both MPs and both had served in Iraq. We planned to be together forever. When our unit was called up, we went to Afghanistan together. We generally worked as escorts for VIPs, sometimes to one of our camps, sometimes to meet with one of the warlords. We didn't work together often, but one day the MP assigned with Jen to escort a VIP to meet with a warlord had an appendicitis attack and I filled in for him. We were coming back from that meeting when our convoy stopped. I got out to investigate, and Jen stayed with the VIP. It turned out to be a flat tire.

"I was walking back to our vehicle, stopping to let everyone know we'd be going again in about five minutes, when we were attacked. I was desperate to get back to Jen, but they were spraying us with bullets and I had to hunker down behind one of the trucks. Just as quickly as they'd appeared, they withdrew and suddenly it was silent except for the screams of the wounded. When I got back to our Humvee it was engulfed in flames with Jen and the VIP inside. Maybe if I'd stayed with her, I could have saved her."

"Or maybe you would have been killed too."

"I would have preferred that. At the time, at least." Quincy stared straight ahead, remembering. She covered her face, but Lindy could see the tears running between her fingers. She went into the bathroom and returned with a box of tissues. She sat next to her, put an arm over her shoulder, and pulled her close. At first Quincy resisted, then she gave in and turned so she was sobbing on Lindy's shoulder.

"I'm so sorry, Quincy. Sorry about Jen and sorry I made you relive that."

The sobbing stopped and Quincy pulled away. Lindy handed her a tissue but didn't speak.

"I thought I'd cried that out of my system." She looked sheepish.

"I'd be surprised if you ever got it out of your system, Quincy. It sounds like an unspeakable horror to feel so helpless, unable to protect your lover when you were right there." Lindy took Quincy's hand. "I imagine you're also feeling pretty vulnerable after what happened tonight."

Quincy dried her tears and blew her nose. "The scene at the accident was so horrible it brought back memories of Jen."

Lindy gazed at Quincy. "Is Jen the reason you were willing to die for a stranger tonight?"

"Maybe." Quincy shrugged. "When I looked into the eyes of Grace, the woman trapped in a burning car, I saw she knew I couldn't get her out, that she would burn to death or be blown up. I saw her fear. But her thoughts were for her children and her husband. She begged me to save them, then she tried to get me to run so I wouldn't be blown up with her. It was *her* courage, I think, that gave me the courage to try to save her, even knowing I might die with her if I failed."

Lindy retrieved the socks she'd taken off Quincy. "Well, the world is definitely a better place because of you, especially because you were successful and saved both your lives tonight. And I'll bet Grace would agree." Lindy rubbed Quincy's chilled feet, then batted Quincy's hands away as she slipped the socks on for her.

Sitting close on the sofa, they talked until the sky began to brighten. Exhausted emotionally and physically, Quincy finally dozed off.

Lindy's thoughts were firing a mile a minute. She couldn't wrap her mind around how you dealt with being so close but unable to save someone you loved, how you lived with the memories. She felt drawn to this brave and obviously distraught woman and hoped her presence was helping her cope. All her internal alarms were blasting, though, and no matter how attracted she felt, she needed to keep her distance. She'd learned—the hard way—not to ignore them.

Lindy's eyes were getting heavy when Quincy started thrashing and moaning and muttering, "No, no, let me go, I have to get her." Lindy called Quincy's name trying to wake her, but she was so deep in her dream she didn't respond. Quincy continued to relive the horror.

Lindy wrapped her arms tightly around the writhing woman and pulled her on top of her. Quincy's flailing arms came close to clobbering her, but the close contact seemed to do the trick and she soon settled back into sleep. Quincy's weight plus her light snores lulled Lindy into sleep shortly thereafter.

CHAPTER FIVE

Quincy's eyes popped open at the sound of the door chime. She blinked. Was she dreaming? Had she picked up this blond stranger who was holding her and staring into her eyes? Had they had sex on the sofa?

Then she remembered. The accident. Maggie's. Lindy. The dancing woman with the beautiful smile and the seductive hazel eyes who drove her home and stayed because she couldn't bear to be alone. She'd somehow pinned the woman down. How embarrassing.

"Good morning." Quincy shifted her gaze, then floundered, trying to get up without touching her. Finally she rolled off, managing to get to her knees on the floor next to the sofa. *What a klutz.* "Sorry. I hope I didn't hurt you." She got to her feet.

Lindy stretched. "You might have crunched a couple of bones, but let's see if I can stand." She extended her hand. The doorbell chimed again. Quincy took Lindy's hand and pulled her into a sitting position. Lindy stretched. Quincy did a couple of bends from the waist to stretch her achy body. The doorbell rang again. "Be right back."

Quincy was surprised to see Connie Trubeck on her porch, stamping her feet and blowing on her hands. She opened the door and let her into the entry hall.

"Geez, it's colder than a polar bear's tits this morning." She unzipped her coat. "Sorry if I woke you."

Quincy pushed her fingers through her hair and tugged her T-shirt down and her sweats up. "Is something wrong, Connie?"

The chief studied Quincy. "How are you feeling this morning? Any problems sleeping or eating? Any bad dreams or more flashbacks? I'm sorry I had to send you home alone, but you know I couldn't leave the scene."

"I'm okay." Her concerned gaze made Quincy uncomfortable. She'd seen it before in Afghanistan when as her commanding officer Connie was constantly evaluating her mental fitness.

Connie shook her head. "I've never seen anything like that accident. Twenty-six cars and three semis were involved. And who knows how many more would have piled on if you hadn't had a cool head and thought to set the flares. They're still going through the wreckage to confirm we have everyone, but thirty people besides the twelve you saved were injured and another twenty-seven died. What you did last night was brave and foolish, but I'm proud of you."

"Thanks."

"Have you eaten? I'd like to take you out for breakfast if you're up for it."

"Why don't you come in?"

The chief followed Quincy into the living room and stopped short seeing Lindy sitting on the sofa.

"Oh, sorry, I didn't realize—"

"It's okay, Connie. This is Lindy, um, a…friend, who stayed with me last night so I wouldn't have to be alone. Lindy, this is Chief of Police Connie Trubeck."

Lindy stood and shook the chief's hand. Chief Trubeck smiled. "Nice to meet you." The chief addressed Quincy. "Well, you seem okay and I see you're busy, so I'll get out of your hair in a minute. The other reason I stopped by was to tell you that the people you saved, especially Grace, are clamoring to see you. And making a lot of noise about a medal and a promotion for you. Would you be willing to go to the hospital sometime today?"

Clamoring? A medal? Quincy paled. She was still feeling vulnerable from having risked her life to save Grace, from the memories of Jen. All the attention, all the emotion would be overwhelming. "Um, maybe I could stop by some time next week when things quiet down?"

The chief put an arm over Quincy's shoulder. "I know you hate this kind of shit, but the department has been under fire and there's been talk about budget cuts, so I'd appreciate it if you would make the effort to visit and face the press."

"The press?" Quincy's stomach turned.

"You're a hero, Quince. Reporters are desperate to talk to you. I've already received a ton of official requests to interview you, but they've also been nosing around trying to find your home address so they can get a piece of you. In my opinion, it will be easier to hold a press conference and answer all the questions at once."

"I can't, Connie. I don't want to deal with the memories or the press right now." She felt Lindy's eyes on her. Some hero.

"I know this isn't your cup of tea even under the best of circumstances. And ordinarily, I wouldn't pressure you but the department really needs some positive public relations after Lewis's fuck-up of the domestic two weeks ago."

"Are you ordering me to do it?"

Connie frowned. "I would never do that to you, Quincy. I'm sorry. I got caught up in the needs of the department and forgot about your needs." She started buttoning her coat. "I feel like a shit but in my defense, I thought this would help me push through your promotion to detective."

"You think the press conference will protect me from the reporters?"

Connie shrugged. "I can't promise that, but maybe if they hear the story from you they'll leave you alone. In any case, I'll do whatever I can to protect you."

Connie was thinking about what was best for her and the department while she was only thinking about herself. What a jerk. Maybe she should—

"Would it help to have some support? Gina is away, but I'll bet Amelia would go with you." She shot a glance at Lindy. "Or maybe Lindy would go?"

Quincy took a deep breath. Having Lindy there would make it easier, but Lindy hadn't signed on for life. "Lindy and I need to talk, but even if she can't make it I'll do it. My car is still buried at Maggie's." She turned to Lindy. "I assume you'll drop me at the hospital?"

Lindy smiled. "No problem."

"In either case, we need to have breakfast and I need to shower and dress. And if Lindy decides to come with me, she'll need to go home to change clothes. How are the roads?"

"The main roads are clear, side streets not so much, but the heavy snow on trees that still have all their leaves caused lots of trees to fall and branches to break off, so some streets are blocked. Be careful driving. I'll look for you at the hospital sometime this afternoon. And, Quince, would you wear your uniform even though you're not actually on duty today?"

Damn, she didn't want to be the poster girl for the department, but then that was what this was all about, wasn't it? "Sure, Connie. Should I call you when I'm on the way?"

The chief grinned. "That would be great. I'll see you there." She turned toward the door.

"Wait a minute, Chief." Quincy retrieved the bag with Grace's jewelry. "When she thought she was going to die, Grace gave me all the jewelry she was wearing and her wallet to give to her husband, but as you know I wasn't thinking too clearly when you arrived and I forgot." She handed the bag to Connie.

"It's good you held on to it rather than sending it to the hospital with him. I'll see that they get it." She nodded at Lindy. "Nice to meet you."

They stood there in the silence after her departure. "Lindy, I appreciate what you did last night, but I can't ask—"

"Why not?" Lindy planted her hands on her hips. "If you want me to go with you, why can't you ask?"

Quincy pivoted to face her and looked down into hazel eyes sparking with challenge. "You're right. Would you accompany me to the hospital?"

Lindy's smile was brilliant. "I'd love to." She picked up Quincy's hands and examined them. "They look a little better, but maybe we can get a better cream for your hands and feet while we're there."

Quincy fingered the tie on her sweats. "I'm not sure how I came to be sleeping on top of you. I hope I didn't force...I mean I hope I didn't do anything you didn't want me...to."

"No worries, sugah, you were a perfect lady. You had a nightmare and I couldn't wake you, so I pulled you down on top of me hoping the contact would calm you. And it did."

"Sorry." She rocked on her heels. "Did I say anything?"

"Just a couple of phrases. 'Let me go, I need to save her,' that kind of thing. Were you dreaming about Grace?"

Quincy shook her head. "It was Jen. I began having nightmares after she died, always a version of what happened. But it's been a couple of years since I had one. I guess the accident triggered the memories and those triggered the dream." She ran her fingers through her hair. "We'd better get moving. Why don't I take you out for breakfast, then go home with you so you can change?"

"I can shower and change here." Lindy flushed. "I keep a suitcase with a couple of days' worth of clothes in my car." She avoided Quincy's gaze. "It's not what you think. I don't do casual sexual things. It's just that sometimes I need to get away, to be alone, and when I get the feeling, I just want to go."

"Hey, you don't owe me an explanation."

Lindy dug in her purse and pulled out her car keys. "I'm going to get my suitcase from the car. I'll be right back."

"You take the first shower. I'll make coffee."

When Lindy came into the kitchen after her shower, she was wearing fitted jeans and a pale green V-neck sweater that brought out the flecks of gold and green in her eyes. She'd applied a little eye makeup and lip gloss, Quincy saw, and her golden hair framed her face like a halo of light and flowed over her shoulders and down her back. Somehow she managed to look sexy and wholesome at the same time. She helped herself to coffee.

Quincy put her cup down and went into her bedroom to shower. After she dried off, she retrieved her underwear and socks from her dresser where everything was folded and grouped together by type. There was something about an organized closet and neat drawers that comforted her and made her feel in control. She stared into her closet. She had four everyday uniforms. One was at the dry cleaner, and two were hanging in the closet. On Monday she'd pick up the one at the dry cleaner and drop off the one from yesterday. She eyed the dress uniform hanging next to the others then decided her everyday uniform would do. She was able to pull on the uniform pants, a T-shirt instead of a bra, and her uniform shirt. Her shoes were still wet, so she slipped into her boots and found Lindy in the living room reading a lesbian romance.

"Would you help me finish dressing?"

"Sure. I wondered if you had another uniform." After buttoning Quincy's pants and shirt, fixing her tie, and tightening her belt, Lindy got on her knees and laced Quincy's boots. She stood. "Ready?"

At the door, Lindy buttoned Quincy's uniform jacket, then slipped into her own jacket and snow boots while Quincy put on her official dress winter coat. Lindy buttoned the coat and stepped back, eyeing Quincy. "Very spiffy, Officer Adams."

"Thank you, ma'am." Quincy handed Lindy the house keys, picked up her hat, and followed Lindy out. It had stopped snowing, but the snow on the ground swirled in the gusting wind, biting and lowering visibility even though the sun was shining brightly. They made a dash for the car. "Man, this weather is weird. We never have snow and this kind of cold so early in October. I'm really feeling it."

Lindy put on her sunglasses, started the car, and turned on the heat. "Climate change, I guess. And you were pretty exposed last night so maybe your body is still adjusting. Are you warm enough?"

"I'll be fine as soon as the car heats up. And breakfast will help."

Heads turned as they were seated at the diner. The waitress arrived with a pot of coffee and took their orders: a spinach, feta and tomato omelet with bacon and home fries for Quincy and the Quinoa Bowl breakfast salad with kale, red cabbage, mixed grains, a fried egg, avocado, and a spicy cashew dressing for Lindy.

Quincy's eyebrows rose. "You eat *salad* for breakfast?"

Lindy laughed. "Obviously. I'm a vegetarian tending toward vegan but not strict about the vegan part. Is that a problem for you?"

Quincy looked down. "Sorry. I didn't mean to be offensive. Do you mind that I ordered bacon?"

"Of course not." She gently kicked Quincy's leg. "I'm not the meat police."

The waitress delivered their meals and refilled their coffee cups. Quincy hesitated, then seeing Lindy's grin, attacked her omelet and bacon.

As they ate, people stopped at the table. Some commented on her bravery and thanked her for saving all those people. A few asked to take pictures with her. Others brought by a copy of the newspaper and asked her to autograph the picture of her on the front page. She didn't remember seeing a photographer at the scene, but in the photo she had a blanket over her shoulders, smoke streaks on her face, and her sweat- or maybe snow-soaked hair was plastered to her head. She looked exhausted. She would have preferred to not have her picture there at all, but at least it wasn't a glamour shot; it showed the reality of the accident.

Quincy was polite and thanked everyone, even though they were interrupting her breakfast.

In a quiet moment when Quincy had nearly finished eating, Lindy spoke. "How does it feel to be a hero?"

"Embarrassing. I'm no hero. Any officer would have done the same."

"Not true. Accept it. You are a hero. Clearly, the public thinks so. And we both know most officers would have run when Grace told them to, if not before."

Quincy looked up into Lindy's eyes. "Maybe."

Sipping her coffee and munching on her last piece of bacon, Quincy watched Lindy eat. She chewed slowly and seemed to savor each bite. Was that what they called mindful eating? They were so different. She ate quickly, a habit acquired as a soldier; being a cop on patrol had reinforced it.

The waitress cleared their dishes. "No rush, relax, and enjoy your coffee as long as you like and don't worry about the check. A customer paid it."

They sat next to each other to read the newspaper someone had left on their table. According to the story about the accident, twenty-nine cars and trucks had been involved and Quincy had been the first and only responder on the scene for almost twenty minutes.

Lindy gasped at the photos of the cars and semis stacked on each other. "How horrible. I never imagined it like that. How did anyone survive?" She stared at the photo of several burned-out vehicles.

Quincy pointed to a car with blackened sides that looked as if someone had used a can opener on it. "That's Grace's car."

Lindy had tears in her eyes when she looked up at Quincy. "You really are my superhero. Is it all right if I say I'm proud of you even though we've only known each other about twelve hours?" She kissed Quincy on the cheek.

CHAPTER SIX

They arrived at Hackensack University Hospital at one and, as the chief had arranged when Quincy called to say they were on the way, she met them at the Emergency Room entrance.

"Hackensack is a major trauma center for the region so the emergency room is always crowded," she explained as they moved into the building. "It was absolutely wild last night when we brought in those injured in the pileup, but luckily they had extra staff on. All the pileup victims have been released, moved up to rooms, or sent to the morgue. The people you see here now are everyday trauma victims brought in for treatment from the surrounding area. I'm sure the storm added to the load with accidents and heart attacks from shoveling."

The chief escorted them through the crowded ER waiting room and into the crowded ER-patient treatment area. Patients on gurneys lined the hallways, some being attended by a nurse or an aide or a doctor, but others appeared to be waiting for treatment or test results. They dodged carts and wheelchairs and moving beds headed for X-rays or other tests and doctors and nurses dashing from patient to patient. Finally they exited out to the elevators that would take them up to the patient rooms.

The chief had a list of names and rooms. When they arrived at the first room, a woman wearing a business suit was waiting in the hall. The chief greeted her. "Ms. Cheryl Wallace, Vice President of Public Relations for the hospital, let me introduce Officer Adams and her friend Lindy."

Wallace took Quincy's hand. "I'm pleased to meet you, Officer Adams. And you too, Lindy. Welcome to Hackensack University Hospital. I'll be accompanying you today as a representative of the hospital. And if you don't mind, our hospital photographer will join us. I've already met with the people you'll be seeing, and they've all signed waivers allowing us to photograph them. I hope you will as well." She held out a clipboard and pen.

Quincy took the clipboard. "How will you use the pictures, Ms. Wallace?" She knew her irritation came through loud and clear, but she really didn't care.

Wallace's smile didn't reach her eyes. "I'm not sure yet but probably in publicity releases and perhaps brochures, maybe posters in the lobby, things like that. Is there a problem?"

Quincy addressed the chief. "Can we talk privately?" She walked down the hall. The chief followed. "Taking pictures with injured people to benefit the hospital is a lot different than just meeting them. I didn't sign up to be used by the hospital and I don't think it's fair to use people who are probably emotionally and physically vulnerable to make the hospital look good." She crossed her arms. "I won't sign."

Connie hesitated, then shook her head. "I apologize Quince. I should be protecting you and the people you rescued instead of getting caught up in department PR." She strode over to Wallace. "You can accompany us, but we won't need the photographer."

Quincy handed the clipboard back to Wallace.

Surprise and annoyance flashed on Wallace's face, but she didn't comment. She slipped the clipboard in the humongous bag hanging on her shoulder and waved over a young man who had been leaning on the nearby nurses' station. "We won't need you after all, Elroy." She turned to the chief. "Anything else or can we proceed?"

"We're ready." She looked at her list. "Yvonne and Syd Bloom. She's sixty-three, he's seventy. They both have airbag trauma and smoke inhalation. He has bruised ribs and a broken leg, and she has whiplash and a concussion." The chief lifted her hand to knock. "Shall we?"

The older couple. Quincy remembered her shock seeing the woman's short white hair and thinking, for a second, that she was Mama. At first she didn't see any movement of their chests and she'd thought they were dead, but when she touched their carotids, they both had pulses and were breathing shallowly. She huffed a breath. "Let's do it."

The chief knocked, then opened the door. The visitors surrounding the two beds turned to them.

The chief placed a hand on Quincy's shoulder. "Mr. and Mrs. Bloom, I promised to bring you the officer who pulled you from your burning car and here is Officer Quincy Adams. And this is her friend Lindy. I believe you've already met Ms. Wallace."

There was a bit of commotion as everyone spoke at once, but then Mr. Bloom put his hand up. "Quiet, please." He reached for Quincy's hand. "We were told that if you hadn't come along, the smoke would have killed us. What can we say except thank you? Thank you for being there. Thank you for being brave and saving us." He burst into tears. One of the visitors put her arm around him. "It's okay, Dad." She bit her lip. "He's right. We can never repay you."

Quincy took his hand. She looked at Mr. Bloom and then at his wife and saw their happiness. She choked up, feeling a warm connection she hadn't expected to feel toward total strangers. She cleared her throat. "I'm glad you both are all right. Just be happy in your lives, that's all the repayment I need." Intent on communicating with the Blooms she was only vaguely aware of the chief and Wallace but totally aware of Lindy standing nearby but out of the way. Before they could leave, everyone in the room hugged and thanked Quincy. She was passed from person to person and, though she was embarrassed, her focus was on Lindy who was observing everything with a big smile on her face.

Out in the hall, Lindy squeezed Quincy's hand while the chief checked her list. "Next up is Carl Lewis, forty years old. Broken leg, broken arm, two broken ribs, and smoke inhalation."

She tried to picture Lewis but she couldn't.

The people in Lewis' room were laughing and talking, but everyone quieted and moved away from the bed when they entered. They stared at each other. Now she remembered him. Getting him out of the car had been rough and once he was on the ground she'd realized she couldn't carry him. She'd pulled the rubber mat from the back of his SUV, rolled his rear on to it, grabbed him under the arms, and dragged him to the safe place. The mat helped some, but it was slow going in the deep snow.

"Hi, I'm Chief Trubeck. As I promised, I brought Officer Adams. That's her friend Lindy behind her. I believe you know Ms. Wallace."

Tears filled the eyes of the big man in the bed. "I'm not so good with words or feelings so I guess thank you will have to do."

All eyes turned to Quincy. "You're welcome. I'm glad I was there."

"I bet I'm more glad." Carl swiped at his eyes. "I don't remember the crash, but I remember waking up in pain and being unable to move. The car was filling with smoke and I thought I was going to die. Then next thing I knew I was in the ambulance. They said a cop had rescued me, but they didn't say a lady cop. How the hell did you move me? I'm six-four and weigh two hundred eighty pounds. I must have been dead weight." He put his good hand out.

Quincy stepped closer and clasped his hand. "Adrenaline, I guess. I knew if I didn't get you out you would die from the smoke or the fire so I didn't think about it." She smiled. "You're probably the reason for the pain in my back."

Quincy's joke broke the tension.

"Hey, go to a chiropractor on me. As many sessions as you need." Carl squeezed her hand. "This is my wife Katie." He tilted his head toward the woman standing next to him. "And those two twerps over there with my mom and dad are eleven-year-old Carly and nine-year-old Daria. See, kids, I told you girls can do and be anything they want."

Katie hugged Quincy. "I don't know how you did it. God must have helped with the lifting." A sob escaped. "Thank you."

"You're welcome." She hadn't expected to feel this emotional, but the pressure of his hand in hers, the hug, the tears, Carl using her to as a role model for his daughters, the appreciation of his friends and family all brought home to her the magnitude of what she'd done for this family. She sniffed and used her sleeve to dry her eyes. She smiled at the wide-eyed girls who would continue to have their dad in their lives because of her.

Chief Trubeck cleared her throat. "Sorry to interrupt, but we need to move on if were going to have time to see everyone."

"Wait." Carl put his hand up. "Officer Adams, would you take a picture with me and my family?"

Quincy nodded. This was personal for Carl and his family. She wouldn't deny them a picture, but she could try to control what happened to it. "Just one camera. And can I ask that you keep this private and not make it available to the press or any outside agency?"

"Don't worry. It's just for us. I, we, want to remember you and what you did for us." Carl grinned. "You're safe with us."

She moved to the bed and took his hand.

Katie handed her phone to one of the women, then moved next to Quincy and motioned for their daughters to stand in front of Quincy.

After the woman snapped two pictures, everyone in the room hugged Quincy or shook her hand. By the time they were in the hall tears filled her eyes. "I don't know if I can do any more of this without breaking down. I'm overwhelmed by the love and appreciation of everyone and the thought that they might have died if I'd decided to go home instead of heading to the accident."

The chief put a hand on Quincy's shoulder, then walked away, giving her some space. Wallace followed.

Lindy put a hand on Quincy's cheek, frowned, and then yelled over her shoulder. "Hey, this is private. We said no pictures. If you took a picture, we'll sue you and the hospital."

Quincy turned as the hospital photographer slinked away.

Lindy glared until he was far enough away so he couldn't hear their conversation.

"I can see how hard this is for you." Lindy dried Quincy's tears with a tissue. "But they need to say thank you. You've already done so much, they don't expect anything else from you. So just say 'you're welcome.'"

"Sorry to be such a baby, but the feelings are so intense, it's hard."

Lindy patted her check. "You're not being a baby. Superheroes always feel things intensely. Besides, this is emotional for everybody. I'm not even involved, and I was all teary in there. And wondering how *did* you get that huge guy out of the car and far enough away to be safe."

"Hell, I was wondering about that myself." Quincy laughed. "Thanks, Lindy." She looked around. "Where did the chief go?"

Lindy leaned and whispered. "I think she might have needed a minute to get her emotions under control. All you warrior types have trouble showing your feelings."

The chief rounded the corner with her list in hand. She studied Quincy. "I've made it clear to Ms. Wallace that Mr. Finn is not to take any photos of you, with or without patients. If you're ready, next room is just down that hall."

Quincy and Lindy followed the chief. Wallace trailed behind.

"So we have the DiLeos, Maisie, forty-three years old, Bonnie, twenty-four, and Bella, one year. All suffering from smoke inhalation. According to them, Maisie was driving and Bonnie was in the backseat on the side that was hit. The baby was properly buckled into her car seat in the front and is mostly okay except for the smoke. Maisie has abrasions on her face, a broken shoulder, and bruised ribs. Bonnie has three broken ribs, a broken hand and arm, and a broken femur."

This room, too, was crowded with family. The injured women were in bed, the baby was in the arms of a woman seated near the mom, and several men and women were standing chatting.

The chief again introduced herself, Quincy, Lindy, and Wallace.

Quincy moved between the beds. "Hi, Mrs. DiLeo. I don't know if you remember meeting me at the scene of the accident. How are you feeling?"

"No, I don't remember you. Are you the one who—" She burst into tears. "I was sure we were going to die. I couldn't wake Bonnie, Bella was crying. I must have passed out. And when I opened my eyes, I was sure you were an angel gently carrying me to safety through the smoke and flames and falling snow to heaven. The next time I woke Bonnie and Bella were next to me in the snow."

The chief stepped closer. "Yes. Officer Adams is the one who pulled you all out of the burning car."

"I didn't know your shoulder was broken," Quincy said. "I'm sorry if I hurt you when I got you out."

Quincy saw Bonnie DiLeo's gaze jump from her to Lindy and back to her as if assessing who Lindy really was. The young woman smiled. "I'm sure sorry I was unconscious when you were holding me in your arms, Officer Adams. If I had known my rescuer was so good looking maybe I'd have tried harder to stay awake." She licked her lips. "Come closer, sweetheart. I'm in no shape to jump your bones right now, but I'd love to give you a kiss to thank you properly." She coughed and, unable to stop, reached for the oxygen.

The others in the room laughed uneasily at her flirtatious words and the tone of her voice.

Quincy made eye contact with Lindy and was pleased to see annoyance on her face. She felt relieved when Lindy moved behind her and put an arm around her waist. Feeling protected,

Quincy took Bonnie's good hand. "I hope you're doing okay, Ms. DiLeo."

Maisie's voice was barely a whisper. "Ignore my daughter, officer. I think she's had too many painkillers. We're doing a whole lot better than we would have if you hadn't rescued us."

The oxygen mask was in place and Bonnie's eyes were closed. Quincy hoped she was sleeping.

Bella made a happy sound, wriggled, and extended her arms toward Quincy.

"I think she likes you." The woman holding Bella stood and handed her to Quincy.

"Hi there. Do you remember me?" Quincy jiggled the girl, who settled into her arms as if she belonged there. She kissed Bella's head, taking in her sweet baby fragrance. Her weight was comforting. Her heart opened when Bella snuggled, wrapping her arms around Quincy's neck and laying her head on her shoulder, as if they belonged together. Quincy filled with an emotion she'd never felt before. It must be what maternal love felt like. She'd saved this baby's life, had given her the chance to grow up, a future that she wouldn't have had. It was as if she'd given birth to her. "How is she doing?"

"She's uncomfortable still from the smoke, but she's a whole lot better than the two of us." Maisie's laugh degenerated into coughing. "She has a few bruises from being bounced around, but she was facing the seat and not the dashboard so the car seat protected her from the air bag. And you moved her out in time. Thank God." She started crying again.

"Sorry, but we have to get moving," the chief said. "We have other people to see."

"Don't go. I want…I'm so tired…" Bonnie roused briefly and then drifted off again.

Happy to avoid the blatant flirting, Quincy handed the baby back. "Take care and get well." She managed to get away without hugging anyone this time but felt the loss of the small body.

In the hall, Lindy punched Quincy's arm. "I think Bonnie fell for you on sight."

"Nah, her mom was right about the drugs. In any case, she's not my type." Quincy stared into Lindy's eyes.

Lindy flushed. She patted Quincy's cheek. "Seems like there was family chemistry there. Bella seemed taken with you too. Do you like kids? You seemed comfortable holding her."

"I don't know about family chemistry, but Bella and I seemed to click. I do like kids. And I liked holding Bella. A lot."

Connie cleared her throat. "Shall we move on, ladies? This is the last room." She read from her notes. "The Walcotts. Grace, thirty-six, Mike, thirty-nine, ten-year-old Katie, eight-year-old Toni, six-year-old Felix, and eighteen-month-old Annie. Katie has a broken wrist and bruises, but the other kids are just bruised. The whole family has smoke inhalation issues."

Lindy clasped Quincy's shoulder. "I didn't realize you saved so many children."

Quincy flushed. "Yeah, well, whoever was in the cars. I mean, I didn't pick or choose or anything." She brushed some non-existent dust from her uniform and avoided Lindy's gaze.

"Mike has facial bruises, a concussion, two broken ribs, and a broken arm. Grace has a black eye, facial abrasions, four broken ribs, a broken wrist, and a broken pelvis. Her right leg has a clean break, but her left leg was crushed. The doctors set the bones that could be set last night so she has a wrist cast and a leg cast, her ribs are taped, but nothing could be done for her pelvis. It has to heal by itself. The first of several operations to repair her crushed leg is scheduled for tomorrow. Grace is in a great deal of pain from the ribs, pelvis, and crushed leg so she's on a self-administered morphine pump and may not be coherent. Ready?"

Connie pulled the door open. All eyes turned toward them as they entered.

"Good afternoon. I've brought Officer Adams as you requested. And her friend Lindy. You know Ms. Wallace."

Quincy recognized Grace and her husband Mike lying side by side in the two hospital beds that had been pushed together. The two older children sat on the ends of their parents' beds, one with a cast on her wrist, and the two younger children were in the laps of the two women sitting on the side of the room, probably their grandmothers. Two older men stood nearby. Quincy choked up again. But this time pride was mixed in with the heavy emotion she'd been feeling today. How lucky for her that she had been able to rescue this entire beautiful family, and the others they'd just visited, from a fiery death. If she achieved nothing else in her life, she'd given twelve men, woman and children a chance to live and contribute to the world.

Though she seemed groggy, Grace extended her arms to Quincy, and, responding to a gentle push from Lindy, Quincy hugged her gingerly.

"Officer Adams, how can I ever repay you?" Her words were slurred. Quincy assumed she'd given herself a shot of morphine before they arrived. Tears streamed down Grace's face.

Quincy tried but was unable to stop her own tears. "Please call me Quincy. And knowing that you're alive and enjoying your family is repayment enough."

Mike touched Grace's chest to calm her. "It might be enough for you, Quincy, but you're looking at six lives that would have gone up in flames if it weren't for you. Our bones and bruises will heal with time, but without you there would be no time."

Grace took a tissue from the box on the bed near her hand. She dried her tears and blew her nose. "Accept the fact that I will," she started to drift, "spend the rest of my life trying to thank you for the gifts you've given me."

Mike placed his hand over Grace's. "She's right, Quincy. And this woman has a mind like a steel trap. Believe me: she means what she says. But she's not the only one who's grateful. Words aren't adequate, but I too thank you for your bravery. The kids are too young to really appreciate what you've done for us, but as they get older they too will thank you." He brushed his eyes. "Let me introduce Grace's mom Irene and her dad Nelson and my parents, Karen and Paul Walcott."

Grace's mother struggled for control. "Nelson and I thank you for…" She started crying. Her husband patted her shoulder and nodded rather than attempting to speak. Mike's mom buried her face in her grandson's neck, but the shaking of her shoulders and her gulps for breath conveyed her feelings.

Quincy flushed and rocked on the balls of her feet. Lindy touched her arm and whispered a reminder in her ear. "'You're welcome' is all you have to say, Quincy."

Lindy was right. Words were inadequate for Grace and her family to express what being alive meant to them. And words couldn't express what saving them meant to her. Her heart sang with joy at having given them their lives to live.

"You're welcome." Quincy grinned. "Don't you love happy endings?"

The laughter broke the tension and cooled the emotion in the room, and everyone, including her, relaxed. "So where do you live?"

Grace had dozed off, but Mike and the parents chatted with Quincy for a while, exchanging mundane information. As they started to leave, Quincy remembered Grace's jewelry. "What should we do with Grace's jewelry and her wallet?"

Mike frowned. "What?"

"When she thought the car was going to explode, Grace gave me all her jewelry so the girls would have it."

The chief stepped forward. "I have it locked up at the station."

Mike laughed. "Leave it to Grace to be organized even when she's looking death in the eye." He thought for a few seconds. "It's probably best not to have the jewelry with us in the hospital. Quincy, why don't you bring everything to us when we go home? That will guarantee you'll come and see us."

"Don't worry. I feel like I have a stake in seeing you and Grace recover. If it's okay, I'd like to visit again before you go home." After they left the room Quincy took Lindy's hand. "It really is overwhelming." She dabbed at her tears with the tissue Lindy supplied. "Thanks for being here."

"You're welcome. But I should be thanking you for sharing this with me."

They were side-by-side leaning against the wall when the chief walked away from Ms. Wallace and joined them in the hall. She followed their lead and leaned back on the wall next to Quincy, then pulled her into a one-armed hug. "You okay? Ready to face the press?"

"I've never done a press conference before. I'm nervous."

"I'll do my best to control the situation. All you have to do is describe what happened, why you were there, how you decided who to save, things like that. All the cameras can be overwhelming but ignore them and pretend you're talking to me or to Lindy."

When Quincy had regained her composure, Connie signaled Ms. Wallace and she led them down the hall to face the press. Just before they entered, Lindy dropped Quincy's hand. "I'll stand where you can see me." The chief spoke to the officer at the door, and she escorted Lindy into the room, then to a spot against the wall, close to the podium.

A minute later Quincy and Chief Trubeck entered along with Ms. Wallace and three doctors. Ms. Wallace introduced everyone, then launched into a description of the trauma designation of Hackensack University Hospital, going on and on about its capabilities and the awards it had received. Finally, she turned the meeting over to the three doctors, who talked about the conditions in the ER last night before and after the injured from the pileup were brought in and offered statistics on the handling of cases.

Quincy knew Wallace's job was to promote the hospital, but she was milking it. And, judging by their shifting and whispering, the press wasn't the least bit interested in her or the doctor's statistics. Quincy and everyone else knew they were here to hear her story. She kept her gaze over the heads of the reporters and photographers, avoiding eye contact. From time to time, she glanced at Lindy, and each time she was rewarded with a smile. At last the statistical review was over and Wallace asked for questions. The room was deadly quiet.

"Well then, let me introduce Chief of Police Trubeck."

Quincy stood at attention as the chief described the 911 calls they had received, how dispatch had sent out the request for assistance, but all cars were engaged with other accidents. She went on to say that the first responder was Officer Quincy Adams, who had just gone off duty and was on her way home. The chief described what she found when she arrived at the scene of the accident then introduced Quincy and asked her to talk about what happened. Quincy took a breath and stepped up to the microphone. Focusing on Lindy, she spoke briefly about being the first on the scene, seeing the number of people injured, and deciding that those whose cars were on fire had to be the priority. "We're trained to respond to this kind of thing. I simply did what any officer would do."

The double doors behind Quincy swung open, drawing all eyes to them, and a petite Asian woman walked in. It was Grace's mother. For a few seconds she seemed stunned by the lights and the crowd, but then she stepped next to Quincy and lowered the microphone.

"I'm Irene Lee, Grace Walcott's mother. Officer Adams saved the lives of my daughter and son-in-law and my four grandchildren. Grace and Mike would have come themselves," she said quietly, "but Grace is heavily medicated to deal with the pain of her multiple injuries and Mike has a concussion and needs to be quiet." After a pause, she continued.

"I have to correct what Officer Adams just said. Not every officer would have the courage or whatever it takes for someone to risk their life to save a woman trapped in a car that's about to explode, to risk their life to save a woman from being burned alive." A sob escaped Mrs. Lee. "She was willing to die trying to save Grace. That is bravery."

She smiled. "Officer Adams is a hero, my hero, our family's hero. But she didn't save only my daughter and her family. She also saved six other people who were injured or unconscious in their burning vehicles. She deserves a medal and a raise and a promotion and…I don't know. How much are the lives of twelve men, women, and children worth?"

She swiped at her tears. "Our family will spend the rest of our lives trying to repay her." She pulled Quincy down for a hug and kissed her forehead. "Thank you." She walked out as cameras rolled and lights flashed. Quincy took the few seconds Mrs. Lee was the focus to get control of her emotions. The last thing she wanted was to cry in front of the cameras.

As the double doors swung closed, attention switched back to Quincy, and she was barraged with questions. She tried to answer each honestly. Finally, one of the reporters went to the heart of the matter. "Grace's car was close to exploding and if it had blown, it would have taken you with it. What made you do it?"

Quincy met Lindy's eyes. She looked around the room where every eye and every camera was focused on her, then took a deep breath.

"She was so brave. Though she knew she was going to die, her first thoughts were for her family and, once they were safe, for me. She tried to get me to leave her, to save myself. Maybe I was inspired by her bravery. Maybe I'd rather die than live with standing by and watching a brave woman burn to death." She shrugged. "I'm not really sure."

The room went dead silent, then the reporters stood and clapped. Chief Trubeck stepped in. "Okay, that's it. Thank you, everyone." She signaled Lindy to follow and escorted Quincy out of the room while Ms. Wallace tried to gain control of the meeting again. The three of them ducked into a supply closet to evade the reporters following them. Quincy was shaking. Lindy put an arm around her waist and the chief put a hand on her shoulder. They tensed at the sound of the reporters milling about in the hall outside the closet cursing the fact that Quincy had disappeared. Ten minutes later it was quiet in the hallway and Lindy peeked out. "They're gone." She touched Quincy's shoulder. "If you're ready to leave, let's see if we can get something for your hands and feet in the emergency room and, at the same time, give the reporters time to leave the building."

"That's probably a good idea," the chief said.

"I was hoping the press conference would satisfy them," Quincy said. "What else could I possibly tell them?"

"Maybe it will. But it looks like feeding the beast only made it hungrier. I'm going to station a car outside your apartment building so if, or should I say when, the reporters find out where you live, we can keep them from following you."

Lindy opened the closet door and looked around again to confirm that the reporters were definitely gone. "All clear."

"Wait." Connie put her arm up to stop them. "You're in Lindy's car and if we're not careful Lindy will be dragged into this circus."

Lindy paled.

The last thing Quincy wanted was to involve Lindy in this craziness. "What can we do?"

"Are you okay exchanging cars, Lindy? This way if they spot you and look up the license plate, they'll find me, not you. And when you're ready to leave we can do another exchange."

"It sounds like a plan." Lindy passed her car keys to the chief. "It's a blue Subaru parked back by the fence."

The chief handed her car keys to Lindy. "Quincy knows it. It's my SUV and it's right outside the emergency room doors." She led them back to the ER, grabbed a nurse she knew, and explained what they needed for Quincy's hands and feet.

"Thanks for your support, Lindy." She clasped Quincy on the shoulder. "I've got to find Ms. Wallace and make nice, then get back to the station. You did great today." She paused. "Are you okay? I know the emotional meetings with the people you saved and the press conference was a lot of stress to pile on top of the stress of the accident. And being hounded certainly doesn't help." She leaned close so only Quincy could hear. "Any more flashbacks?"

Quincy pulled away. "I'm a little wrung out, but no. No flashbacks. I'm sure it was a one-time thing. No need to worry."

"I do worry." Connie squeezed her shoulder. "Take care. Call me if you need me. If you can, start on the report I asked for. I'll see you Monday if you're up to it, otherwise come in Tuesday."

While they were leaning against a wall outside the crush in the ER waiting for the nurse to gather the supplies, Quincy pulled Lindy into a hug. "Thank you. Without your support I doubt I'd have made it through the night, forget visiting with everyone and doing a press conference."

Lindy looked up at her with the sweetest smile, but whatever she was about to say got lost in a series of flashes from a camera. The photographer, a young woman, grinned. "Can I get your name, miss, and your relation to Officer Adams?"

Lindy lunged for the camera and the young woman backed away, holding it against her chest. "If you print that picture, I'll sue you for invasion of privacy. Officer Adams may be a public figure, but I'm certainly not. And isn't it illegal to take pictures in the ER?"

"Sorry, you're in the hall and you're not patients. You look fabulous together. You'll like the pictures, I promise." The photographer backed up until she hit the exit door, then dashed out.

Quincy grinned. "Wow, you're awesome when you're pissed. And great reflexes. I was stunned, but you reacted immediately. I'm impressed. Are you really going to sue? Are you reluctant to be tagged a lesbian?"

Lindy straightened her blouse. "No to suing. And I'm an open lesbian, so no problem there. I just don't like to be ambushed."

"Well, now you see the downside of associating with today's person enjoying her fifteen minutes of fame."

Lindy pinched Quincy's cheek. "You're worth it."

"Ouch, that hurt." Quincy touched her face.

"Come on, officer. You're tougher than that."

Ten minutes later, a nurse handed Lindy a bag with tubes of cream and bandages, then explained how to use them. The parking lot was clear so they dashed to the car—without a press escort, to their great relief.

Before she started the car, Lindy turned to Quincy. "I was thinking of picking up some Indian food for lunch and heading back to your apartment. Okay?"

"Sounds like a plan." Quincy patted Lindy's knee. "I love Indian. And all vegetarian is fine for me."

While Quincy set the table, Lindy unpacked their lunch, describing each dish as she removed its cover: vegetable samosa, crisp pastry turnovers filled with vegetables; begun bhorta, eggplant, herbs, sautéed onions & tomatoes; alu mattor gobi, potatoes, peas and cauliflower in masala sauce; vegetable kurma, mixed vegetables in cream with almonds and sweet spices; rice; and garlic naan, Indian bread.

She held up the last container. "And special for you, lamb biryani. Lamb with basmati rice, raisins, and almonds."

Quincy's mouth watered as the heady fragrance of the spices filled the kitchen. "What a feast. How many guests are we expecting?"

"Leftovers are always good." Lindy inhaled and sighed as she joined Quincy at the table. "I get full on just the smell of all the spices."

"Not me. I'm starving." Quincy served Lindy a little of each vegetarian dish, then helped herself to the lamb biryani and some of the vegetables. "Thanks for the meat, but I'm okay with all vegetarian sometimes."

Once again she observed Lindy eating slowly, seeming to savor each bite.

Lindy gazed at Quincy. "You deserve something special." In between bites, Lindy commented on the morning. "You've made some friends for life, you know, the people you saved. Especially Grace. She seems really determined to show her gratitude."

Quincy helped herself to another serving of biryani. "Grace is brave, clearheaded, and fiercely protective of her family. She's also strong-minded. I like that. I admire her. I think we could be friends."

"I'm glad to hear you're not put off by strong-minded women."

"Because you're strong-minded?" Quincy waited and was rewarded with a nod and a shy smile.

"Some might even say stubborn, especially when others try to tell me what to do."

"Thought so. What will you do if that photographer publishes our picture?"

Lindy shrugged. "Probably give her a piece of my mind, then demand she give me a copy." She stood. "I'll clean up." Moving to some inner music, she transferred the leftovers into Quincy's glass containers, stacked them in the refrigerator, then began to empty the dishwasher to make room for their dirty dishes and silverware.

Quincy studied her as she worked. Lindy seemed to glow in the sunshine streaming in through the windows over the sink, her hair more gold than blond. *My guardian angel bathed in a shaft of golden light from the heavens.* Quincy smiled at the thought. She'd been…"blessed" was the word that came to mind, with the presence of this woman—beautiful on the inside and outside—when she most needed someone to soothe and care for her, someone to help her feel the joy in life. Lindy said she believed in some higher power. Maybe that was it.

Quincy ran a hand through her hair, then folded and refolded her napkin. "I really appreciate your taking care of me, Lindy, but if there's something else you have to or want to do today, my friend Amelia doesn't work Saturdays, so I can go to her house if I need company."

Lindy looked up from the dishwasher and pushed her hair out of her eyes. She chewed her lip. "Unless you're tired of me, I'd love to keep you company again tonight. Be honest, Quincy."

"Please stay." She tossed her napkin on the table. "Now I know you can protect me from attacks by photographers I feel even safer than before."

Lindy stuck out her tongue. "Whatever it takes, my hero." She turned her attention back to the dirty dishes and finished loading the dishwasher. "I thought I'd run to Shop Rite to pick up what we need for dinner and breakfast. Don't get nervous. Even though I'm a vegetarian I can make you a steak or chops or anything you want. Do you want to come?"

"If you don't mind, I'll stay home and get a leg up on the report the chief asked me to write about the accident. And whatever you cook for yourself is fine with me." Quincy cleared her throat. "Do you have enough clothes so you can leave for work from here Monday?"

Lindy narrowed her eyes and looked long and hard at her. "Is this going to turn into the lesbians moving-in-together-after-the-second-date thing?"

"No, of course—"

"Because I would count this whole weekend as only one date, so it's too early."

"What?" Quincy was stunned.

Lindy grinned. "Just playing with you, sugah."

CHAPTER SEVEN

Quincy and her friend Amelia were both drying their eyes when Lindy walked in with the groceries.

"Sorry, the door wasn't locked, but I should have knocked."

Quincy got up. "Don't apologize, I left it open for you." She took the shopping bags from Lindy. "Lindy, this is my best friend Amelia. Amelia, this is my new friend Lindy. Amelia doesn't own a TV so she didn't see any coverage of the accident last night, but she received calls from friends after the press conference this afternoon and, assuming I was probably sinking fast, she dashed over to take care of me. Just a sec. Let me put these in the kitchen."

"Hi, Amelia." Lindy extended her hand. Amelia stood and, ignoring her hand, pulled her into a hug. "I'm so happy to meet you, Lindy, and I'm grateful you were here for Quincy."

"Thank you." Lindy blushed. "But I didn't do anything special."

"I heard that." Quincy spoke as she returned from the kitchen. "Don't believe her, Amelia, it was very special. She's a very special lady." She put an arm around Amelia. "You don't need to worry about me being alone. Lindy has volunteered to stay with me the rest of the weekend."

Amelia raised her eyebrows. "Have you been holding out on me, Quince?"

"What?" Quincy's voice went up an octave. "No. We just met last night. There's nothing…I mean we're just friends." She looked at Lindy for confirmation.

Lindy's grin was mischievous. "At least for now."

"Whoa." Amelia punched Quincy's arm. "I'll leave you two to it."

Quincy hugged Amelia. "No pressure, huh?"

"No pressure. I just wanted to be sure you were okay and not brooding by yourself. And I see things are fine on both counts, so I'll go home and eat the fine dinner Jackson is cooking for me." She kissed Lindy's cheek. "Nice to meet you. And thanks for taking such good care of my friend." Quincy walked Amelia to the door.

"Enjoy the weekend." As she walked out, Amelia elbowed Quincy and whispered, "You lucky girl."

Amelia was right. She was lucky. She'd never met anyone as caring and sweet and sexy and funny and…

Grinning, Quincy went into the kitchen. "You missed all the action. Some other friends stopped by to say they'd seen the news conference and wanted to make sure I didn't need anything. And Maggie called to see how I was doing."

"Can't say I'm sorry I missed them." Lindy looked up from the shopping she was unpacking. "I mean it was nice meeting Amelia, but it's not like I need to be introduced to your whole social circle."

Quincy hesitated, not sure how to take that remark. Was Lindy shy or was she afraid of getting too involved in her life? "They just dropped by to see if I'm okay. Like Amelia." Why did she feel like she had to apologize for having friends who care?

"I got more Social Teas." Lindy held up the box as she emptied the bag. "So how do you and Amelia know each other?"

Quincy laughed. "The short version is I saved her from five white boys who were about to beat her up on her first day as a second grader at Fairmont Elementary School and we've been best friends ever since. Amelia loves to tell the story so ask her the next time we're together."

Lindy stacked the groceries in the cabinet, closed the door, and leaned against the counter. "So saving people is nothing new for you?"

The question surprised Quincy. Her first thought was *Some hero—wasn't even able to save the woman I loved.* But as she considered it, she thought of the times she'd intervened to protect others growing up, about her medals from Iraq and Afghanistan, and times on the job where one way or another she'd saved people from themselves or from a dangerous situation. "I've never thought of it that way, but it does seem to be a motif in my life."

Lindy opened the refrigerator. "I figured."

"You figured what?"

Lindy pulled out a cauliflower, garlic, parsley, and salad ingredients, then moved the crushed red pepper, pine nuts, sundried tomatoes, and box of raisins from the counter to the table as well. She faced Quincy again. "Since we met less than twenty-four hours ago, it's presumptuous of me to assume I know you. But serving in Afghanistan and Iraq and being a police officer shows an ongoing commitment to working for the greater good. And in the short time I've been with you I've learned you feel deeply, are sensitive, kind, and gentle, and you care about people and they care back. While you were heroic last night, I don't think a person becomes those things overnight, so I figured that's who you are. My very own superhero."

Quincy stared at her. "*Your* superhero?"

Lindy opened a drawer, selected a paring knife and a larger chef's knife, and put both on the table. "Yes. I've never known one before. But I think the people whose lives you saved last night probably feel the same way, so maybe you're everyone's superhero."

Quincy shook her head and waved her hands, brushing the idea away. "I'm not a superhero, just someone who doesn't like to see people hurt."

"A lot of people feel that way, Quincy, but very few put their life on the line the way you did. And I'll bet you have some medals in a drawer somewhere that attest to the fact that last night wasn't the first time."

Quincy blew out a breath, thinking again of her medals and citations. "Thanks for the vote of confidence."

Lindy moved to the other side of the table, closer to Quincy. She placed her hands on either side of Quincy's face. "Uh-oh. If I go on like this I'm afraid your head soon won't fit through that doorway, so I'm going to concentrate on making dinner now."

"Excellent idea." Quincy sat at the table while Lindy checked the ingredients she'd set out, filled a pasta pot with water and put a flame under it, then selected serving bowls for the pasta and the salad and a basket for the bread.

"Would you mind if I turn on your radio and listen to music while I cook?"

"Be my guest." Quincy pointed.

Quincy smiled when Adele came on. She could live with that. She picked up her pen and turned to work on her report, but her attention kept sliding to Lindy who was singing, dancing, snapping her fingers, and waving her knife while she prepped and cooked dinner. She moved as unselfconsciously and gracefully in the kitchen as she did on the dance floor, shifting with ease between cutting the cauliflower into florets, chopping garlic, sundried tomatoes, and parsley, and measuring out pine nuts and raisins. Quincy tried not to stare, but watching Lindy cook was like watching a choreographed dance, every movement fluid, no movement wasted. Her singing along was a bonus.

Lindy cooked the cauliflower in the boiling water, then removed it from the pot and tossed in a half pound of the *orecchiette*, pasta shaped like little ears. She heated extra-virgin olive oil in a frying pan, sautéed the garlic, crushed red pepper, sundried tomatoes, raisins, and pine nuts for a few minutes, and then added the cauliflower. When the pasta was ready, she drained it and placed it in a bowl, stirred in the contents of the frying pan, and sprinkled it all with fresh parsley. Lindy placed the pasta, the salad of arugula, pear, gorgonzola cheese, and toasted pecans, and a crusty loaf of Italian bread on the table.

"Red wine, beer, or seltzer, Quincy?"

"A beer, please."

She retrieved a bottle of Sam Adams from the fridge, filled a glass with seltzer for herself, then sat and served each of them.

Quincy tasted the pasta, then the salad. "This is delicious, Lindy. My mouth feels alive with the contrasting tastes, hot and sweet, tangy and savory. You're spoiling me."

Lindy pushed her hair behind her ears. "Nothing wrong with a little spoiling, sugah." She watched Quincy eat for a minute. "So how are you feeling about meeting Grace and all the other people you saved, about the press conference, about being seen as a hero?" She forked up some pasta.

Quincy chewed as she considered the question. "Um, 'overwhelmed' sums it up pretty well, I think." She finished her pasta. "But not so overwhelmed I've lost my appetite apparently. This is really good. Were you planning on leftovers for lunch or may I have seconds when I'm ready?"

"Eat as much as you want." Lindy pushed the bowl closer to Quincy. "Can you take in that what you did was heroic?"

Quincy rubbed her neck. Lindy seemed intent on forcing her to deal with this hero thing. "It feels to me like I was doing my job, but at the hospital today I understood that I've given the people I rescued, especially the children, the gift of life which they might not have had if I'd gone straight home that night. I feel proud of that. I suppose if I was looking at someone else who had done that, I would consider them a hero. So I can see how the people I pulled out of those vehicles would think I was a hero." She helped herself to more pasta but didn't pick up her fork. "But it's embarrassing with everyone, you know, focusing on me."

Lindy pointed to Quincy's plate. "Better eat that before it gets cold." She turned her attention to her own food, eating in her careful way. After a few minutes of silence, she looked up.

"Since you'll probably have to deal with being a hero for the next couple of weeks, try to enjoy the attention."

"That was delicious." Quincy leaned back and waited for Lindy to finish her meal. "I'll clean up." She stood. Her phone rang. Mama's ringtone. "That's my grandmother. Leave everything and I'll clean up after I take this." She sat again, knowing this would not be quick. "Hi, Mama. I was wondering how long it would take your intelligence network to contact you."

Lindy stood. "Take your time." She began to clean up.

Quincy nodded as she listened to her grandmother. "I'm fine, Mama. Not even a scratch. How are you?"

She held the phone away from her ear as her grandmother shouted. "How could I be? I come home from an afternoon on the golf course and dinner out to find my voice mail filled with messages about my only granddaughter almost getting blown up. What were you thinking? You could have died!" Her always calm, collected grandmother's voice broke on a sob.

Lindy had stopped moving to listen.

Quincy winked at Lindy. "Really, I'm fine, Mama. I apologize for not calling. I'm sorry to cause you pain. But in the moment, I was only thinking about saving a brave woman, a mother of four, so her children wouldn't have to grow up without her."

"What did I do wrong? Why did you grow up having to save people? Did I make you eat too many vegetables?"

Quincy grinned. *First Lindy, then Mama.* At least Mama's sense of humor was intact.

Lindy was wide-eyed and seemed to be struggling to keep from laughing.

Quincy stood and paced. "You didn't do anything wrong, Mama. You're my role model. You saved so many children from self-destructing over the years. We just go about saving people in different ways."

Mama sighed. "In any case, as soon as I can get a reservation I'm going to fly up and see for myself that you're all in one piece."

"Don't bother coming now. Let's just stick to our plans for Thanksgiving. Amelia was just here. Call her, she'll confirm I'm okay." Quincy listened. "Love you, too." She disconnected and sat back. "You probably figured out my mama was upset."

Lindy turned from the sink. "So *she* agrees that you're a hero?"

"She wondered why I'm always saving people." Quincy laughed. "She thinks it's because she fed me too many veggies."

Lindy laughed. "She sounds nice. Is she coming?"

"Amelia will assure her that I'm okay and tell her about you, so I'm pretty sure she'll realize you're taking good care of me."

They finished cleaning up together then Lindy went into the bathroom to change into PJs. When Lindy came into the living room, Quincy smiled. She looked cute in her very large, faded long-sleeved T-shirt and tights.

Lindy looked down at her outfit. "What are you smiling about, Quincy?"

"I like the look. Comfortable and homey. Makes you look young."

"Oh, so I usually look old?"

"No, no. You just look younger and…relaxed and pretty."

Lindy turned red. "So are we going to watch a movie or not?"

"Okay, let me change."

Lindy eyed Quincy's loose-fitting yoga pants and tee. "I figured you for a boxer girl."

"Only in the warmer weather." Quincy dropped on the sofa next to Lindy. "So what should we watch?"

"I'd prefer something light, a comedy but not a romance. What's available?"

Quincy paged through the Netflix options. "How about *Late Night*? It's a workplace comedy starring Emma Thompson. It doesn't look like a romance is involved."

"It sounds perfect."

The movie was funny, and it felt good to laugh. It also felt good to be sitting close to Lindy on the sofa sharing the light moments after the stress of the last twenty-four hours. Several times during the movie Quincy glanced at Lindy. And each time, Lindy was looking at her. She was tempted to put an arm around her, but she didn't want to assume anything, so she quashed the impulse.

After the movie Lindy rubbed the cream the nurse had supplied on Quincy's hands and feet.

"That feels wonderful." Quincy yawned. "I don't think my body could take another night on the sofa. Are you okay with sleeping in my bed tonight?"

"As friends?"

Quincy blushed. "Of course, I wouldn't…um, yes, as friends. Usually when I wake up and go back to sleep, the nightmare recurs, but I think being held by you after the nightmare last night allowed me to sleep without dreaming."

Lindy frowned. "So I'm just a warm body?"

Quincy took her hands. "Lindy, you are so much more than a warm body to me. I appreciate your taking care of me, physically and emotionally. I appreciate your friendship. I appreciate your staying with me and supporting me. But most of all, I appreciate that you've opened your heart to me and helped me reconnect with the joy of being alive. And you've done all of that without the pseudo-connection of sex."

"'Pseudo-connection,' huh?" Lindy moved closer for a hug. "Okay, my hero, let's go to bed."

Lindy brushed her teeth and crawled into bed. Quincy did the same.

They were on their backs, side-by-side, but not close. Lindy touched Quincy's arm. "Hey, I thought you wanted contact."

"I thought you'd never ask." Quincy rolled into Lindy's arms. Then, lulled by the gentle rise and fall of Lindy's chest, the warmth of Lindy's breath on her forehead, and the gentle rasp of her breathing, she fell into a dreamless sleep.

Quincy woke first, watched Lindy sleep for a few minutes, then eased out of bed to take a shower. With hot water streaming over her, she thought about Lindy asleep in her bed and wondered at the strangeness of it all. It was confusing. Deciding it was okay to die, but living. Finding a peace she didn't know she'd lost. And finding Lindy, a warm, caring, strong woman she hadn't known she wanted. Did Lindy feel the same connection or was she just being nice?

She pulled on sweats and socks, then moved into the kitchen to mix the batter for cottage cheese pancakes. By the time Lindy appeared dressed in jeans and a flannel shirt, Quincy had cut up strawberries and a mango, put out the powdered sugar and maple syrup, and poured herself a cup of coffee.

"Morning." Lindy didn't meet her eyes. "I smell coffee."

It was weird. On the one hand they were intimate. On the other hand, they were virtual strangers. Lindy had given her so much in such a short time, and she didn't want them to be awkward with each other.

Quincy wanted to hug Lindy, but she wasn't sure the contact would be welcome. Lindy seemed comfortable touching her, but Quincy's gut told her to tread carefully.

"Good morning. How about a hug and some pancakes?"

Lindy stared for a few seconds. "A hug would be great. And I love pancakes."

Quincy opened her arms, Lindy moved in and wrapped her arms around Quincy's waist. They embraced for a moment, then Lindy pulled away. Quincy moved to the table. "I hope cottage cheese pancakes are okay?"

"Cottage cheese pancakes sound wonderful." Lindy met her eyes and smiled. Quincy felt as if the sun had just moved into the kitchen. "Is the coffee ready?"

"Sit, let me serve you this morning. Milk and sugar?"

"Yes, light and sweet."

Quincy placed the coffee in front of Lindy, then she put the flame under the griddle and began to cook the pancakes. "The sun is out and it's still cold, but I'm feeling a little stir-crazy with no exercise. I doubt they've plowed the park, but would you be up for taking a walk in the snow today?" Quincy took the plate of pancakes out of the oven, picked up the butter, and joined Lindy.

"The outdoors beckons to me in any season as long as I'm dressed for it. I might need an extra layer from you, but I'd love to take a walk."

They continued to chat as they ate, then, like an old married couple who had been doing it for years, they cleaned the kitchen together before getting ready for their walk. The silk thermals, sweatshirt, leg warmers, and heavy-duty gloves Quincy gave Lindy were all big but fit well enough to keep her warm.

Lindy stopped short as she stepped out of the house. "Uh-oh, the press has found you. What do we do?"

Quincy stepped outside to see for herself. This was crazy. Her neighbors would be pissed at the vans and cars clogging the road that wove through the apartment complex. "Come back in. Let me call Connie." She pulled out her cell and found Connie's number in her contacts. "Good morning, Connie. Lindy and I were hoping to go for a walk this morning, but the press is out in full force. I don't think one car is going to be able to control them." She listened. "Okay. Thanks." She disconnected. "A couple of cars will be here in a few minutes."

Eight minutes later, Quincy's phone rang. She nodded and disconnected. "Okay. They have the press blocked and we can go." She zipped her coat again and watched Lindy do the same. "Maybe you should use that fur hood so if they have a telephoto lens they won't get much of your face."

"Good idea." Lindy pulled the hood over. She blew the fake fur out of her mouth. "I never wear this thing because it falls over my face, but I guess that's good now."

As they settled in the car, Quincy gave Lindy directions. "Make a left onto Essex Street, then another left onto Prospect. Go a couple of blocks and turn on Central Avenue and I'll direct you from there."

CHAPTER EIGHT

Once it was clear they'd escaped without a press entourage, Quincy directed Lindy to Van Saun Park in Paramus. The main roads were plowed, but lots of cars along the way were still buried under mounds of snow. As Lindy made her way through a narrow path between abandoned cars, Quincy shook her head. "I'm not looking forward to tomorrow with the roads like this. There'll be lots of accidents, delays, and grumpy drivers. Will the snow make your job harder?"

Lindy hesitated before answering but decided it was okay. "Yes. I'm a scheduler for a trucking company and I'll have to do a lot of juggling of routes and shifting of loads to keep things moving this week."

Quincy opened her mouth, probably to ask a question about her job, but then remained quiet. Lindy was relieved that Quincy seemed willing to let her take the lead and didn't press.

The parking lot at the park was clear, but, as Quincy had predicted, the paths hadn't been shoveled and the roads hadn't been plowed. Undeterred, they trudged along, talking about books and music and movies and travel, about Quincy's friends, about dreams, about everything and anything. Except the elephant lumbering along between them, her personal life.

She did reveal some impersonal stuff about books and music. They discovered they'd both recently read and loved the same novels—*The Seven Husbands of Evelyn Hugo* and *Eleanor Oliphant is Completely Fine*. And she'd shared that she liked music from the sixties and the seventies better than most current stuff. And that Marvin Gaye was one of her favorite artists. She also told Quincy something that only Sarah and Babs knew—that she was taking college courses at night in order to become an elementary school teacher.

As they walked past the playground and the closed zoo, they heard the sounds of excited screams and laughter. It turned out to be kids and adults sledding down the hill and trudging back up to do it all over again. They watched a few minutes, then Lindy decided this was her opportunity to fulfill a desire. She picked up some snow and lobbed it at Quincy, who yelped in surprise when it hit her.

Quincy didn't hesitate to retaliate. She packed some snow into a ball and held it out to Lindy. "This is a snowball, Ms. Southern Lady, not that pitiful handful you tossed."

While Lindy scooped up more snow, Quincy threw her snowball and hit her in the chest. They chased each other, throwing snowballs and dashing away screaming and laughing. Finally, a breathless Quincy raised her hands. "I surrender."

Lindy put her hands in the air like a winning boxer and danced around Quincy for a few seconds, then out of breath herself she leaned into Quincy.

"Do you know how to make a snowman?"

"Of course. Come on, I'll show you."

They rolled three snowballs, one large for the body, one medium for the chest, and a small one for the head, then searched for sticks for the arms and stones for the eyes, ears and mouth. As they proudly surveyed their work, a couple stopped to admire the snowman and the woman asked if they would like a picture with him.

Lindy grinned. "Yes." She loved the idea of capturing this moment in a photo. She didn't think she'd ever felt so free and alive.

Quincy smiled at Lindy. "Me too, definitely."

They handed their phones to the woman. She snapped pictures of them arm and arm standing proudly next to their creation, then handed their phones back and ambled away with her companion.

Quincy looked at the photo. "Wow, we look good and so does our snowman."

Lindy looked at her phone and smiled. "Yeah, we do, don't we?" She shivered. "Now that we stopped moving, I'm getting cold. We should go." She wrapped her arms around herself.

"We can't leave without making snow angels." Quincy walked to a fresh patch of snow, lay down on her back, and moved her arms up and down along the ground. Lindy snapped a picture. Quincy stood and admired her creation.

"Wow, that's great." Lindy followed suit, then stood and took pictures of both their snow angels. "Do people name their snow angels?"

"Not that I know of."

Lindy got down on her knees. "I'm going to name mine." She wrote "Quincy" in the snow above her snow angel. "It's only fitting since you taught me how to make her."

She looked up, forgetting to hide her feelings, her attraction to sweet, kind, and sexy Quincy, then caught herself. She'd done it again, sending mixed messages, subtly putting out her desire for Quincy while holding her at arm's length. The poor thing looked flummoxed. What could Quincy say? How could the poor woman decode the confusing messages? Lindy looked away, suddenly overcome by a longing to be close to Quincy, to get to know her better. But that couldn't be. "And you are my superhero."

Quincy hesitated, then bowed. "I accept the honor, milady." She pulled Lindy up. "Now let's go get warm."

Lindy hoped Quincy would put her arm around her, but she didn't. She'd trained her well.

They'd walked an hour, had a fifteen-minute snowball fight, built a snowman, and spent a few minutes rolling in the snow making snow angels and now they were both shivering. They hurried to Lindy's car. She turned the heat to high.

"That was the most fun I've had in a long time. That was my first-ever snowball fight, first-ever snowman, and first-ever snow angel. Thank you." Lindy glanced in the mirror. Her face was flushed and she looked relaxed and happy. And she was. "I've achieved a new level of social skills."

Quincy rubbed her hands together and laughed. "I'm happy we had some exercise, happy I made you happy. I'm thrilled to be your first. I mean snow playmate, of course."

Lindy punched Quincy's arm. "Think you're cute, huh?" She started the car. "Maybe you are…"

She hadn't meant to speak that thought out loud. She stared straight ahead as she drove out of the lot. She knew Quincy heard since she'd swiveled to get a look at Lindy's face but she didn't comment.

At Maggie's, they worked up a sweat digging Quincy's car out of the snow. Now hungry as well as wet again, they drove in separate cars to Lindy's favorite diner on Route 4 for lunch.

Back at Quincy's apartment, they spent the rest of the afternoon on the sofa, talking companionably and reading. The evening was pretty much the same as the night before, except the house filled with the fragrance of bubbling tomato sauce and sautéed garlic as Lindy prepared eggplant parmesan and broccoli with garlic and olive oil. Quincy made the salad.

After dinner, Quincy sat back. "I never imagined I'd enjoy vegetarian meals, but I have. You are a wonderful cook. Is it a health or a religious thing for you?"

"Neither. I just can't bring myself to eat animals." Lindy smiled. "I'm enjoying cooking for you. I'm glad you're enjoying eating."

"I'll clean up. You go relax and prepare yourself because I'm challenging you to a game of Scrabble later."

Quincy watched Lindy stroll into the living room, then turned to the dirty dishes. As she loaded the dishwasher then scrubbed the pots, images of their afternoon in the snow flashed in her mind. She couldn't remember the last time she'd played and had so much fun. Maybe next time they'd bring a sled.

Would there be a next time? Judging by how she was feeling and how Lindy seemed to feel about her, it seemed likely. She smiled. Bring on the snow.

Before joining Lindy to play Scrabble, Quincy took a few minutes to lay out her uniform, underwear, and socks for tomorrow. She sighed. What a colorful, emotional, and exciting weekend. Going back on patrol tomorrow would seem like being in a black and white still photo in comparison.

After a weekend of connection and conversation, the silence Monday morning as they ate the omelets Quincy cooked was uncomfortable. Except for quick glances, they barely looked at each other. Quincy worried about being alone tonight, about the nightmares returning, but mostly about letting go of the first woman since Jen to spark a desire for something more.

Quincy cleared her throat. "The press is outside again this morning. I spoke to Connie earlier and she wants you to drive to the emergency room parking lot at Hackensack Hospital, park, and wait for her. When you leave I'll call her and she'll find you in the lot so you can exchange cars."

Lindy nodded. "Connie is a good friend. You're lucky to have her."

"I am. She's been there for me every single time."

It wasn't until they were cleaning up that it occurred to Quincy that Lindy was probably as nervous as she was about parting after the intense connection of the weekend. When they were pulling on boots to go their separate ways, Quincy cleared her throat.

"Lindy, would you have dinner with me one night this week? A date."

Lindy paled. "A date?" She looked up from tying her boot. "Like if we just met and you liked me and wanted to ask me out?"

"Yes, that kind of date." Quincy held her breath.

"No." Lindy looked down as she tied her other boot.

Quincy's face was on fire. Had she done or said something to put Lindy off? Or was she so needy she'd projected her feelings onto Lindy? Was she so desperate that she'd mistaken Lindy's kindness and generosity for attraction? *Gross.* Clearly, Lindy wasn't feeling as close to her as she was feeling to Lindy.

"I'm sorry if I—"

"Don't." Lindy put a finger on Quincy's lips. "It's not you." Her eyes filled. "I can't."

Quincy needed to be clear. "Can't or won't?"

"Can't." Lindy sounded sad.

"Is there someone else?"

"No." Lindy took a deep breath. "Look, I had a good time with you. But I need to be alone. Believe me, I would end up hurting you, and I like you too much to do that."

"Do you think you might change your mind?" Damn, she sounded like she was begging.

Lindy looked sad. "I doubt it. But give me your phone number and I'll call you if I do." She fumbled in her pocket for her phone.

Quincy dictated her number and, sensing Lindy wanted control, she didn't ask for her number in return. "Give me a call when you feel like getting together." She hoped she sounded casual, hoped her confusion and hurt didn't come through.

Lindy reached for her coat, but Quincy grabbed it first and held it for her. Lindy slipped her arms into the sleeves, turned to face Quincy, and zipped her coat.

Lindy's body was tense and her jaw tight, but she was still beautiful. Her joy, her gentle soul, her inner and outer beauty called to Quincy. She hoped she didn't look as lost and helpless as she felt.

"It's been wonderful spending time with you, Quincy. I hope I helped." She touched Quincy's face. "You're a remarkable woman and I know there's a special someone waiting out there for you." She kissed Quincy's cheek, then bolted out the door.

Quincy's hand went to her cheek. She stepped out onto the landing and watched Lindy run to her car, pleased to see the press hemmed in by police cars. Hopefully, seeing her in uniform would distract them and they would ignore Lindy when she drove Connie's car out. Before she got in the car, Lindy turned. Their eyes locked for a few seconds. Had Lindy changed her mind? No. With a tense smile and a quick wave, she got in the car, and pulled out of the parking space. A police car followed her out of the lot.

Quincy's eyes filled. What had she expected? How pathetic. Wanting to date someone who probably just felt sorry for her. She reached for her coat, then realized she was crying. Wouldn't do for the big hero to have a tearstained face. She put her coat down, washed her face, and then left for work. At least the hollowed-out version of her did.

CHAPTER NINE

Pretending she hadn't noticed Quincy's tears, not wanting Quincy to see hers, Lindy forced a smile, waved, and drove out of the slick driveway as fast as she could. Her gaze bounced between the road and the rearview mirror. She wasn't sure whether she feared or hoped Quincy was following her. How had she gotten herself into this pickle? She could have said no when Maggie asked her to drive Quincy home, but she was touched by Quincy's bravery and wanted to do something nice for her.

She also could have said no when Quincy asked her to go to the hospital with her. But she didn't. *That* was the mistake. She knew it at the time. And she'd compounded her error by offering to stay the whole weekend. But she wanted to be with her. At Maggie's it was Quincy the hero, her bravery, and her vulnerability that had attracted Lindy, but as they spent time together it was Quincy the person, her kindness, her honesty, and her strength that drew her in. She dried her face with the sleeve of her coat, but the tears kept coming.

She'd enjoyed the time with Quincy, comforting her, caring for her, laughing and talking with her. All of it. And she didn't want it to end this morning. But what did she have to offer such a brave and strong woman, a real hero, someone ready to sacrifice herself on the battlefield for her country and for a woman she didn't even know? It could never be more. She couldn't deal with more. Quincy would eventually see the real her and be repulsed. And while her intention had been to do a good thing, she'd ended up hurting Quincy. Brave, sweet Quincy didn't deserve that. A sob escaped. As usual, she'd screwed up. This was why she didn't do people.

She glanced in the rearview mirror. A police car was behind her and she didn't see any media vans. It was a miracle that she hadn't been identified. What a horror that would have been. Poor Quincy, having to deal with that pressure along with everything else. The police station must be close because Connie arrived a few minutes after her. They got out, exchanged keys, and before Lindy could turn away, Connie pulled her into a hug. "Thanks for taking care of Quincy, Lindy. It looks like we were able to preserve your anonymity. See you soon."

Lindy parked at the far end of the parking lot for DiMonte Trucking, pulled out her phone, and went through the pictures they'd taken when they were frolicking in the park—Quincy hands on knees out of breath but laughing after their snowball fight, the snowman, the two of them with the snowman, their snow angels. *Frolicking*. A word she would have never applied to herself anytime in her twenty-seven years of life. Yet they had definitely frolicked. She hadn't ever laughed so much, hadn't ever felt so happy, hadn't ever felt so in the moment with someone.

Even through the tears blurring her eyes she could see Quincy looked happy too. This was the Quincy she wanted to remember, not the pained Quincy she'd left without explanation this morning. A tear bounced off her screen. Damn, she needed to pull herself together so she could deal with the teasing of the guys in the office without going into a screaming rage or, worse, breaking into tears.

She jumped at a tap on her window. Babs. She must have been waiting to talk before work. She put her phone in her pocket. Babs slid onto the passenger seat. Lindy stared straight ahead until Babs gently touched her cheek and turned her face.

"Did that cop hurt you, honey?"

She smiled through her tears, sniffed. "Not the way you mean, Babsie. I'm just sad because I really like her. And I could tell she felt it too. But I can't."

"I wondered at you going with a stranger. Maybe it's time to talk to someone about that, honey." Babs took Lindy's hand in hers. "You have so much to offer. I hate seeing you separate yourself from everyone because you're afraid of getting hurt again. I hate seeing you so lonely."

"I'm not lonely. In case you haven't noticed, I'm happy to spend time by myself. I have you and our group of friends when I want to be social and dance and play, and I can do it without complications or demands for things I can't provide." She pulled a tissue out, dried her eyes, then fished in her bag for makeup. They needed to go into work soon.

"You should talk to someone, a therapist."

"Been there, done that. That's where I figured out that being alone works best for me." She pulled the visor mirror down and started to patch up her face.

"That was a long time ago. Maybe you've changed. Maybe you need something different."

"I talk to you."

"We're best friends, we share stories. And I share feelings. You, not so much. If you like this cop and you think she likes you, then you need to figure out whether you want a relationship and how to make it happen. Otherwise, you're doomed to be alone forever. As much as I love you, I can't help you with that."

"Hello? Are you listening to me? I know what I want and I've made it happen. I don't need any more therapy to know that a relationship with her, or anyone, is out of the question for me." Lindy threw her makeup into her bag. "Let's go. We're going to be late." She opened her door.

"Lindy." The tone of Babs' voice stopped her short. "Sometimes your stubbornness gets in your way."

"I like to think of it as knowing what I want and need rather than stubbornness. You know, Babs, it's possible to be sad about this and still not want to take what she's offering."

As they walked toward the office, Babs put a hand on Lindy's arm. "Did you watch the TV coverage of that press conference on Saturday?"

"No, why?"

"I don't know if any of the Neanderthals who work here saw it, but there was a second or two showing the cop's eyes on you. It was hot. And, speaking of hot, there's a picture of the two of you in today's *Bergen News*. You're in profile, but anybody who really looks will recognize you. So be prepared."

"Great. I'm going to kill that photographer."

"Have you seen the picture?"

"No. Why?"

Babs snorted. "You sure look like you definitely want what that cop is offering." She bumped Lindy's shoulder. "I left the paper at the apartment. You can judge for yourself tonight. Unless one of these jerks pushes it in your face today."

"She's more than a cop, Babs. Her name is Quincy."

CHAPTER TEN

Trailed by a long line of media vans, Quincy approached the police station from Central Avenue as usual. She winced at the number of vans bearing the logos of New York and New Jersey TV stations that were already there, parked haphazardly along the piles of snow lining the curb. Clearly, it wasn't just the local media anymore. Connie had warned her to expect even more media coverage today, but the size of the crowd of reporters and the number of cameras contained behind barriers across the street from the station house surprised her.

She parked in the lot, but she was shaking and sucking in air so fast she was unable to move. She closed her eyes and suddenly heard Lindy's husky voice. "You can do this, sugah. You've faced more dangerous enemies than these twerps. You're my superhero."

Some superhero, sitting in her car hyperventilating at the thought of facing the press.

But Lindy was right. She could do this. She focused on inhaling slowly through her nose with her mouth closed and exhaling slowly through pressed lips. It took a few minutes to get her breathing under control and another minute to psych herself to leave the safety of the car. As soon as she stepped out, cameras swiveled toward her, lights flashed, reporters called her name and hurled questions at her. Quincy smiled and waved as she dashed into the station.

She gave silent thanks to Connie for making sure Lindy's privacy was protected and for shielding them from the press this weekend, allowing them to enjoy each other and their wonderful walk in the park. The private time with Lindy had been wonderful. She hadn't felt so peaceful, so whole, since spending extended time alone with Jen after Iraq.

She stopped short. Was it bad she hadn't thought of Jen in the last twenty-four hours? The good news was that being with Lindy had rekindled the desire for the life she'd left behind in Afghanistan. The bad news was she needed to forget Lindy and move on with her life.

It was warmer than it had been over the weekend, but it was still nippy. She hoped the cold would encourage the press to leave now that they'd seen her. She looked out the window. Nope. They seemed to be settling in. A number of reporters were talking into microphones with cameras focused on them. Morning news updates, she guessed.

Having a gaggle of reporters trailing her and yelling questions would complicate patrolling today. She needed to ask whether she could disperse them or arrest members of the press if necessary.

She shook her head and headed for the morning meeting to get her assignment. Everyone she passed offered words of appreciation or congratulation or asked how she was feeling. She got lots of slaps on the back, some hugs, and a few guys pretending to faint as they sighed and murmured, "My hero." She grinned. She definitely preferred the jokes to the emotional stuff she'd received at the hospital Saturday.

When she reached the door to the meeting room, her friend and fellow officer Gina Lawson, pulled her into a hug. "God, Quincy, I was down in Maryland visiting Heather and the girls.

I got in late last night, so I had no idea until this morning." Gina held her at arm's length and examined her. "Are you really okay?"

"Other than hating all the press attention, I'm good." She put a hand on the doorknob. "Though it started with a disaster, the weekend was, um, life changing for me, but in the end it didn't turn out as I'd hoped. If our assigned sectors are close enough today, let's meet for lunch and I'll fill you in."

Gina gripped Quincy's arm. "Just a second, lady. You can't drop a bomb like that and expect me to wait until lunchtime to hear about it. Explain."

Milly, the chief's assistant, interrupted. "Adams, orders are for you to skip the morning meeting. The chief wants to see you in her office now."

Quincy turned to Gina, raised her shoulders, and extended her hands. "Sorry, I guess you'll have to wait. I'll call later to set up something."

"Yeah, you really look sorry." Gina pushed her toward the chief's office. "Better go when the boss calls."

Chief Trubeck was on the phone, listening and thumbing through a document on her desk. She waved Quincy into one of the chairs facing her. "Paragraph fourteen section A covers it." She listened a few more minutes. "Agreed." She hung up. "Sorry about that." She took her glasses off and studied Quincy. "How are you today?"

"I'm okay but I'm not looking forward to being shadowed by the press while I'm on patrol. Or anytime actually."

"Uh-huh. And if I might get personal, how is the beautiful Lindy?"

Oh, shit. The last thing Quincy wanted to talk about was being dumped this morning. "She was good when we said goodbye this morning."

Connie studied her. "You two seemed very connected for two people who'd just met the night before."

Quincy wondered where this was going. Connie was always strictly business in the office. "Yes, we were. We did connect."

Connie smiled. "About time you found someone."

Found someone? "I didn't find someone, Connie. It was a great weekend, but it's not like we got together. She's not interested."

"She sure looked interested to me."

Quincy shrugged. "Before she left this morning, I asked her out on a date. She flat-out said no. When I pushed, she took my number and said she would call if she changed her mind, but it was clear she didn't want to give me *her* number."

Connie looked sympathetic. "I'm sorry, Quince, you deserve better. But I wouldn't give up on her if I were you. I'd say she just needs some time."

Time for what? She'd been more intimate with Lindy than some of the women she'd had sex with in the last few years. She'd thought Lindy felt it too. But obviously she was wrong. Why was Connie so positive they'd get together? Was it just that she wanted Quincy to be happy and was hoping Lindy was the one? Or something else?

"What makes you think she just needs more time?"

"What I saw between you on Saturday. And the photo of the two of you."

"What photo?"

"I guess you haven't seen today's *Bergen Daily News*." Connie smiled. "Let's talk about it later, after you see it."

She turned her attention to some papers on her desk, and when she looked up, her demeanor had changed. She looked grim. "I'm worried about you, Quince, worried that you're not fit for duty after the trauma of Friday night. I'm removing you from patrol."

"What the fuck?" Quincy jumped up. Some hero. Dumped by Lindy this morning. Now she was being punished because she went to the scene of the accident Friday night instead of going home. She tried to rein in her fury, knowing it might not be helping her cause.

"I don't understand, Chief Trubeck." She drew out Connie's official title. "You thought I was healthy enough to be the public relations face of the department Saturday, but now I'm not fit for duty? I'll admit I was stressed Friday night and used Jen's name by mistake, but I saved twelve people, for fuck's sake."

She glared at Connie. "I want my union rep here. I don't recall anything like this in the regulations."

Connie sighed. She moved to the front of her desk, perched on the edge, almost knee to knee with Quincy, and made eye contact.

"There is no regulation, Quincy. It's my call and I don't make it easily. I struggled with the decision all weekend. I'll wait for your union rep to get here if that's what you want, but I was there Friday night. I heard you refer to Grace as Jen, I saw the desperation in your eyes before you realized you'd saved Grace. And I've seen enough flashbacks to know you were having one. I know you've struggled with guilt about not saving Jen. I know you put your life on hold the day she died. And I also know you've never really dealt with her death. I'll bet the nightmares are back and you're not sleeping."

Quincy looked away. Of course Connie would know. She'd been their commanding officer. And unlike many commanding officers, she'd supported their relationship. She'd stood by Quincy after Jen's death, allowing her time to grieve.

"I went through it with you in Afghanistan and I understand you had to slam the door on the memory in order to survive. But I also know you left a good part of yourself behind that door and now that it's cracked open you need to deal with Jen's death. And your life."

"So what? I'm suspended? I'm fired? I have to see the department shrink?" Quincy blinked back the tears.

"None of the above right now. You'll be off patrol for a couple of weeks, partly because of the media circus and the danger it poses to you if you're on the streets and partly because you need to deal with what happened in Afghanistan, with Jen's death. We both know flashbacks occur in stressful situations, and you and those around you could be in danger if you're fighting something in your head when you're in a potentially life-threatening confrontation on the job."

"I haven't been able to deal with this for five years. So I'm supposed to magically do it now?" She snapped her fingers. "Just like that?"

"I'd like you to consider going to a PTSD support group for veterans at the VA. That way you would have support from other veterans who understand what you're dealing with. It would be separate from the department so there would be no mention of it in your file. I won't violate your privacy, Quincy, but I trust you to use the time to work through Jen's death. If you don't want to do it on your own with a PTSD group, the department will pay for therapy and your file will indicate you requested the therapy to deal with the stress of Friday night. It won't say anything about flashbacks or Afghanistan."

This couldn't be happening. Her life was fine. She'd put Afghanistan behind her. So what if the wound had never quite healed? Why change her life now, why rip the scab off and confront the guilt and anger and pain she'd buried? Especially now that Lindy had dumped her?

"And if I refuse?"

She didn't mean to be confrontational, but damn it, she was angry. She got that Connie was trying to take care of her, but she just wanted to go back to the way things were before Friday night, back to spending time with friends, back to her quiet life.

Connie straightened and held her eyes. "This isn't a request. It's an order, officer."

"Yes, ma'am." This was Chief Trubeck talking, not her friend Connie. There were consequences for disobeying an order. She'd never done it before and she wasn't going to start now. She forced herself to meet Connie's eyes. "How long?"

"I'm thinking two or three weeks working here at the station, but I'm willing to extend it if you feel you need the time." Chief Trubeck met Quincy's eyes. "I'm sorry, Quincy. I won't stand by and watch you sink into a deep depression again."

"Yes, ma'am." Quincy sat. She stared at her hands, not sure whether to apologize. Most of the department loved working with Connie because she took care of her people. Besides that, she and Connie were friends, and Quincy knew Connie would do everything she could do without compromising her principles to avoid adding to the stress of the accident.

"What should I say if anybody asks why I'm suddenly stuck in the office?"

"Tell them it's to avoid being harassed by the media." Chief Trubeck cleared her throat. "Are we okay, Quincy?"

Quincy straightened. "Yes, ma'am." She realized Connie had been prepared for her negative reaction but did it anyway. A good commanding officer. A good friend. The tension left her body.

Connie visibly relaxed. "So are you ready for some good news?"

Quincy stretched her legs. First thing today she'd had Lindy dumping her and now Connie was assigning her to desk duty and forcing her to deal with Jen's death, something she'd avoided for a long time. Hell yes, she wanted some good news. "I sure could use some."

Connie grabbed some papers off her desk and waved them. "I've started the paperwork for your promotion to detective. Given the city's financial situation and our tight budget, it won't be an easy sell, but I promise I'll put the full force of my position behind it. If it comes through, it'll mean a raise, no more uniforms, no more patrols, and did I say, no more being outside in the snow and cold all day."

Quincy sat back, stunned. The chief and several people at the hospital had mentioned promotion on Saturday, but she'd shrugged it off as wishful thinking given the budgetary problems the city was facing. Her goal when she joined the department had been to become a detective, and now she was close. Her eyes filled again. Damn, she wasn't usually so weepy.

"Thanks, Connie. I'm thrilled."

"The promotion is well-deserved even without the heroics of Friday night, but all the good press makes it a much, much easier sell. I'll do my best."

The chief pulled Quincy into a hug. "I'm so glad you managed to put that fire out, my friend." She kissed Quincy's cheek. "I hope you know I'm always available to talk as your chief or as your friend." She stepped back. "I don't have anything specific in mind for you to do today so take it easy. I'd take you out to lunch, but I have to prepare for the City Council meeting this evening."

"It's okay. I was planning to meet Gina for lunch wherever she is today."

"I'm giving you a couple of days to relax and unwind, so stay home, come in late, leave early, do whatever you feel like, then I'll have a couple of projects for you."

Everyone wanted a word with her today, it seemed, so it took a while to make her way from the chief's office to her desk. She sank into her chair, eyed the package sitting there, then called the mailroom. Reassured it had been checked for safety, she tore it open. And grinned. *Maybe this is what Connie was talking about.* The photographer had truly captured a beautiful moment between her and Lindy and had framed two of her photos to highlight her work. She picked up the handwritten note.

> *Dear Officer Adams ,*
> *You are my hero and I'm sorry for upsetting you and your friend. I did check and I do have the right to publish her picture with you. These pictures are gorgeous, if I say so myself, but I've paid attention to your friend's wishes and for today's paper I've used one that focuses more on you.*
>
> *The pictures capture the beauty and tenderness I saw between you and I hope you both will accept them as a peace offering.*
>
> *Sincerely,*
>
> *Patsy Mackenzie*
> *Photographer, Bergen Daily News*

Thank you, Ms. Patsy Mackenzie. Now she had a good reason to get in touch with Lindy. As she was stowing the pictures in her drawer, though, it dawned on her that she had no idea how to do that. She didn't know her last name or where she lived or worked. She hadn't even thought to get her license plate. *What an ass!*

Had the newspaper possibly identified Lindy? It wasn't hard to find a copy of the day's *Bergen Daily News* in the station. Sure enough, the photo Patsy Mackenzie took was on the front page. As promised, it showed her full face and Lindy in profile, making it difficult to identify her. The caption didn't name her, listing her only as a friend supporting the "hero officer," but the intense connection between them was as obvious in this photo as it was in the other two. Maybe Connie was right.

She could try Maggie, but if Maggie didn't know how to contact her, she'd have no choice but to wait for Lindy to call. Hopefully, as Connie had suggested, she only needed some time to process the weekend.

Sighing, she turned her attention to finishing her report of Friday night's accident. She tried, but her mind flitted between thoughts of Lindy and Jen and Connie's order to deal with Jen's death. She'd never considered herself a threat to anyone because of the flashbacks that occurred from time to time, but she understood now how she might be.

Flashbacks often occurred when under stress, not a good idea for a police officer who at any time might be called on to use her weapon in a stressful situation. She wasn't sure whether it was the specific situation, a woman trapped in a burning car, or whether she might flashback under other conditions, but she owed it to Connie, to her colleagues, and to the public to work it out.

CHAPTER ELEVEN

Gina, Quincy's closest lesbian friend and the only friend other than Amelia she shared her feelings with, eyed her as she approached their favorite booth in their favorite diner. "I hope it's not me you want to punch."

"What?" Quincy stopped midway in her slide into the booth facing Gina. "Am I that obvious?"

Gina fiddled with the straw in her Coke. "You are to me. What's going on, Quince?"

Before she could answer the waitress appeared. "Tuna on rye and black coffee as usual?"

Quincy nodded, then moved around to sit next to Gina, hoping to keep their conversation private. "Connie put me on desk duty for the next few weeks. Maybe longer. Because of them." She dipped her head toward the parking lot where the antennas of the TV vans that had tailed her from the station were visible and then at the three reporters who had followed her into the diner and were seated a few tables away.

She lowered her voice. "I flashed back to Afghanistan Friday night, and you know Connie sees all so she caught it. She says I put my life on hold when Jen died and I need to work through her death, because the flashbacks could endanger me and everyone around me if they occurred during a confrontation."

Gina looked away, took a breath, then nodded. "I think she's right."

"What?" Quincy reacted from the gut and made no effort to hide her anger.

"Not about hurting someone." Gina grasped Quincy's arm. "Don't get pissed at me too, but you haven't been yourself since you came back from Afghanistan. It's almost like you've been underwater or behind a glass wall. Visible but muffled. Here but not here. You know what I mean?"

Quincy kept her eyes on the paper napkin she was shredding.

"I'm sorry if you don't want to hear it, Quince, but we've been friends for a long time and I remember when you used to smile and laugh, when you were vibrant and alive, not muffled and shuffling through life." Gina squeezed Quincy's arm. "Needing help doesn't mean you're weak."

The waitress dropped their lunches off. Quincy sipped her coffee. "Yeah, I know." She took a bite of her sandwich. Gina concentrated on the stew she'd ordered.

So two of her friends agreed she needed to work on her feelings about Jen's death. And if Gina felt that way, she knew she'd probably discussed it with Amelia, who, no doubt, agreed as well. They were right. She'd left her heart and part of her soul on a dusty road in Afghanistan and had come home filled with guilt and a certainty that she didn't deserve to enjoy life. "Muffled and shuffling" summed up how she felt most of the time. But being with Lindy had reminded her of the joy in living, reminded her that happiness was possible. Perhaps it wouldn't happen with Lindy, but her response to Lindy gave her hope for the future. Still…

"I don't want to go back there. I'm afraid I'll fall apart again if I let myself feel the way I felt then."

Gina nodded. "I get it, Quince. Dealing with my feelings about Heather leaving me has been painful, but talking about it in therapy has allowed me to move on. I know our situations aren't really comparable, but I don't think you'll ever move past losing Jen the way you did without facing up to it." She picked up her fork and stabbed a piece of meat in her stew. "Is the chief sending you to see the department shrink?"

"No. She wants me to check out PTSD support groups for veterans."

"Good idea. I'm sure plenty of other vets are dealing with similar issues. I promise I'll be there for you in any way you need."

"Thanks." Quincy dabbed her eyes with her napkin. "And thanks for being honest with me." She smiled. "On a more positive note, Connie put me in for a promotion to detective. She thinks there's a good chance it will be approved because of the publicity and the support of the people I saved."

Gina lifted her Coke as if to toast. "Congratulations. You'll make a great detective." She waited patiently as a couple of patrons recognized Quincy and stopped by to say a few words, then she put a copy of the *Bergen Daily News* on the table.

"Okay, no more pussyfooting around. Time to spill every detail of your heroic evening, especially where you found this beauty and how this came to be the front page picture for the latest news about the accident."

"I promise a brain dump, but humor me and tell me first how it went with Heather this weekend."

Like the spouses of many police officers, Heather had resented Gina's shift work and her reluctance to discuss her job, and she hated the fear she felt every single day that Gina might not come home, that she might be killed on the job. But most of all she was angered by Gina's emotional unavailability and her unwillingness to go into therapy. Gina was devastated when Heather ended their relationship a year ago, and after the breakup she went into therapy to work on those issues. They had been together for five years and Gina loved Heather's daughters, now six and eight, as her own, and the girls considered Gina their other mom.

Luckily, Heather understood the importance of the relationship to Gina and the girls and encouraged her to see them on a regular basis. But six months ago Heather moved to Maryland to be close to her family, and since Gina had no legal standing with the girls, there was nothing she could do to stop her. Now Gina made the four plus-hour drive each way to see the girls in Maryland every other weekend unless she was working. Happily, Heather was supportive of that and occasionally made the drive north to relieve Gina.

Gina's smile dimmed. "It was okay. I stayed at Heather's. We had a heart-to-heart Saturday night after the kids were asleep. She still loves me and wants me in her life, but she's not in love with me. In fact, she's attracted to a lesbian she met at a PTA meeting and wants to start dating. Driving home, I realized I've been treading water waiting for her to take me back."

She took a deep breath. "But the girls are great. We did some fun things. And they loved the books you sent them. Heather and I are going to work out a schedule for them to spend time with me here, so that part is good. And she agreed to come here for the Thanksgiving weekend so the four of us can spend the holiday together."

Quincy hugged her. "I know it hurts now, but we both know how difficult it is for police marriages. Heather is clear that she can't deal with it, so it's probably better for you in the long run that she cut you loose. You need and deserve someone who understands and supports you. We both know if you open yourself up, the ladies will flock to you." Out of the corner of her eye she saw the reporters jotting notes.

"Yeah, yeah." Gina dried her tears. "I know you're right about Heather, but it still hurts. On the other hand, you hear so many horror stories about lesbians being denied access to the children they've raised, I'm lucky she's supports and encourages my relationship with the girls. But enough about me. I'm dying to hear about your weekend."

"Just so you know, those reporters," Quincy lifted her chin in the direction of their table, "are going to think you're my girlfriend." Gina was a couple of inches shorter than she and light to her dark: short blond hair, laughing blue eyes, a pale complexion, a strong jaw, and a wiry build. In a nutshell, she was a handsome dyke with a great sense of humor. "Not that I mind."

Gina laughed. "I've been called a lot worse things. So tell me already."

Quincy told her about the accident, about her despair after she'd left the scene, about watching Lindy, about Maggie arranging for Lindy to drive her home, about how Lindy had comforted her and helped her understand what she was feeling, and about how Lindy had encouraged her to think about life rather than death.

"Lindy pulled me back from the edge and warmed places that have been frozen since Jen died. She made me feel hopeful and open in way that I haven't since I met Jen." Quincy smiled, remembering. "She's a great cook. And she's fun to be with. I can't even imagine where I'd be if she hadn't been there with me through the weekend."

She unwrapped the photographs Patty Mackenzie had taken of the two of them at the hospital and put them on the table so Gina could see them but the reporters couldn't. "The photographer who took the picture that's in the newspaper also snapped these Saturday at the hospital after we visited the people I pulled out of the burning vehicles."

Gina shook her head. "Geez, Quince, own it, own your bravery. How about saying we visited the people 'whose lives I saved.'" She studied the pictures. "These are even better than the one in the newspaper. You both look like you're in love. When do I meet her?"

Quincy sighed. "There's more." She described how they'd parted in the morning and how hollow she'd felt.

Gina squeezed Quincy's arm. "Sorry, I just thought—"

"It's okay, Gina. After I talked to Connie, then saw these pictures, I realized I wasn't crazy, that Lindy was feeling what I was feeling. She wouldn't talk about herself, so I have no idea how to contact her or what her life is like. She said there was no one else, but for all I know she's in a bad relationship and carries a packed suitcase in case she has to make a quick escape. In any case, I hope Connie is right, that maybe she just needs some time. In the meantime, I'll work on my own problems. How's that for a good attitude?" She sipped her coffee.

"It's great. I like Ms. Positivity much better than Ms. Muffle and Shuffle."

Standing in front of the diner a little while later, they embraced despite the cameras pointed at them.

"This should confuse them, first the picture with Lindy and now me." Gina straightened her uniform. "I'm hoping you're able to work through the Jen stuff, Quince. She would want you to move on. Let me know if you need anything. And I'm rooting for this thing with Lindy to work out."

"I hope so too. She's the reason I'm thinking that dealing with Afghanistan is a good thing."

CHAPTER TWELVE

Quincy was pondering her conversations with Connie and Gina and struggling with the idea of letting herself feel what she'd felt that day in Afghanistan when Connie stopped by her desk that afternoon.

"I really don't have anything for you today so take the rest of the day off."

As the chief turned toward her office, Quincy reached for her coat. She glanced out the window. There were still some TV vans and some cameras outside. She needed a diversion. "Chief."

Connie looked back.

"Um, is there some way I can leave without them following me?" She pointed to the window.

Connie frowned. "I didn't realize they were still here. Give me a moment." She looked around, spoke to a few officers, and headed out the door. The officers grabbed their coats and scrambled to follow her. Quincy watched Connie cross the street and speak to the press contingent still behind the barrier.

After a few minutes, the officers cleared them out and Connie returned to the office.

"Just to be safe, take my car and go." She handed Quincy her keys. "Give me your keys. If you haven't brought my car back before I leave, I'll track you down and do the exchange."

"Thanks, Chief." She sprinted for the door. Happy to be out of the stuffy station, she inhaled the crisp cold air and stood in the brilliant sunshine for a minute before getting into the chief's car. At the exit to the parking lot, she turned toward her apartment, then on impulse continued on to Van Saun Park. A walk would clear her head.

The walkways still had not been shoveled and staying upright on the snow-packed paths required some concentration, but her mind was free enough for memories to creep in, memories of talking with Lindy as they strode through the snow, of their laughing snowball fight in the icy cold just yesterday, and older memories of laughing and talking with Jen as they strode through the stinking heat of the desert.

Two very different women. Two different aches. The ache of guilt and loss for Jen and the ache for what might have been with Lindy. She removed her glove to dry the tears streaming from her eyes, surprised to find them frozen. Fitting. Since Jen died, she'd been frozen inside, looking out at the world but not really in it. She let the tears flow. She missed Jen, her laughing and teasing, the caring and the love, but after five years the missing felt more like a dull ache.

And now she would miss Lindy. They'd only had a weekend together, but it had been intimate and caring and playful, and it felt...loving. She stopped to admire their snowman and to stare at their snow angels and she wondered again why Lindy had named hers Quincy.

Perhaps missing Lindy would be a dull ache someday, but right now it was a sharp pain. She walked until the sun dimmed and a wind came up. Then, shivering, she headed for the parking lot. She needed to talk to Amelia. As soon as she was back in her car, she texted her.

Need to talk ☹

Amelia texted right back.
F2F better. Come to dinner at 6:30 ♥

She felt better already. She had time to go home, shower, and change into comfortable clothes but not enough time to sink deeper into the sadness. On the way she stopped at the station to swap cars, then picked up a bottle of red wine and arrived at Amelia's a little before six thirty.

Amelia's husband, Jackson, a computer expert, worked at home and did all the cooking, so Quincy wasn't surprised to find him putting the finishing touches on the dinner of beef stroganoff, egg noodles, broccoli, and salad. "Good timing. I'll be ready in fifteen." He hugged her and handed her a glass of wine as Amelia came into the kitchen to greet her.

Right on schedule, Jackson served dinner. He'd read the newspaper reports, but he wanted to hear her take on the accident so, as they ate, he peppered Quincy with questions. When she'd told him all, he grinned.

"Now I want to know all about this mysterious woman Amelia mentioned." He left the room and came back waving the newspaper. "Is she the woman making goo-goo eyes at you in this picture?"

"I don't know about goo-goo eyes, but that's the woman Amelia met." Quincy told him about bringing Lindy home but didn't mention how she and Lindy had parted that morning. Then she changed the topic and they chatted a little about Jackson's latest project. When they finished eating, he stood and kissed Quincy's cheek. "As always it's been great seeing you, Quincy, but I have work to do." He kissed Amelia, then left for his home office and the computer program he was developing for a client.

Amelia looked up from loading the dishwasher. "Talk to me. You look miserable."

Quincy rinsed the last dish before answering. She knew she'd have to go over all of this with Amelia, but she didn't mind because Amelia always helped her clarify her thoughts.

"Lindy's not interested in seeing me again. Or at least that's the impression I got from what she said this morning. Give me a second, there's something I want to show you." She dried her hands and retrieved the package with the photos she'd brought in with her. "Connie thinks she just needs some time."

Amelia closed the dishwasher. "She certainly seemed into you Saturday afternoon when I saw you. And it sure looks that way in the picture in the newspaper."

"But she gave me a definite no when I asked her to go out on a date with me. She said she needs to be alone, that she can't see me. I kind of forced her to take my number, but she didn't offer hers. Yet…" Quincy handed Amelia both the photos she'd brought with her.

Amelia looked at one then the other. "Nice. Very nice. I would say definitely interested. Tell me what happened. How did you *force* her to take your number?" She handed the photos back to Quincy.

"When she said she couldn't see me I groveled a bit and asked if she might change her mind. She said she doubted she would, but if I gave her my number she would call if she did." Quincy could see Amelia holding back a smile. "Okay, so maybe I didn't exactly force her."

After hearing the whole story, Amelia agreed with Connie that Lindy probably just needed some time. They were sitting in the living room finishing their wine when Quincy told Amelia about Connie's observing her flashback Friday night, about hearing her call Grace Jen, and ordering her to deal with it by attending a PTSD group for veterans or see the department therapist.

"I was angry when Connie said I'd closed a door after Jen and left part of myself behind it. Then Gina said I've been cut off since I came home. And—"

Amelia rolled her eyes.

"I suppose you agree, smarty pants?" Quincy shook her head. "Let me guess. You three have discussed this more than once?"

"We're your friends, Quince. We care. You've been muted, not yourself, since you came back from Afghanistan, but whenever one of us tried to bring it up you got angry and denied it. We miss the old Quincy."

Grace had cracked the door open, Lindy had pushed it a little wider, and Quincy could almost hear it slowly swinging open all the way. She was feeling exposed.

"Well, then, you'll be glad to know that when I was walking earlier, I realized I've been frozen inside." She sniffed. "I'm afraid, Meelie. I'm afraid I'll break if I let myself go back there. But the nightmares have returned, and the way I felt with Lindy reminded me what life used to feel like. Of what it could be." She swiped at her tears. "I want to open the door, but I don't want talking about it to drag on for years."

Amelia slid closer and slipped her arm around Quincy's waist. "You'll feel the pain again, but you won't break. I won't let that happen. Neither will your other friends. As for the time, people spend years in therapy because they avoid dealing with the issues that bring them there. If you really want to do this, deal with it head on."

"Connie's idea of a PTSD group for veterans sounds like a good idea," she continued. "You'll be with people who understand what you went through and how it's affecting your life. It seems to me it would be easier to express your fear of breaking to a group that probably has felt the same thing. You can do this. I love you as you are, sweetie, but I remember how you were with Jen, always playful and laughing. It would be wonderful to have that part of you back. I'm sure the VA runs multiple groups. I suggest you go in and talk to the group leaders, find one you feel comfortable with. I have a friend at the VA who runs several groups. I'm not sure they include PTSD, but I could call her if you would like."

By the end of the evening, Quincy had arranged to meet Dr. Giles, Amelia's friend at the VA, and steeled herself to plunge headlong into a PTSD group. Preferably an all-women's group, run by a woman.

CHAPTER THIRTEEN

Lindy studied today's *Bergen Daily News*. Babs subscribed and it was delivered every day. And every time she picked up the damn paper lately there was another article about Quincy and the people she'd rescued. The articles, with pictures of the rescued person and their family, were a not-so-subtle organized effort to get Quincy a medal and a promotion, but they were very effective. Lindy assumed Grace was behind the series.

Today's article featuring Grace was the most dramatic. She described the quiet in the car as she drove through the snow and her family slept, the blast of wind that cleared the snow just long enough for her to see the accident unfolding in front of her, her panic when she put on her brakes and realized she wasn't going to be able to stop. She talked about the dreamlike quality of the heavy snowfall, of trying to steer as the car fishtailed and slid sideways toward the pileup in front of her. Lindy could almost hear the sound of crunching metal as her car rammed the others. And then Grace described seeing in the rearview mirror a huge truck sliding slowly toward them. She was knocked out by the impact, but when she woke she knew she was trapped in the burning car, knew she was going to die.

She told of trying to rouse her husband and the horror of realizing that he and their four children were all unconscious and would die with her. She went on to describe her relief when Quincy appeared and carried her children from the car and placed them far enough from the burning vehicle to ensure that when it blew up they would be safe. She was thrilled that despite his weight Quincy was able to also pull her husband Mike, a former professional football player, from the car and drag him to safety with their children.

Grace was an excellent writer and storyteller because, even knowing the story, Lindy found herself breathless as she read. Grace described her terror watching the flames lick at the gas tank and urging Quincy to run, to save herself. She talked about her shock that Quincy chose to risk her own life in an attempt to save hers.

Lindy could feel Grace's panic and then her relief when the fire was out and she knew she would live. Grace's being overwhelmed and grateful and in awe that Quincy had braved death to save her came through loud and clear throughout the article. And her talking about getting to know Quincy and appreciating her as a person as well as a hero was touching. There were two pictures, one of Grace alone in a wheelchair and another of Mike and the children surrounding Grace. Lindy smiled. They looked happy. She wondered whether Quincy had visited as she'd promised and whether she and Grace had connected. She felt a pang of loss. She missed Quincy.

The last part of the article encouraged the city of Hackensack to reward Quincy with a promotion and a medal for bravery beyond the call of duty. Grace encouraged readers to call City Hall and to write letters and postcards in support of Quincy.

Lindy wiped her tears and reached for her scissors. She carefully cut the article out and added it to all the articles she'd collected about the accident and Quincy. She looked up at the front-page photo of her and Quincy that she'd framed and at the collage of the pictures she'd printed of their day playing in the snow and let the tears flow. She'd get over it eventually, but in the meantime it was painful to think about what might have been with Quincy if she, Lindy, didn't have so many emotional and physical scars. If she wasn't too terrified to ever trust again. Until now being alone had worked for her. She felt safe and was somewhat happy. Quincy made her yearn for more. She just had to resist until it passed.

She heard Babs' key in the lock and quickly moved everything into the drawer in her bedroom. If Babs saw what she was doing, she would give Lindy a lecture about screwing up her life. Babs didn't seem to get that she'd done that long before meeting Quincy.

CHAPTER FOURTEEN

Quincy paced the waiting room. She'd allocated too much time to drive to the Veterans Medical Center in East Orange and had arrived early. Waiting to see Dr. Giles was nerve-wracking. She considered leaving but, confident that not following Connie's orders would not have a happy outcome, she forced herself to endure the torture. The hum of the noise machine outside the office door was comforting, and so was the fact that she couldn't hear voices from the office. She pivoted at the sound of the door opening behind her, not sure whether she was more afraid of facing the veteran in the session before her or Dr. Giles.

A red-haired woman in fatigues acknowledged Quincy with a smile, put on her cap, and walked out the door. The woman who remained was in uniform, a major. Quincy instinctively started to salute.

"At ease, soldier. We don't worry about rank in here."

They stared at each other for a moment.

"Officer Adams, I recognize you from your picture in the news. I'm Dr. Cynthia Giles. Please come in and have a seat."

She swept an arm in front of her and stepped back to make room. Quincy stood while Dr. Giles closed the door and walked around to take what was probably her usual seat, leaving Quincy the choice between the sofa and an easy chair. She sat in the chair opposite Dr. Giles. Amelia hadn't mentioned a word about Giles being an officer or being attractive, some might even say sexy. In her late forties, with wavy brown hair, gentle brown eyes, and a curvy figure even her uniform couldn't hide, she gave off warm, caring vibes and something else, something sensual.

She didn't flinch from Quincy's frank evaluation, but Quincy did when she realized she was ogling the therapist. She lowered her eyes, then crossed her legs and wrapped her arms around herself to cover her discomfort. How did this work? Was she just supposed to start talking about her problems? She looked at the therapist.

Dr. Giles seemed to be assessing her as well, but then their eyes met and the doctor smiled. "May I call you Quincy?"

Relieved to be asked a question she could answer, she nodded. "Please do."

"Amelia tells me you're interested in an all-women's PTSD group." Apparently Amelia's word was good enough for Dr. Giles because she didn't wait for Quincy to confirm. "It just happens that I run the only all-women's PTSD groups at this VA facility. We meet once a week as a group and I meet with everyone in the group privately once a month. Tell me about your service."

Quincy had expected to be asked about her problem, not about her service, so it took her a moment to get started, but she was able to provide a full account without having to mention Jen.

"I also served in Iraq and Afghanistan, as did most of the women in the PTSD groups. If you join us, you'll find that the reasons for PTSD vary, some battlefield, some…personal experience, but all related to time in the military. How long ago did the…event or events occur?"

"About five years ago in Afghanistan."

"Did something happen recently that brought it front and center?"

"Yes. I had a flashback at the accident you mentioned. And my nightmares have come back."

"I see." She made a note. "Did you deal with this in therapy when it happened? Or any time after?"

"No."

"Do you have any reservations about becoming part of a group?"

Quincy shifted, feeling ready to run. "Some. I want to deal with this, but I don't want to spend forever in therapy. How long will this take, Dr. Giles?"

"No need to be formal in here. Call me Cynthia or Major, if you prefer." She rubbed her chin and seemed to be considering the question.

"I have no magic wand, Quincy. You're the key player. The time needed depends on why you're here and how open you are to dealing with what comes up. If you focus, it can take as little as a couple of months. Some women leave right after, but because our experience in the war-time military is unique and not easily understood by those around us, others choose to stay in the group for support. I've had pretty good success with women who overcome their fears and risk reliving the experience that's bothering them. But there's no way to know until you're in it. Sorry I can't be more specific. Any other reservations?"

"I've never been in therapy or any kind of group thing so I'm not sure I'll be able to talk about...about it."

"You're not required to talk about your issue until you're ready, but I will ask you to tell the group about your military experience, much the way you did today. The women are friendly and very supportive of each other so that makes it easier to be honest and open. I have spots in my Wednesday and Friday night groups. If you can make it, I think the Wednesday group would be a good fit. What do you say?"

"What if I don't like it or maybe I can't open up?"

Dr. Giles laughed. "Hey, we don't take prisoners here. It's voluntary. I hope you stay long enough to give it a chance, but you're free to leave at anytime."

"What about confidentiality?"

"I make notes, but they're for my personal use. No one else sees them. The group members agree that what goes on in the group stays in the group. Most of the women acknowledge to family and friends they're in a group for women veterans without saying why. You can discuss with the other members how you want to handle the situation if you run into each other out in the real world. Most just say they know each other from their time in the military. We've never had a problem." She smiled. "Would you like to join the group?"

Quincy rubbed her throbbing temple. Actually, she didn't want to join anything, but she knew there was no going back now that the door was ajar. And she wanted to do it fast, like ripping off a bandage. She took a deep breath. "Yes."

"So I'll see you Wednesday at seven thirty. We meet here in my office. How would you like me to address you in the group?"

"Quincy is fine." She took out her phone and updated her calendar.

Dr. Giles stood. Quincy followed her to the door.

The therapist put a hand on Quincy's shoulder. "I know it feels scary, Quincy, but as a soldier and as a police officer you've faced things a lot scarier than your feelings."

CHAPTER FIFTEEN

For her first evening out with friends since Babs' birthday three weeks earlier, Lindy dressed to be attractive but not seductive. While she wasn't looking for a relationship or even a hookup, she did enjoy the attention she got at Maggie's. And she loved the dancing. But now standing in Maggie's parking lot she was anxious, fluctuating between fearing she would run into Quincy and hoping she would run into Quincy. What would she say? How would she feel seeing her in the flesh again?

In the weeks since that weekend, she hadn't been able to get Quincy out of her mind. Or, judging by the lingering feelings of loss and a longing for something she'd glimpsed with Quincy, out of her heart. For the first time in years, her aloneness did not feel good. *Well, you can't always get what you want*, she reminded herself. *This too shall pass.* But the clichés didn't offer any comfort. Would she ever get back to her safe comfortable, happy life alone?

The *Bergen Daily News* wasn't helping. The latest accident-related article featured Bonnie. It was syrupy and suck-up describing a dramatic rescue by Quincy when she'd in fact said she had no memory of the rescue. It also seemed to hint that she and Quincy were dating. A grainy picture of Quincy holding Bella, the baby, in her arms, accompanied the article. She realized it must have been taken in the hospital when they visited because she was partially in the picture, standing behind Quincy. She was pretty sure no one had asked to take a picture of Quincy with the baby that day and since this was the first time a picture of Quincy appeared in any of the articles, she assumed Bonnie hadn't asked permission to use it. Lindy ground her teeth at the thought of Bonnie The Bitch actively pursuing Quincy. She had no claim on Quincy, no right to be jealous, yet she was. It made her angry and sad and lonely in a way she hadn't been before. She really needed to stop reading the newspaper, to forget Quincy, to stop freaking out about her. She took a deep breath and used her coat sleeve to dry her eyes. *Damn.* She was here to have fun, not dwell on Quincy.

Her eyes darted around the room as she entered Maggie's, but there was no sign of Quincy. Was she sad or happy about that? She couldn't tell. She sat at the table with her group and once again refused to dance with Lisbeth, the only one of their friends who didn't seem to get the message and continually pushed for more. She sipped her seltzer, talked to sharp-eyed Nora who had noticed the tension with Lisbeth, then got up to dance by herself, something that always gave her great pleasure. But she couldn't keep her eyes from going to the mirror hanging over the bar, hoping to catch Quincy sitting there watching her.

Oh, man, this is downright annoying, taking the pleasure out of the music and the dancing. She closed her eyes and danced, but she was unable to settle into the zone. She was about to give up when someone tapped her shoulder. Thinking it was another woman asking her to dance, she opened her eyes with a sharp no ready to puncture whoever couldn't take a hint. But when she found herself face-to-face with Maggie, she flushed and stopped moving. "Uh, hi."

"Hey, Lindy, I was just wondering what happened with Quincy?"

"What do you mean, what happened?" She rolled a strand of her hair between her fingers as she shifted from one foot to the other. "I drove her home like you asked. I even stayed with her because she didn't want to be alone, then the weekend was over, and I went back to my life. I assume she did the same."

Nodding, Maggie rubbed her chin. "So it was okay? I mean staying with her?"

Lindy glanced back at her friends, hoping for rescue. "She was a perfect gentlewoman if that's what you're asking. She's really special and I enjoyed the time we spent together."

"But? I hear a qualification in there."

"But I'm a loner, Maggie. I have a few friends that I spend time with and I'm not looking for anything or anybody else, so I said goodbye Monday morning and that's that."

"I noticed you looking at the bar a lot, so I thought maybe you were looking for her. Sorry to bother you." Maggie turned toward the bar.

Lindy put a hand on Maggie's arm. She had to know. "How is Quincy doing? She was struggling with the whole hero gig and maybe some old issues. Is she all right?"

"I haven't seen her, just talked on the phone. She seems okay, but she's not one to show her feelings. She asked about you, so I wondered what happened."

"By staying with Quincy to take care of her, I went way beyond my comfort zone with strangers. I felt good helping her, but that's it as far as I'm concerned." She felt uneasy, unsure whether she wanted Maggie to give Quincy that message or not.

"Hey, Lindy, let's dance."

She flooded with relief hearing Babs' voice. "Are we done, Maggie?"

"Sure, Lindy, thanks. And thanks for helping Quincy. She says you saved her life."

Yeah, that's me, Lindy, the hero. Not.

Had she saved Quincy? She understood about sliding into darkness and pain, so maybe having someone to talk to and laugh with, someone to take care of her, had saved Quincy from that. It had felt good to her too. But her time with Quincy had disrupted her life and now she was struggling to find the peace she'd had before that weekend. The peace she'd worked really hard to find.

She turned into Babs' arms. "Thanks for coming to my rescue."

"I could see you were uncomfortable. What did she want?"

"She wanted to know what happened with Quincy. They're friends, so I don't know why she's asking me. I didn't know what to say so I told her the truth. She told me Quincy had asked about me."

Babs swung away and they danced that way for a while then came back together. "So Quincy is interested?"

"I knew that, Babs. I just don't know what I can do about it."

Babs spun Lindy. "You could call her and ask her out for coffee or something."

"It's too complicated."

"I don't know, hon." Babs pulled her close. "She's interested. You're interested. It's only as complicated as you want it to be."

"Easy for you to say." Lindy danced away, leaving Babs on her own. Could she call Quincy?

She was aware of Babs watching her as she closed her eyes and reached for the music, reached for the calm, but both eluded her. She couldn't get thoughts of Quincy out of her mind. She opened her eyes and Maggie was staring at her. She spun around and Babs was dancing with Dani but watching her. At their table, Lisbeth was staring with that hungry look on her face. And ringing the dance floor observing her every move was the small group of women who always asked her to dance though she always said no.

She couldn't do this tonight. There was no zone for her. She said goodnight to her friends at the table, kissed Babs, waved to Maggie, and swept out of the bar before anyone could approach her. Time to be alone. Really alone. Another night yearning and crying for what she couldn't have.

CHAPTER SIXTEEN

Quincy was struggling to stay optimistic. Despite having witnessed Jen's death, she had spent months afterward somehow expecting her to walk through the door. The three weeks she'd been waiting for Lindy to call were somewhat easier—because Lindy was alive and going about her life. But they were also unbearable—because Lindy was alive and lived nearby but might not choose to come back to see whether they could have more together. She was on tenterhooks waiting for her phone to ring, and every day that went by made it less likely it would. In her head she'd arbitrarily given Lindy a month to call, but the days dragged. And, though she forced herself to focus on learning during the day, to focus on coaching girls basketball at the Y on Saturdays, and to focus on immersing herself in other worlds, other places, other lives by reading in the evenings, she couldn't stop thinking about how she'd felt with Lindy and wanting more.

Yesterday she'd concluded if Lindy hadn't called by the end of the allotted month, it would mean she wasn't interested. After all they'd only spent that one weekend together. And obviously the weekend meant more to her than it did to Lindy. So, rather than be pathetic she would mail one of the pictures to her and move on.

And then she remembered again that she didn't know Lindy's last name or where she lived or worked. *What an asshole.* She could probably track her down through Maggie, but Lindy had made it pretty clear she didn't want to be contacted and she would respect that. She could set all the deadlines she wanted. But unless she wanted to appear to be stalking Lindy, her only option was to wait. Not something she was particularly good at.

Deadly desk duty wasn't helping. She felt like a trapped animal having to be indoors all day doing boring paperwork. She started to wonder if being a detective was the best job for her. The only positive thing about desk duty was the fixed hours and the freedom to do things like go out to lunch and stay in touch with the people she'd rescued. She'd been welcomed into the families of those she'd rescued and once they got past the hero thing, they'd connected in a deep way, like close family. She and Mama were close and she'd had a happy childhood, but she'd always envied friends with large connected families. Her bond with Grace was the strongest. Despite their lives being so different, they connected on a visceral level and were becoming close friends. Grace was the only one still in the hospital and Quincy stopped by frequently with lunch for the two of them.

As much as she enjoyed the opportunity to socialize, when the chief summoned her to her office she was hopeful she'd be assigned to patrol again. Only the local press showed up from time to time now, usually in response to the articles written by the people she'd rescued. She knocked.

"Come in."

The chief was at her desk. She smiled and waved Quincy to a chair facing her.

"Thanks to the articles in the *Bergen Daily News*, the mayor and council have received a lot of mail and phone calls supporting your promotion. They'll vote on it this week and I'd be very surprised if they didn't approve it. To give you a head start, I've decided to have you shadow John on the Tiffany Maggio investigation."

Quincy felt as if her smile might split her face. She'd been following the disappearance of the twelve-year-old girl in the papers and Detective John Field was part of the countywide kidnapping task force. She'd never dreamed she'd have the opportunity to be involved in something like that.

"You won't be an official member so you won't be allowed to do anything on your own, but you'll learn a lot just by sitting in on meetings and observing how John and the other detectives work the case."

Quincy was so excited she had an impulse to kiss Connie, but they always tried to be professional in the office so she ignored it. "Thank you, Chief. I'm overwhelmed. Is John okay with this or does he feel like he'll be babysitting?"

"He enjoys teaching and he likes and respects you, so he was enthusiastic when I proposed the arrangement. He's already cleared it with the leader of the task force, so you're good to go. Meet with him when he gets back to the station later and figure out a schedule."

She spent the next two hours obsessing about the proper way for a detective to dress. John usually wore a suit, but she didn't own any suits. She called Amelia to discuss it. As a social worker she came into contact with detectives from the surrounding towns, and it seemed to her that the few women detectives she'd worked with usually wore a jacket but not necessarily a suit. She figured it was to cover their guns. Later when she had a chance to talk to her again, Connie said a jacket and slacks would be fine and offered one of her jackets if Quincy didn't have one. But she did.

The next morning Quincy attended her first task force meeting. Since it was led by the FBI and staffed with a combination of FBI agents and detectives from local police departments, she'd expected lots of posturing and infighting. She was pleasantly surprised to find everyone focused on finding the girl and little visible jockeying for power. She listened and took notes.

Life became more interesting as she worked side by side with John, attending task force meetings, taking notes while he questioned witnesses, then writing up the reports. Best of all, he used her as a sounding board for his thoughts on the case and was happy to answer her questions. She loved the work and felt like she was learning and contributing. At night she studied the reports they received from the task force, looking for clues.

But the investigation seemed to be going nowhere, and every day the child wasn't found increased the likelihood she would be murdered—if that hadn't happened already. Quincy, like everyone on the task force, became more and more worried and frustrated. At a rancorous meeting of the group, the task force leaders decided they would review everything from the beginning and have all the witnesses re-interviewed by different detectives to see whether they'd pick up something new.

It was on one of their routine follow-up interviews that Quincy asked a question that led to a break in the case. The woman had been the last person to see the girl before she disappeared. Quincy and John sat down in the woman's living room to go over the facts with her again. Her answers were all the same. Quincy had been reading a book on interview techniques and one of them seemed like it might work with this witness. She exchanged a glance with John and he nodded, seeming to understand that she wanted to ask a question.

"Mrs. Forrest." The woman swiveled to look at Quincy. "I'd like to try something if you're willing."

The woman clutched the neck of her sweater. "Well, it depends on what it is."

Quincy smiled, trying to reassure her. "Would you close your eyes, take a few breaths, and try to picture the day you saw Tiffany on the street?" She watched until the woman relaxed a bit. "What time of day is it and what is the light like?"

"It's afternoon. About three thirty, you know when the kids are on the way home from school. And it was raining off and on, so it's gloomy."

"Is there anyone on the street? What do you see and hear?"

Mrs. Forrest squeezed her eyes tighter as if trying to clear her vision. "Now and then a car. I hear the swoosh as they drive by and laughter, girls laughing."

"Where are you? Can you see Tiffany?"

"I'm standing in front of the movie theater waiting for my friend to arrive. Tiffany is across the street at the bus stop talking to three girls. The rain starts again and her friends run in the direction of the nearby coffee shop. But Tiffany opens her umbrella and waits at the bus stop. She leans into the street and gazes in the direction the bus will come from, then turns and sees me watching her. She waves."

"What is Tiffany wearing?"

"A blue jacket and a red knit hat."

"Okay, continue to focus on the scene and let me know when something changes."

Mrs. Forrest's eyelids fluttered. "My friend arrives. I hug her and I see Tiffany over her shoulder so she's still there."

"Take a minute and look around the street. Was anybody else nearby? Were cars going by? Could you still see Tiffany?"

"We jump back because a car speeds through a puddle on the street next to where we're standing. I look up and notice Tiffany shivering on the other side of the street. My friend suggests we go into the theater and I glance back at Tiffany to see if the bus has arrived. She's leaning in the window of a car."

"What color and make of car? And do you recognize the driver?"

"A man is driving, but I can't see his face. The car is light blue and has a smashed rear fender."

"Did Tiffany get in the car?"

"No. We got in line. I heard a car door slam and looked across the street, but the bus had pulled in, blocking my view of the sidewalk."

"Was the car still there?"

The woman frowned. "No, the car was driving away. Then the bus left and Tiffany was gone. I assume she got on the bus."

Quincy glanced at John. In previous interviews the woman had been adamant that Tiffany had waved and boarded the bus.

"But you didn't actually see her get on the bus or get in the blue car?"

"No." Her eyes popped open. "Oh, God." She covered her face, realizing she'd misled the other detectives who'd interviewed her.

John called it in as she drove to the task force office. Detectives were already sifting through the reports of possible suspects and they came up with two light blue cars, one owned by a neighbor of the Maggio family, the other by a male teacher at the middle school Tiffany attended. The neighbor was an elderly woman. The agent sent to the school to look at the teacher's car confirmed that the rear fender was smashed.

Some of her friends had reported that the teacher paid a lot of attention to Tiffany so he was on the list of suspects, but nothing had tied him to Tiffany after she left school that day. Until now. It took another hour and a half to do the paperwork and assemble a SWAT team to accompany the task force detectives to the isolated farmhouse Greg Balzer rented about twenty miles from Teaneck, where Tiffany lived and Balzer taught school. Quincy was thrilled to be included with the group going to his house. A team was sent to the middle school to bring in Balzer.

Everything was quiet at the farmhouse. They knocked, called out, "FBI. Open the door," and, getting no response, rammed the door and swarmed through the house. Tiffany was found handcuffed to a pipe in the root cellar. She was distraught and dirty but unharmed. Apparently she was just Balzer's latest victim. During the search of the house they found a notebook with the names and pictures of other girls he'd kidnapped and sold to a sex trafficker over the years. It also had enough detail to lead the FBI to the leaders of the group.

Since John was the one officially on the case, he got the credit for getting the details that broke the case from the witness, though he made it clear that Quincy had elicited the information. She didn't care. She'd had enough of being a "hero," and now that the press had lost interest in her the last thing she wanted was to incite them again. The hugs she got from Tiffany and her parents were enough for her. Besides she was truly thankful to John for treating her as an equal and giving her the opportunity to question the witness.

CHAPTER SEVENTEEN

The chief had been lobbying for Quincy's promotion since the day after the accident. And the newspaper articles, instigated by the chief, according to Grace, had stoked public support. So when, as the chief predicted, her promotion and the medal for bravery were announced, Quincy wasn't surprised. Since it came a few days after Tiffany Maggio was rescued, she wondered whether her involvement in solving the case had tipped the scales in her favor.

Tonight, nearly five weeks since the accident, she was being awarded a medal for bravery. She'd hoped for an intimate ceremony with the survivors, her friends, and a few city officials, but they'd booked the high school auditorium, so she was resigned to it being much larger. She'd have skipped it if she could, but she knew it was important to the department and to the people whose lives she'd saved. And, in her head, Lindy urged her to accept that she was a hero.

As often happened when she let her mind drift, memories of the accident morphed into thoughts of Lindy and the weekend they'd spent together. The month deadline she'd set for Lindy to call had passed, and every day that went by made it less likely she would. She hadn't given up hope, though. She'd discussed the issue with Dr. Giles and realized that the month was an arbitrary deadline she'd set. In reality, she had issues that needed to be resolved before she could truly consider being in a healthy relationship, and she was still working on them. Perhaps Lindy needed time too. Hopefully, they would be ready at the same time. Or not. Time would tell.

The ping of an incoming text interrupted Quincy's musings. She stepped out of the shower, quickly dried herself, then responded to Gina.

I'll be ready at 6:45.

She brushed her hair, then checked herself in the full-length mirror. Her dress uniform fit perfectly, her dress shoes were spit-shined to perfection, and her hair was just the right length. She popped her cap on. Not too bad. She wished Lindy could see her.

She laughed. As if it was about looks. Lindy had seen her at her worst, with blood and smoke and despair on her face, and had gone home with her, a stranger, and held and comforted her. She blew out a breath. Tonight was a time to celebrate the lives she'd saved, not mourn the loss of Lindy. She would always be grateful to Lindy for saving her that weekend and reminding her of what life could be. She was ready to accept that she'd lost Lindy for now. At the same time, she was hoping, futile as it might be, that Lindy might show up tonight.

The doorbell rang. Her driver had arrived. When she opened the door, Gina whistled.

"Mighty nice, Officer Adams. You are handsome, in a dark-eyed, dark-haired, olive-skinned, sexy Italian way." She kissed Quincy, a quick brush of the lips. "If we hadn't failed so miserably at sex in high school, I might fall for you."

"Yeah, yeah. We both know we're better friends than we were lovers." Quincy grabbed her dress coat from the hall closet and followed Gina to her car.

Gina grinned as she drove out of the parking lot. "Ready for this?"

"I'm a little nervous, you know, hearing people say sappy things about me, but I'm as ready as I'll ever be."

She gazed out the side window. *I'd be a thousand times better if Lindy was at my side. She'd ground me and with a lifted eyebrow or a smile or a gentle poke in the side help me deal with the praise and the attention.*

Gina glanced away from the road. "Don't worry, you won't be facing this alone. All our friends will be there to support you and keep you real. We need to make sure your halo doesn't get so big you can't fit through normal-sized doorways."

Following Connie's instructions, Quincy entered through a side door at the high school, went through the door to the left, and found the backstage area of the auditorium. *Whoa.* She'd expected the chief and the mayor and maybe some members of the city council, but not all these people. Then the crowd opened, revealing four wheelchairs, one of which rolled toward her. A grinning Grace, pushed by Morgan, her ten-year-old daughter, opened her arms. Quincy leaned down and hugged her, sure it was no coincidence that she was wearing the jewelry she given to Quincy when she'd thought she would die She should have realized her number one fan wouldn't miss this for anything.

The others Quincy had saved, including Grace's husband and children followed, crowding around her, some still in casts and bandages. She hugged everyone, then greeted the other three in wheelchairs—Bonnie DiLeo, Syd Bloom, and Carl Lewis. Bonnie tried to pull Quincy down for a kiss and a hug, but rather than lean over to greet her Quincy took her hand. She'd repeatedly told Bonnie she wasn't interested, but the young woman continued to act as if they were involved.

Grace rescued her by reminding everyone that she and Mike were hosting a huge Thanksgiving dinner in Quincy's honor to thank her for saving their family and that they and their families were invited to come and celebrate with them. In addition to the other people Quincy had saved and their families, Grace and Mike's family and friends, Quincy's friends, and many of the police, fire, EMT, and hospital personnel who were at the scene of the accident would be there. An aide to the mayor interrupted to brief them about where to sit and the order of things, then herded them onto the stage.

Quincy's stomach flipped as she got a look at the packed auditorium. Dr. Giles' voice echoed in her head.

"Own it, Quincy. What you did was exceptional. Saving so many people makes you a hero, but what you did for Grace puts you in the superhero category. Let yourself feel proud."

She stood tall. Having her therapist and the warriors in her PTSD group say this had confirmed what Lindy had said and helped her accept it. And though the medal didn't include it, her pride at having saved Tiffany Maggio allowed her finally to feel proud of saving Grace and the others from death.

The aide directed them to seats, official dignitaries next to the podium on the left, Quincy front and center surrounded by the survivors and their families. Her eyes skimmed the crowd. Her friends lined the front rows. *Wait!* Was that her grandmother seated next to Amelia? She couldn't help the smile that erupted at the sight, but she did manage to keep herself from running off the stage to hug her. No doubt Amelia and Gina had arranged the surprise. She tossed a salute to Mama, then continued to scan the auditorium, hoping to see Lindy.

Hackensack police officers, firefighters, EMTs, nurses, and doctors filled a number of rows behind them, and then there were lots of rows of police in uniforms from surrounding towns. She picked out a row with a beaming Dr. Giles and the members of her PTSD group, all in their military uniforms. And sitting right behind them were Tiffany Maggio, her brother and sister, and her parents. Quincy blinked back tears at seeing them and the familiar faces of former teachers, former classmates, former reserve members, and neighbors as well as faces of many citizens she didn't recognize. She grinned and met Dr. Giles' eyes. The therapist saluted her.

The mayor called for quiet and spoke on behalf of the city and the council members, talking about Quincy's service to the community. Chief of Police Connie Trubeck followed. She described Quincy's military background and what she found when she arrived on the scene the night of the accident. The next speaker was an eyewitness, a woman also injured in the accident, who had watched from her car as Quincy pulled men, women, and children from burning cars, then working against time had put out the fire in the car that looked ready to explode.

Finally, it was Grace's turn. She rolled forward, and using a handheld microphone she spoke about why Quincy deserved this medal and much more, for her extraordinary act of selfless bravery saving her, about her family and the other survivors being alive due to that bravery. By the time she finished the entire auditorium was in tears. Even Quincy.

When the chief called Quincy to the podium to receive the medal, she stood tall and proud listening to what the chief was saying about her and scanning the room, still hoping Lindy had come.

After the chief pinned the medal on her, Quincy took the mike.

"Thank you for this recognition. Saving these twelve people I now consider friends was a gut reaction. It is what I, what we police officers and other first responders are trained to do, and I'm very proud that I did it. But I'm especially proud that I didn't let my fear cripple me, that I didn't run as she urged, that I saved Grace Lee Walcott, one of the bravest people I've ever had the pleasure to know. Grace's death would have been a terrible loss for her family. But I've since learned that Grace is an important leader in the fight against racism and homophobia and for equality, so her loss would also have been a great loss for this community and the world. I'm honored to be honored. Thank you for coming tonight."

The crowd gave her a standing ovation. Right after the mayor closed the meeting, a photographer ran up the steps onto the stage. Quincy recognized Patsy Mackenzie, who had taken the beautiful pictures of her and Lindy at the hospital.

Patsy shouted to be heard. "Hey, can I get a picture of Detective Adams with everyone she saved? Just come and stand around her." While they gathered, Patsy scanned the auditorium, then turned to Quincy. "I thought your girlfriend was coming up here for the pictures?"

"My? Who?" She could only mean Lindy. Was she here? Quincy stepped to the edge of the stage and scanned the crowd leaving the auditorium. No sign of Lindy. Maybe Patsy was mistaken.

"I recognized her right away." Patsy had moved next to Quincy. "I reminded her where we'd met, and she thanked me for not publishing a full-face picture. I asked why she was standing in the back and she said she'd arrived late." Patsy studied Quincy, then seemed to notice her disappointment. "I guess she left right after the ceremony."

Lindy had been here. How had she missed her? Why didn't she stay? Quincy quelled the urge to run out to the parking lot to find her. If Lindy wanted to have real contact, she would have waited. In any case, she'd take it as a good sign that she still cared enough to come to the ceremony.

Patsy led her to the waiting group and arranged them for the first picture, Quincy standing next to Grace, Mike on the other side, and the children clustered around them. As Patsy set up the next shot, Grace took Quincy's hand. "You okay?"

Quincy smiled and started to lie, but she and Grace had spent a lot of time together since the accident and Grace knew about Lindy. "Flustered. Patsy said Lindy was here for the ceremony, but it looks like she left."

Grace squeezed her hand. "So she hasn't forgotten you. Be patient, Quincy. It will work out."

Quincy smiled. "Okay, Ms. Optimist. I think you came into my life to cheer me up."

Grace squeezed her arm. "As I've said, my debt is great. I'll gladly cheer you up and on for the rest of my life. But I'm kind of exhausted tonight, so we won't make the party at Amelia's. I hope you understand."

Before Quincy could respond, they were surrounded by another group gathering for another picture.

"See you at the party later?" Patsy asked Quincy after what felt like hundreds of pictures. "I'd like to buy you a drink."

"I'll be there and I'll be thirsty, but I think the drinks will be free. But could I ask you to take a few more pictures?"

"Sure. It's your night."

Quincy saw Amelia talking to Dr. Giles and the women from her group and assumed she was inviting them to the party she was hosting. She caught Amelia's eye and waved her and Mama to the stage. Mama pulled her into a tight hug. "I'm so proud of you, Quincy. But don't you ever do anything foolish like that again."

"I'm thrilled to see you, Mama." She kissed her mama's cheek. Patsy was snapping away as Grace and the other survivors surrounded them.

"Hey, introduce us to your grandmother, Quincy." It was Grace. "I want to invite her to our Thanksgiving dinner."

Quincy introduced the two women, and they seemed to connect immediately. But then who didn't connect with Grace… or Mama? Another round of photos and lots of conversation, then Amelia and Mama left to go to Amelia's house. Jackson had gone on ahead, but Amelia wanted to be there to greet their guests.

Quincy said her goodbyes to the group onstage, encouraged Grace to go home and rest rather than push herself to go to the party, then turned her attention to the crowd waiting at the bottom of the steps. She was surprised when Gina grabbed her and kissed her. "Whoa, twice in one night?"

Gina's pale skin turned bright red. "Sorry, I'm just so damn proud of you. Don't panic."

It seemed everyone in the world wanted a word and a selfie with her. When she and Gina were finally able to escape, she scanned the parking lot, hoping Lindy had waited to see her. No luck.

Gina was bubbling with excitement as she drove them to Amelia's to meet their friends to celebrate. "Amelia asked me to invite some of the guys to the party, so John and his wife will be there along with some of our patrol buddies." Quincy half listened. She was feeling good about the medal and looking forward to the party, but her mind was on Lindy. Had Patsy told Lindy about the party at Amelia's house? A girl could hope.

But hoping didn't make it true. Quincy took a deep breath and entered the house. She was greeted with cheers, someone handed her a beer, and she was surrounded by friends from all parts of her life. Lindy wasn't there, but Quincy was hugged and kissed and toasted so many times she didn't have time to mourn her absence.

CHAPTER EIGHTEEN

Two blocks away from the high school Lindy pulled into a dead-end street and let the tears come. She'd been trying to shove her feelings away, pretending the time she'd spent with Quincy hadn't had an impact on her, pretending she wanted to go back to her lonely life, pretending she didn't want the chance at the life with a good, kind woman that Quincy offered. So tonight she'd convinced herself to come help Quincy get through the ceremony.

But Quincy looked self-confident, proud, and gorgeous. She didn't need her help. Clearly, *she'd* moved on.

But Lindy hadn't. She'd waited in the hallway until the ceremony started, then leaned against the back wall of the auditorium. Quincy hadn't noticed her, but that photographer recognized her immediately and introduced herself. Assuming she and Quincy were a couple, Patsy asked if she would be going to the party at Amelia's house with Quincy after the ceremony. Patsy was on the stage when Lindy ducked out. Had she told Quincy she was there? Quincy was probably on her way to

Amelia's. The decision whether to go or not was taken out of her hands. She had no idea where Amelia lived, unless… She glanced at her phone.

Seeing Quincy would be nice, but it wouldn't change anything. She knew herself well enough to know she would run again the minute feelings for Quincy bubbled up. As much as she wanted to spend time with her, she cared about her too much to do that to her again, to abandon her again.

Babs was right; she needed help. She should have gone into therapy when Babs suggested it five weeks ago. Had she lost the opportunity to explore a relationship with Quincy? Maybe. She hoped it wasn't too late. But she had work to do before she could approach Quincy. She started the car and headed home.

Babs looked up from the book she was reading. "How was your class?"

Lindy dropped her coat and headed for the refrigerator. She'd barely mentioned Quincy since the Monday after their weekend together but no more evasion; she was ready to share her feelings.

"I cut it. Quincy was awarded a medal tonight and I decided to go to the ceremony instead." She pulled a container of leftover stuffed acorn squash from the refrigerator and heated half of one in the microwave. She filled a glass with Dr. Pepper. "Want a beer?"

"Sure." Babs joined her at the table. "Did you talk to her?"

Lindy shook her head. "No. I watched from the back of the auditorium and left right after the ceremony ended." She arranged her plate, a napkin, silverware, soda, and the beer on the table, then sat and dug into her squash.

Babs studied Lindy's face. "You've been crying."

Lindy shrugged.

"You cut your class to go, so why leave without talking to her?" Babs concentrated on peeling the label off her beer bottle.

Lindy put her fork down. "I thought she might need me to help her deal with the attention and the pressure, but she didn't. I realized I'm the needy one."

"Wow, babe, you haven't mentioned her at all. I believed you when you said you didn't want what she was offering. I feel sort of out of it. Want to talk?"

That's what she loved about Babs. No recriminations. No judgment. Always ready to listen and support.

"Sorry, Babs." Lindy covered Babs' hand and waited for her to make eye contact. "I didn't think talking would help. I was intent on putting Quincy and the weekend behind me and getting back to normal. But the opposite happened. She's been on my mind constantly and instead of enjoying my quiet, isolated life, I've been longing to see her, longing to talk to her, longing to just be with her. I want to show you something."

Lindy went into her bedroom and returned with the framed newspaper picture of her and Quincy, the collage she'd made of pictures from their snow adventure, and the pile of articles about Quincy that she'd clipped. "While I was telling myself I didn't want what Quincy was offering, I was doing this. And tonight I realized that I do want what I think she was offering, but I'm not sure she's still offering it."

Babs picked up the collage and studied it. "You're both glowing. I've never seen you look so…so vibrant. It's almost like you were a different person with her."

"We had so much fun that day, walking, talking, playing in the snow. I can't remember ever feeling so free and alive and happy."

Babs placed the collage on the table. "I haven't met Quincy, but based on these pictures and what you've said about her and the weekend, I would guess she's feeling the loss too. Are you going to call her?"

Lindy surprised herself. She hadn't expected the sob or the tears streaming down her face. "Sorry." She reached for a tissue. "I know I'll run the minute I get close and I think that would be really hurtful to both of us. I'll call Quincy when I can handle intimacy."

Babs sat back. "Really? And how is this transformation going to occur. Self-help book? Osmosis? Magical thinking?"

Lindy brought her hands together in prayer position and bowed her head. "As you suggested weeks ago, oh wise one, therapy is the way to go." Hiding her smirk, Lindy forked some of the no-longer-warm stuffing and squash into her mouth.

Babs stretched, then smacked Lindy lightly on the back of her head. "'Bout time you admitted I'm brilliant."

"It's not just you I have to eat crow with over this. When I told Dr. Crawford I was leaving therapy, she told me I needed to work on my intimacy issues before terminating. So now, after insisting I didn't need intimacy, that my own company was enough for me, I have to admit she was right."

"You're so stubborn." Babs burst out laughing. "This Quincy person won't know what hit her if you get together." She kissed the top of Lindy's head. "Let me know what I can do to help. And don't keep anything else from me." She grinned. "Hoo-ha, Lindy wants a girlfriend." She wiggled her behind, then boogied to the living room.

Lindy stared after Babs. Is that what she wanted? A girlfriend? A relationship? As she washed her dinner dishes, she remembered the pleasure she'd felt taking care of Quincy, doing little things like putting cream on her hands and feet, helping her dress, and supporting her when she was anxious about meeting the people she saved. And how much she'd enjoyed the simple domesticity of shopping, cooking dinner, cleaning up after, and reading together in the evening. Yeah. She wanted all of that. And more. She wanted love and affection and respect.

CHAPTER NINETEEN

With her mind still back in her therapist's office, Lindy pushed her cart through the aisles of the supermarket picking up the items she needed for dinner. Up to now she and Dr. Crawford had explored her low self-esteem and her fear of intimacy. But today, for the first time, they'd focused on the weekend she'd spent with Quincy. She browsed the pasta shelves looking for the *orecchiette* she always made with the cauliflower dish she planned to cook tonight. She warmed, remembering how much Quincy had loved her cooking and this dish in particular. Was that memory the source of her sudden desire to make it tonight? Whatever. If she didn't get moving, she'd be too tired to cook when she got home. She pulled a box of the pasta off the shelf, leaned over to place it in her cart, then shoved the cart forward without looking. And hit something. Or rather somebody. Hard. She raised her head. *Oh, shit.* The man in front of her was holding onto his cart and hopping on one leg.

She rushed to his side and took his arm. "I'm so sorry."

The man glanced down at her. He stilled. Their eyes met. Lindy's heart flipped. Not a man. Quincy.

"Hi." Quincy leaned over rubbing her leg.

"Jeez, I'm sorry." This wasn't the way Lindy wanted their second meeting to go. Her fantasy had been a little more romantic. "I was daydreaming. Is your leg—?"

Quincy continued to rub. "I'll live. What are you doing in my Shop Rite?"

Quincy sounded annoyed. *Screw her.*

"*Your* Shop Rite?" She snorted. "I'm not stalking you if that's what you mean?"

Quincy put her hands up. "Sorry, sorry. I'm just surprised to see you in my neighborhood store. Have you moved?"

"That's better, sugah. Since you asked, I'm seeing someone who lives near here."

"Oh." Quincy paled and seemed to deflate. "You're seeing someone?"

That's not what she meant. Though she liked the fact that her seeing someone upset Quincy, she didn't want to leave her with the wrong impression. "My therapist's office is a couple of blocks away. I often shop here after my therapy sessions."

"Oh. I thought…" Quincy seemed to relax. "So how have you been?"

Lindy became aware of grumbling behind them and realized they were making it difficult for other shoppers to get by. "I think we'd better move. Can you walk?"

Quincy glanced behind them. "Yeah, my leg is good. Want to grab a cup of coffee? There's a place with tables near the deli counter."

"Sure."

Lindy found a table while Quincy went to get their coffees. To keep her eyes from devouring Quincy, she feigned great interest in what Quincy had in her shopping cart. And started laughing.

Then, seeing the weird look on Quincy's face when she deposited their coffees on the table, she doubled over.

"What?" Quincy looked mystified. "Are you losing it?"

Lindy took a deep breath, then another, and dried her eyes. "Look at our shopping carts."

It took Quincy a few seconds to notice that they contained exactly the same items.

"I've been trying to make your recipe for cauliflower and 'little ears' pasta since that weekend, but I can't seem to get it right. I really like it. And I always think of you when I eat it." She flushed. "Would you write the recipe down for me?"

Lindy was touched. "Sure. But it's not a recipe with precise measurements. You kind of have to play around with it until it suits your taste." She removed a pen and notebook from her backpack.

Orecchiette Pasta with Cauliflower
There's nothing hard and fast about this recipe, fiddle with the measurements and the ingredients until you find what you enjoy.

½ lb pasta – orecchiette or shells or any desired
1 head of cauliflower, cut into florets
¼ cup extra virgin olive oil
6 – 8 cloves of chopped garlic (about 2 TBSP), or to taste
¼ cup of pine nuts (more or less to taste)
¼ cup raisins
2 TBSP sundried tomatoes, chopped
¼ cup chopped parsley
¼ TSP crushed hot pepper (more or less as desired)

1. Boil water for pasta. Throw in the cauliflower and cook until a knife easily pierces.
2. Remove the cauliflower, bring the water back to a boil and cook the pasta according to directions.
3. Heat the oil over medium heat in a sauté pan. Add the hot pepper and the garlic and cook until the garlic softens.
4. Add pine nuts, raisins and tomatoes; cook until the nuts start to brown.
5. Add the cauliflower and cook it until it's as soft as you like.
6. When the pasta is done, drain. (Optional: Some people like

to add a half or a cup of the pasta water to the sauce; be sure to reserve it before draining.)

7. When the cauliflower is done, stir the pasta into the pan with the other ingredients. Stir in the pasta water, if using. Sprinkle with parsley and serve.

"Here you go." Lindy handed the recipe to Quincy. "I'm glad you got something out of the weekend."

Quincy met Lindy's eyes. "I got a lot more than a recipe out of that weekend."

Quincy's directness and open honesty stirred up the guilt always swirling in Lindy. "I'm sorry I left the way I did that morning."

Quincy opened her mouth to speak, but Lindy put a finger on her lips. "Let me finish, please. It was cowardly. But I was freaked out by…by the intimacy and the thought of what continuing to see you would mean." There she'd said it. Dr. Crawford would be happy.

"I have issues. I have lots of scars—internal and external. Some of them were put there by the people who should have loved and protected me, who should have taught me to trust but who offered only hate and violence as they tried to crush my spirit, accused me of *their* sins, and punished me for them. Others I made possible by choosing the wrong women to love. Fourteen years of rigid religious upbringing taught me that I'm worthless, that I have to accept what I'm given, and that I have no rights. I'm ashamed. I've been weak and I've put up with things I shouldn't have, even though Sarah, my good mom, the one who saved me from a life of prostitution, told me time and again that I'm better than that. That's why I'm in therapy."

Quincy was quiet for so long Lindy thought she'd upset her. "Well, I have issues too, about Jen and letting go of her. I flashed back to Jen in Afghanistan when I was saving Grace and the chief recognized it. She was afraid it might happen again if I was under stress and that I might harm myself, or others, and ordered me to get help. So I'm going to a PTSD group once a week and I meet privately with the therapist at least once a month. And, I'm surprised to say, it's helping me. But I still have work to do. So I guess we're two peas in a pod, as they say."

Lindy sipped her coffee and played with the stirrer. "Did the photographer tell you I was there the night you received the medal?"

"She thinks we're a couple, so she wondered if you were going to join me on stage for the pictures she was taking. I was pleased to hear you were there but disappointed that you didn't stay around to talk to me."

"It was a nice ceremony. I enjoyed the speeches, especially yours and Grace's. I was happy to see Grace recuperating so well. And you looked really relaxed and confident. Have you finally accepted your hero status?"

"You noticed that? My therapist and the group finished what you started and helped me come to terms with it. Where were you sitting?"

"I stood against the wall in the back during the ceremony, then I moved to the hall just outside the auditorium and watched. I saw you kiss a woman in uniform when you left the stage. She had her arm around you. Your girlfriend?"

"To quote someone I met in a bar one snowy night, 'she's a girl and she's a friend, but she's not my girlfriend.' That was Gina. An old friend. I'm still single." She put her hand over Lindy's, stopping her fidgeting. "So why did you come and then leave without saying hello?"

Lindy struggled for a few minutes trying to figure out how forthcoming to be, then decided to be honest. "Seeing you brought up a lot of feelings, Quincy. I couldn't stay." She brushed a tear away. "Sorry. It was painful. It forced me to confront my behavior. Actually, I started therapy right after that."

"Wow. I'm sorry I caused you so much pain."

Sweet Quincy, always ready to be the savior. "It's not you, my superhero. It's all me."

They were silent amidst the shopping carts zipping past, the chatter from people crowding the deli counter, and loud conversations from a group of men at a nearby table. Quincy sipped her now-cold coffee and pushed it aside. "I don't want to scare you again, but I'd still like to take you out on a real date. Do you want to have dinner now?"

Lindy shook her head. "I can't, Quincy. I'd just screw things up again."

Quincy stiffened. "Oh, sorry."

Lindy reached for Quincy's hands, then looked into her eyes. "I want to. I'd still like to call you for that date when I've taken care of...when I'm able to."

"Okay." Quincy stood and opened her arms. "I can wait." Lindy stepped in for a hug. They went to the cash registers to complete their purchases and waved goodbye as they exited the store.

Lindy was excited. She wanted to turn around and go right back to Dr. Crawford's office, but she reminded herself that the therapist had other patients. Luckily it was Tuesday, so she only had to wait until Thursday to share.

CHAPTER TWENTY

Lindy was smiling as she approached her car. She hit the fob on her keys to open the doors and the trunk and only then noticed the woman leaning against her car, arms folded and a smirk on her face. Lindy froze.

Melanie was thinner and shabbier than Lindy had ever seen her, her hair was lifeless, and her clothing was wrinkled and dirty. She shifted from foot to foot, swiped her dripping nose, scratched her arms.

"So is this where you shop now? It took you so long to shop I figured you were doing one of the checkout girls in the backroom."

Lindy ignored the insult. She knew the signs. Melanie needed a fix and could easily get violent. It wasn't the first time her ex had accosted her in a parking lot, but it had been a while and it had never happened so far from her apartment. Lindy scanned the lot, but nobody was near them. Why hadn't she asked Quincy to walk her to her car?

She turned to run, hoping to make it to the safety of the supermarket, but stumbled on the snowy ground. Melanie caught her arm, swung her against the car, pulled her arm back, and pushed it up. She tried to pull away, but Melanie forced the trapped arm higher, bringing tears to Lindy's eyes.

"Stop, please, you're hurting me."

Melanie wrapped her free arm around Lindy's neck and squeezed. She smelled of unwashed clothes, an unwashed body, and foul breath. In comparison the reek of alcohol on her jacket was almost pleasant. "You don't look too happy to see me, baby," she breathed in Lindy's ear.

Lindy tried to pull away, but Melanie tightened the chokehold and forced her closer against the car. "Let me go." She opened her mouth to scream, but Melanie pulled tighter, cutting off her breath.

"Don't make a sound. I promise I'll hurt that pretty little roommate of yours if you get away." Lindy relaxed, indicating she wouldn't try to run.

"We belong together, baby. Make sex great again." Her breath was hot in Lindy's ear. She cackled at her attempted imitation of the catch phrase of the other crazy, the orange president. Tears stung Lindy's eyes as Melanie began to grind herself against her backside, pushing her into the side of the car, forcing her twisted arm up in the process but loosening the arm around Lindy's neck.

"No." Lindy pushed back against Melanie, trying to free her neck. "I'm done with you." Melanie pulled her arm tighter, cutting off Lindy's air again.

She's going to kill me this time.

Lindy thrashed in Melanie's embrace, fighting even as she felt herself start to black out. She thought she saw the headlights of a car flash on them, but maybe the light was the result of fading in and out of consciousness as Melanie alternated cutting off her air and loosening her chokehold.

"Police. Step away from the lady."

Lindy staggered at the sudden loss of support, but strong arms caught her before she went down. Wheezing, trying to take in air, Lindy opened her eyes. It was Quincy who was clutching Lindy to her breast. She was also pointing a gun at Melanie, who seemed surprised to find herself sitting on a pile of snow.

"Hands up." This was Quincy in command mode.

Melanie stared at Quincy, then slowly raised her hands. "Who the fuck are you?"

"Detective Quincy Adams at your service."

"Hey, we're friends, Detective. Ex-lovers having a conversation. You know how it is." She was wrong if she thought the smile she flashed made her look harmless. In fact, the missing and rotted teeth it revealed gave her a demented look.

Quincy glanced at Lindy. "Is that true?"

Feeling safe in Quincy's arms, Lindy blurted out. "Not for a long time. She just wants money for drugs. And she's violating an order of protection. She's not allowed to come close to me."

The woman on the ground paled. "It was mistake, officer. I was surprised to see her here and I forgot about the court order."

"Let me see some identification. Remember I have a gun pointed at you, so remove it slowly and hand it to me."

Quincy released Lindy and reached for the wallet the woman extended with a shaking hand. She glanced at the driver's license. "Melanie Kowalski. Are you following Ms…this lady?"

"It's Lindy James, officer."

"No. I swear. I stopped by to shop and I spotted her car. I thought we could talk, maybe get back together. Can I get up?"

"Yes, but don't try anything."

She tried to stand, fell over onto her hands and knees, scratched at her torso, and dragged her dripping nose across the sleeve of her filthy jacket, then managed to get on her feet. "I guess I got a little upset. I didn't mean anything."

Quincy holstered her gun, used her phone to take a picture of the ID, and handed it back. Melanie's hands were shaking so hard it took her several attempts to get the wallet into the pocket of her jeans. "Ms. James says she has a restraining order against you. Is that true?"

Melanie shot a nasty look at Lindy. "Yeah, it's true, but—"

"There are no buts about a restraining order, Ms. Kowalski. Do you understand what it means?"

"Yeah." Melanie's shoulders slumped. "I just thought she might help me out with a couple of bucks for old times sake."

"It didn't look like you were asking for anything. It seemed like you were assaulting her." Quincy looked from Melanie to Lindy. "Do you want me to arrest her?"

Lindy shook her head. "But I swear this is the last time I save your ass, Melanie. Just stay away from me."

Quincy straightened to her full height and stood close so Melanie had to look up to see her face. "Stay away from Ms. James or I'll personally come after you. Now get out of here before I decide to run you in."

Melanie glanced at Lindy, then turned and stumbled to her car. They watched her burn rubber leaving the parking lot.

Quincy pulled Lindy into her arms. "Are you okay?"

Lindy held on tight. "Yes. Or I will be. Thank you." She shuddered. "I'm sorry you had to see that."

"I'm sorry you have a drug addict in your life."

Lindy flushed. "I'm not…I don't do drugs. Or alcohol."

"You don't have to explain."

Lindy gazed at her. "I'm nervous about going home right away. Does the offer to have dinner with you still stand?"

Quincy grinned down at her. "It certainly does."

They agreed they would save the fancy restaurant for a real date, so Quincy followed Lindy's car to the diner they'd gone to during their weekend together.

After they ordered, Lindy went to the ladies' room to wash up. Quincy sipped her coffee, thinking about what she'd witnessed. She believed Lindy didn't do drugs or alcohol. But she had lots of questions. When they had coffee earlier, she'd talked about being weak and scarred and being made to do things she didn't want to do. Was she talking about drugs? Is that what she was working on in therapy? How did she hook up with an addict like Melanie?

Lindy returned and fiddled with her Dr. Pepper, stripping the paper off the straw. Finally, she drank some, then gazed at Quincy. "Aren't you going to ask me about Melanie?"

Quincy shook her head. "You made it pretty clear that your personal life is off limits. I respect your wishes."

The waitress arrived with Quincy's burger with fried onions and a side of sweet potato fries and Lindy's salad with quinoa, walnuts, grilled vegetables, and goat cheese. After checking they had everything they needed, she moved to take orders at a nearby table.

Lindy chewed her lip. "I feel I owe you an explanation."

"You don't owe me anything, Lindy." Quincy put ketchup on her burger. "I know all I need to know about Melanie. If you'll let me, I'll do what I can to keep you safe from her." She bit into the burger.

Lindy gazed at Quincy. "I need to tell you." She took a fry off Quincy's plate.

Quincy nodded. Was the potato Lindy's way of reminding her of the intimacy they'd shared during their weekend together? Maybe. But she obviously needed to talk. Quincy would listen.

"When my adopted mother Sarah sold her bookstore, she wanted me to move to Florida with her, but I didn't want to leave everything I knew, the friends I'd made. So I opted to stay in Atlanta. Before she left, Sarah made sure I was settled into a room in a hotel for girls and I was earning enough to support myself with two part-time jobs, one as a salesgirl at a department store and one working nights at a burger joint. About a year later, Melanie was hired as the bartender at the burger place. She was older than me so I was flattered when she started flirting and then asked me out. Six weeks later we were a couple." She stopped to take a bite of her salad.

Since Lindy wanted to share, Quincy decided to satisfy her curiosity. "Was she your first?"

"No. When I was sixteen I came out with a college student working at Sarah's bookstore for the summer. She was sweet and loving, but it was lust, not love, for both of us. After that, I was with a couple of other girls, but the only one I was somewhat serious about only lasted a few months before Sarah helped me see she was abusive and I broke up with her. Melanie was the one I really fell for. You would never know it now, but she was beautiful with a lush mane of dark hair and piercing black eyes, full of life and fun to be with. She was the most adventurous sex partner I'd had and I," she lowered her eyes, "was enthralled." She speared a piece of avocado.

"Anyway, we'd been together about four months when she said she was moving to New Jersey in two days and asked me to go with her. She said she had a friend we could stay with, but I would have to pay for the bus tickets. Stupid me had no idea she had to get away fast because she was deeply in debt to her dealer. I knew she did some drugs because she was always offering me cocaine and marijuana and pills, sometimes insisting I try them, but I always refused. Naïve as I was, I had no idea she was hooked and buying on credit. Anyway, I quit my jobs, packed my few belongings, said goodbye to my roommates and friends, and followed her to Lodi.

"Once we were here, we got jobs and our own apartment. Things were good for a while, but then she started getting fired from one job after another. It was never her fault. She missed work because the schedule was wrong, the other bartender stole from her register, a customer picked a fight, things like that. At first, she always got another job, but eventually no one would hire her. And it almost didn't matter whether she worked or not since she never had any money. I was supporting us both and giving her money while she spiraled down and down. It took me a while to recognize what was happening and more time to get away, but I finally left and went into therapy to deal with the whole experience. On the advice of my therapist, I took out the restraining order.

"Without me paying the rent, Mel got evicted. At first, she stayed with friends, then with family, and when neither friends nor family would have anything to do with her, she began to sleep in her car. Recently, she started coming after me. At first insisting we get together again and then just wanting money."

Lindy had kept her eyes on her salad the whole time she talked about the relationship, but now she took a deep breath and met Quincy's gaze. "So now you know. And that's all I'm prepared to say now about my relationship with Melanie. Except I swear I've never used drugs and, though I've tasted alcohol a couple of times, I don't like the taste so I don't drink."

"Thank you for trusting me with that. I know it can't be easy to talk about." Quincy extended a sweet potato fry as a peace offering.

Lindy ate the potato, then smiled. "Thank you for being there tonight, my superhero."

Quincy offered another potato. "You have my cell number. If you'll let me, I'll be there if she bothers you again. Call me any time of day or night."

"Thank you." Seeming lost in thought, Lindy chewed the potato slowly. "I'd like to give you my cell so you can be in touch if you need me for some reason."

Quincy sensed that Lindy trusting her with her cell number was a milestone of sorts, but she had no illusions. Lindy wasn't ready for a relationship with her or anybody else, but she was reaching out to connect. There was hope. She keyed the number Lindy dictated into her cell. "So."

Lindy fidgeted with her silverware. "So, could I ask you to follow me home in case Mel has decided to ignore your warning?"

"Anytime." Quincy grinned. Was it a show of trust that Lindy was willing to let her know where she lived? Or just fear? In any case, having Lindy's cell and her address made Quincy feel more in control. And hopeful.

CHAPTER TWENTY-ONE

Quincy and Grace had become close after the accident, mainly because Grace was intent on showing Quincy her appreciation every day in every way. But Quincy also felt a closeness to Grace and her family that surprised her, as did the ease with which Grace was able to read her feelings and her thoughts, something even her closest friends weren't always able to do. This weekly coffee hour/lunch was something they'd instituted while Grace was still in the hospital and wanting to make sure Quincy didn't fade out of her life.

It was a week before Thanksgiving and Grace had asked Quincy to review the list of people she'd invited to what she was calling The First Annual Thank You, Quincy Adams, Thanksgiving Celebration. In addition to Grace and her family, it included the other people Quincy saved that night and their families, her mama, who was driving up from North Carolina, some of Mama's friends who had been involved in raising Quincy, Heather, Gina's ex, and her daughters who were coming up north for the holiday, plus every friend of Quincy's she could track down. About seventy people had confirmed their attendance.

"Other than my mother and father, it looks complete to me," said Quincy after reviewing the list.

"I tried Quincy, but they're in the jungle and can only be reached by canoe and a mountain trek." She grinned. "I'm not up to it physically yet, otherwise I would have gone and brought them back."

Quincy had no doubt she was speaking the truth. "I know, Grace. You've got everyone close to me. And then some. Don't worry about them."

Grace leaned across the table, reached for Quincy's hand, and peered into her eyes. It was her way of making sure she had your full attention before asking the question, making the statement or issuing the order on her mind at the moment. Quincy figured Grace had developed this as an offensive play against being overlooked in discussions with bigger, louder men who believed what they had to say was more important than a diminutive Asian-American woman with a soft voice. Woe to those who underestimated the powerhouse that was Grace Lee Walcott.

Quincy sipped her coffee and waited for Grace to say what was on her mind.

"So I was thinking," Grace enunciated carefully, "that one important person is missing from the list."

Quincy dropped her eyes to the list, then met Grace's gaze. "Other than my parents, the only people missing are the doctor who delivered me and the grandparents and uncles I've never met."

"Maybe next year." Grace squeezed her hand. "I was actually thinking of someone who was involved, an important player."

"Who? I can't—you mean Lindy?" The day after she'd rescued Lindy from Melanie was the day of their weekly lunch and Grace had guessed that Quincy had seen Lindy again. Something about Quincy's "happier vibes," Grace had said, and Quincy had told her all, including that she now had Lindy's cell number.

"Yes. She needs to be with us Quincy. You saved us. She saved you. It's only right."

"I can't invite her, Grace. I need to back off while she figures out what she wants."

"But I can invite her. It's my house, my dinner, my guests. A lot of them. So you and she won't even have to talk if you don't want. She can bring whomever she wants with her. She can say no, Quincy, but I need to ask. All you have to do is give me her number."

Quincy knew this was not a game for Grace. She was intent on celebrating and honoring those involved in the rescue operation and had reached out to everyone she could identify. Some were coming, some had other plans. But in some deep, inexplicable way, Grace really did need to have all the important players from that night with her to celebrate her and her family's life. Hoping this wouldn't make Lindy shy away again, Quincy took out her phone and gave Grace Lindy's number.

Grace stretched out on the chaise longue in front of the fireplace that evening, thinking about what to say to Lindy. She really did feel Lindy was an important player in the event and wanted to include her for that reason. But, she admitted to herself, she wanted to make Quincy happy. If she managed to bring Lindy and Quincy together, she would feel she was making an infinitesimal payment on the debt she owed Quincy. She keyed Lindy's number. As expected, it went to voice mail. Why would anyone answer a call from an unknown number? "This is Lindy. Sorry I missed you. Please leave a message after the beep."

Grace had been heavily medicated the day they'd met so Lindy's soft Southern drawl and husky voice were a surprise. "Hi, Lindy, this is Grace Lee Walcott. I don't know if you remember meeting me in the hospital, but I'm one of the people your friend Quincy rescued. I'd like to speak to you for a moment, so if you can, please call me back. Thanks."

Confident that Lindy would return the call, Grace watched the flickering flames of the fireplace and thought again of what might have happened had Quincy not risked her own life to put out the fire and her car had exploded. She was in pain a lot of the time, but they said it would eventually lessen, and it reminded her she was alive, that life was fragile, that it was important to live the best life you could and do whatever you could to make the lives of those around you as good as they could be. She would do everything possible to get Lindy to the Thanksgiving celebration.

The ringing of her phone jolted her from her thoughts. Lindy's name flashed on the screen. "Hi, Grace speaking."

"Hi, Grace, this is Lindy returning your call. I do remember you from the hospital. How are you feeling?"

"A lot better than the day we met, but I still have a couple of operations to go, so I'll be healing for a while. I'm calling to invite you to The First Annual Thank You, Quincy Adams, Thanksgiving Celebration. My husband Mike and I are hosting Thanksgiving dinner for Quincy, her family and friends, and as many people involved in saving us and our children as we can get to come."

"But I wasn't—"

"You were. Quincy saved us. And after many talks with Quincy, I believe you saved her. Please come. Do you have plans?"

"I was planning to go out to the diner with my roommate and her girlfriend."

"No, no, no. The three of you must come to my house. I insist. And, Lindy, I know you and Quincy are taking space to figure things out, but—" She heard Lindy gasp. "Sorry. Quincy and I have become close since the accident and we talk. Anyway, there will be sixty or seventy people here and you won't have to spend time together unless you want to."

"I don't know, Grace. I'll have to think about it and talk to Babs, my roommate. Can I let you know?"

"No need to call. I'm catering for a hundred, so there will be plenty of food and drink. Just show up and celebrate life with us. I'll text you the details and directions."

CHAPTER TWENTY-TWO

It was about an hour drive to Grace's house in Bedminster from their apartment in Lodi, the last bit up a very long winding driveway lined with trees. Lindy's jaw dropped when they rounded a curve and the house appeared. It was gorgeous. Wood and glass snuggled into the landscape as if it had always been there, overlooking a lake and well-tended land that seemed to go on forever.

"Oh. My. God. Babs. I never stopped to think about the cost of catering for a hundred people. Grace and Mike must be very rich."

Grace's text had said, "It's informal, wear comfortable clothes." She'd been worried about seeing Quincy, now she worried she'd be out of place in her jeans and sweater. "I feel underdressed. Do you think we should leave?"

"Nah. She said dress comfortably. Besides, I want to see what the inside of the house looks like."

"I don't know—" Her car door opened.

"Happy Thanksgiving." An attendant offered her a hand. "I'll park your car. Go right in." He gestured to the front door. "Someone will help you once you're inside." She exchanged her keys for a ticket, squared her shoulders, and walked up the stairs with Babs and Dani. At the door they stopped to take in the view.

"Holy shit," Dani said. "Do you think this is their property or a park?"

"Based on the house, I bet it all belongs to them." Babs clutched Lindy's arm. "Imagine how beautiful this must be when the trees and flowers are blooming. Did you know Quincy had fancy friends like this?"

"I don't know how friendly they are. Grace said she and Quincy are close, but I don't know how Quincy feels about them. She didn't know them before she saved their lives." Lindy reached for the doorknob. "I'm nervous."

"Me too." Babs giggled. "But, hey, we're invited, so we have every right to be here."

"Happy Thanksgiving. Please come in." A woman dressed in black pants and a white shirt stood in the doorway. "I need the name of whomever received the invitation, please." She confirmed that Lindy's name was on the list, took their coats, and gave them numbers to retrieve them later. "Just follow the noise to the Great Room."

"The great room?" Babs elbowed Lindy. "What the fuck is a great room?"

Lindy chewed her lip. Grace and Mike seemed down-to-earth in the hospital, but how much can you tell about a bandaged and doped-up person lying in a hospital bed. But Quincy was a regular person. And they'd been invited. They'd be fine. She straightened again and led her friends in search of the crowd they could hear rumbling somewhere along this hallway. She inhaled, savoring the smells of turkey and apple pie and who knew what else was cooking. Though she wouldn't eat the turkey, smelling it cooking brought back happy memories of the only Thanksgivings she'd ever celebrated, those with Sarah and her family and friends.

It was breathtaking. Truly a great room. Fires blazed in huge fireplaces at either end of the room framing a wall of windows that overlooked the lake, the huge lawn, and the woods. Several bars and long tables were scattered around the multiple seating areas. Men and women sat and stood in clusters talking while waiters circulated with drinks and trays of hors d'oeuvres.

"Wow, I feel like I'm in a movie," Babs said, her voice filled with awe. Dani took her hand.

Uneasy at the three of them gawking like the yokels they were, Lindy poked Babs. "I take you nice places, don't I?"

Before Babs could respond, another woman in black slacks and white shirt approached and asked their names. And when Grace rolled up in her wheelchair, the woman introduced them.

"Welcome, Babs and Dani and Lindy." Grace took each of their hands as she said their names. "I'm so glad you could join our celebration." She held on to Lindy's hand. "I thought I recognized you when you walked in, but I was kind of doped up the day we met so I couldn't be sure. I'm happy you decided to come."

Lindy relaxed. Grace's friendly welcome and her down-to-earth manner eased her anxiety and she could feel Babs and Dani relaxing as well. "Thanks for inviting us. We're a little overwhelmed by your beautiful house. Is the property yours or is it a park?"

Grace laughed. "You might have guessed we're very lucky people. Not only do we have all this, but Quincy saved our lives so we can enjoy it. The property is all ours, but we try to share with the community by having events here, and in the summer we host a day camp for inner-city children who wouldn't otherwise have access to a pool or lake and other fun activities."

Lindy tried to keep her eyes on Grace as she welcomed them, but she couldn't help scanning the room for Quincy. She was surprised when Grace pulled her down and whispered in her ear. "Quincy is talking to a group of people by the windows to your right. Her back is to you."

"What?" Lindy was surprised Grace noticed her looking for Quincy. "I wasn't…" She started to deny she was looking for Quincy, but as she straightened her head she turned to her right. She flushed. She didn't think she'd been that obvious. She was going to have to watch herself around Grace.

Grace smiled but didn't comment. She nodded to the woman pushing her wheelchair. "Come along. Let me make sure you get drinks and something to eat. Then I'll introduce the three of you to a few people. We'll probably serve dinner in about an hour." She took them to a bar where Lindy ordered Dr. Pepper but settled for seltzer and lime, and Babs and Dani selected from an assortment of high-end beers. Grace directed her aide to go to a group near the fireplace but signaled her to stop by a woman standing alone in the center of the room. Grace introduced the three of them to Heather. "This is one of Quincy's friends."

Grace's aide put her hand to her ear. "Mike wants to see you, Grace."

"Right. Sorry I have to dash." As she rolled away she promised, "I'll send some hors d'oeuvres in a minute." A waiter appeared almost immediately and offered coconut-coated shrimps on skewers. Babs waved to someone in a group standing near the fire. "Ooh, Chita is in that group with Maggie." She touched Lindy's arm. "I hope you ladies don't mind. We see some friends over there."

"Go ahead," Lindy said, exchanging a glance with Heather. Curious about why Grace had introduced them, given most of the people in the room were Quincy's friends. "So what's your connection to this event, Heather?"

"Quincy is a very good friend and the best friend of my ex, Gina. I live in Maryland, but I had planned to spend Thanksgiving in New Jersey with Gina so when this was organized she asked if I minded having Thanksgiving here instead of at her house. Pretty classy place, huh?"

"I'll say." Lindy accepted a tiny quiche from the server. "It's nice that you're still close to your ex."

"While I had my problems with Gina, she was a great mom and a great co-parent for my two daughters, who were one and three when we got together. They're six and eight now. She adores them and they feel the same so I can't just walk away. And, speaking of the devil, she went downstairs to make sure they're happy and here she comes."

The attractive blond butch sauntering toward them appeared relaxed, but her eyes bounced between Lindy and Heather, as if gauging their connection. "It's like day camp down there. The girls are having a great time." She turned to Lindy. "I'm Gina. I don't believe we've met, but I recognize you from pictures Quincy showed me. You're Lindy, who took care of Quincy, right?"

Her easily summoned flush rushed to her neck and face. "Yes. That Lindy." Gina was the woman in uniform who had kissed Quincy at the awards ceremony. Quincy had said they were just friends so why was she feeling jealous?

"Took care of Quincy when?" Heather looked at Gina and getting no answer, turned to Lindy.

"The night of the accident. I drove Quincy home from Maggie's. She'd gone there because—"

"Because I could feel myself going down that old black hole you and Gina rescued me from a couple of times, Heather."

They all swiveled to look at Quincy. She was glowing. "Lindy, I'm so glad you came. I tried to talk Grace out of inviting you, but—"

"You didn't want me to come, sugah?"

"What? No. I mean yes. I wanted you to come, but I didn't think you would want to. Grace said you could say no."

"And she was right. But I said yes and I'm here. Are you sure that's all right with you?"

Gina cleared her throat. "Excuse us. We're going to talk to some people we missed before."

Quincy and Lindy stared at each other after they left, then Lindy laughed. Quincy wrapped her arms around Lindy. "I'm really glad you came. Come let me introduce you to my friends. Don't be embarrassed. They've already heard the story of you saving me. Just relax. Let's be thankful and enjoy this day."

Lindy leaned into Quincy, enjoying the closeness. But she didn't want Quincy to get the wrong idea. She pulled away. "Just remember we're not a couple. My being here doesn't mean I've figured things out."

"Whoa. I'm not trying to rush you. I know what we agreed to, what we are to each other at this time. But you're the one who comforted me when I most needed it. So maybe I'm silly, but I'm happy to spend time with you. And I assume you have a little bit of the same feeling or you wouldn't be here today."

Lindy blew out a breath. "Sorry, I'm nervous. Meeting all your friends is kind of scary. And I've never been involved with this kind of…wealth. I'm not sure I know how to act in this…" She waved a hand indicating the enormous room. "It's kind of overwhelming."

Quincy gazed around the spectacular room. "I felt the same way the first time I came here. But there wasn't time to check Grace and Mike's financials when I rescued them, and this is what they came with. Grace is a managing director at Goldfarb Black Investments, Mike is the head of a hedge fund, and, for better or worse, they're my friends now. Besides, they don't really live here."

"You mean they have another house?"

"They use this room and the meeting rooms and industrial kitchen downstairs for entertaining large groups of clients and potential clients and also for the many community events they support. But, if you walk through there," Quincy pointed to the rear, "to their living quarters, it's beautiful and luxurious but on a scale that people like me and you can relate to. They really are wonderful, genuine people. You'll like them when you get to know them."

"Grace seems like a regular person, so I'll take your word for it."

"Did you come alone today?"

"No. Babs and Dani came with me. They're talking to Maggie over there." Lindy lifted her chin in the direction of the cluster of lesbians around Maggie. "Babs is my best friend and roommate. Dani is her girlfriend."

Quincy studied the group of women. "Would you rather I didn't meet—"

"Sorry. I thought you knew her from Maggie's, but of course you didn't speak to anyone but me. Babs is the reason I was at Maggie's that night. We were celebrating her birthday." Lindy waved Babs and Dani over.

Lindy suddenly felt anxious. Introducing Quincy to Babs was inviting Quincy into her life. She caught herself. Having met Melanie, Quincy was already in her life. And she was here at this Thanksgiving Dinner celebrating Quincy so she was in Quincy's life. Too late. "Babs and Dani, I'd like you to meet my friend Quincy. Quincy, this is Babs." She put an arm around Babs' waist. "And this," she touched Dani's arm, "is Dani. They're a couple, in case you can't tell."

"I'm happy to meet you both. I gather you were at the bar the night of the accident, and though I was staring at your table, the only one I saw was Lindy. Let's make some time to talk later. Maybe over dessert. But for now I have many guests to greet." Quincy extended her arm. "Shall we mosey around?"

Lindy took the offered arm. Mosey was no exaggeration; they couldn't walk two feet without being stopped. Quincy introduced her to everyone, not that she'd remember the names. She'd expected to feel shy and awkward, but she was enjoying being on Quincy's arm and meeting other people who cared about her. While she was turning "other people" and "cared about" over in her mind, she came face-to-face with the tall, white-haired woman she recognized as Quincy's grandmother. She tensed.

"About time you got around to me, Quincy." She pulled Lindy into a hug.

Lindy relaxed into the warmth of the embrace and the comfort of the woman's fresh fragrance, a combination of shampoo and perfume. "I'm Leigh Summers, Quincy's grandmother. I know you're Lindy. And I so appreciate you taking care of my granddaughter when she needed someone to hold her."

Lindy's face was on fire. Somehow, meeting Quincy's grandmother seemed more personal, more intimate than meeting her friends. She didn't know what to say.

"You're embarrassing her, Mama."

Lindy pulled herself together. "No, it's all right, Quincy. I'm happy to meet you too, Mrs. Summers. And I was happy to spend the weekend with Quincy. I hope she didn't tell you too many bad things about me."

"Please call me Leigh, everyone does. You may rest assured, Quincy has only said good things about you. I'm happy you decided to come today to celebrate her and the people she saved."

Lindy smiled. "I'm glad I came. Everyone has been so warm and welcoming. Did you drive up?"

They chatted a while, then Leigh was summoned by a group of older women who seemed deep into a serious discussion.

They watched Leigh walk away. "She's very nice, Quincy."

"Yes, she is." Quincy gazed at Leigh and her group of friends for a few seconds, then she scanned the room. "If we don't touch base with the dyke contingent by the fireplace Maggie will have my head."

She steered them to the group of women standing with Maggie, Babs, and Dani and introduced Lindy to the women she didn't know. Quincy was hugged, kissed, and teased by several of the women, obviously old friends. She introduced Lindy as her friend and she was welcomed, but some of the regulars from Maggie's seemed puzzled by her presence. Maggie hastened to explain how on the night of the accident she'd introduced Lindy and was responsible for getting Lindy to drive the exhausted hero home.

"Uh-oh, here comes trouble," Quincy whispered and moved closer to Lindy. "She won't take no for an answer."

"Who?" Lindy followed Quincy's gaze. Bonnie, the bitch, in her wheelchair, was headed straight for them. "You're not interested?"

Quincy laughed. "Not a chance."

Lindy slid her arm around Quincy's waist.

Bonnie glanced at Lindy but focused her megawatt smile on Quincy. "There you are. I've been looking all over for you." She extended her hand as if expecting Quincy to take it and walk away from Lindy. "Bella is asking for you."

"Oh, has she started talking since I saw her?" Lindy shifted so she was between Bonnie and Quincy.

"I'm sorry." Bonnie scowled at Lindy. "How do you know anything about my daughter?"

"I met Bella when Quincy and I visited you and your mom in the hospital after the accident. In your drugged state you chose to ignore me and flirt with Quincy. You're not still on drugs, are you? Or are you so desperate that it doesn't matter to you that she's already involved with someone?" Lindy heard the gasp from the women behind her but held her ground.

Bonnie put her hands on her hips. "Is that true, Quincy?"

"Yes. I've been trying to tell you nicely, but somehow you don't seem to hear what I'm saying."

Bonnie's face darkened. She opened her mouth but was interrupted by the sudden squawking of a microphone followed by Grace's voice.

"Hello. We'll be serving dinner in a minute, but before we begin I want to say a few words."

"Take me away," Bonnie commanded the boy pushing her wheelchair.

"It's kind of hard to flounce away in a wheelchair, but Bonnie managed." Lindy squeezed Quincy's waist. "I doubt she'll bother you again."

"Thanks. It's been unpleasant."

"Mike and I appreciate you all coming to The First Annual Thank You, Quincy Adams, Thanksgiving Celebration on such short notice. I won't embarrass Quincy by asking her to come up here and say something, but today is for you, Quincy. You saved my family and those of many others here today and nothing we can say or do will ever fully convey our gratitude. So thank you." The crowd cheered, whistled, and applauded.

Lindy poked Quincy. "Wave or they'll never stop."

Quincy followed orders and everyone quieted down. She squeezed Lindy's shoulder. "See this is why I need you around. You know how to handle these things."

"Is that the only reason you need me around, sugah?" The words were out of her mouth before her brain had a chance to edit them. She couldn't seem to help flirting with Quincy.

Quincy's grin was mischievous. "Well, since you asked—"

"One more thing before I let you eat," Grace said. "You've all heard me say a thousand times, I will be thanking Quincy for saving me and my family every single day for the rest of my life. I intend to do that publicly every year on Thanksgiving Day as long as Quincy is willing to show up here. So you'll all receive invitations, but please be sure to add the annual Thanksgiving Celebration to your calendar every year until further notice. Now dinner will be served. There are tables in various parts of the room, and all contain turkey and all the fixings. There's plenty of food so help yourselves to as much as you like. Dessert will be served later. Happy Thanksgiving."

When Lindy and Quincy got to one of the tables, Lindy was pleased to see vegetarian options that went beyond just the side vegetable dishes. Grace had thought of everyone. They filled their plates and joined Grace and Mike, Mama, Amelia, Jackson, Gina, Heather, John, Quincy's partner on the job, and his wife Gloria at a grouping of seats near one of the huge windows,

Lindy, like everyone, concentrated on eating for a few minutes, then looked up to find Maggie staring at them from across the room. She had been aware earlier that Maggie was focused on them as they moved about but thought nothing of it. Now it was making her uncomfortable, so she shifted slightly trying to block Maggie's view of her.

"What is it?" Quincy seemed to sense her discomfort.

"Maggie hasn't taken her eyes off of us. I think she's decided we're a couple and she owns us because she asked me to give you a ride home that night. I think she's planning our wedding in the bar."

Quincy laughed. "Is it that she thinks we're a couple or that she thinks she owns us or that she's planning our wedding in her bar that you're objecting to?"

"All of the above. I've never thought about getting married, but if I did, it certainly wouldn't be in a bar, sugah."

"I know your wedding wouldn't be in a church. So where *would* you get married?"

Lindy had never thought about it, but she liked the beauty of this place. She looked around. This room was beautiful in and of itself and with flowers and wedding decorations it would be stunning. She gazed out the windows at the clear blue of the sky, the sun sparking off the lake and the light coating of snow on the grounds, the deep green of the pine trees, and she imagined how magnificent the grounds would be in the summer. Religion and churches were the creations of men for men. In nature she felt the hand of a higher force at work. Outside in the beauty of nature is where she would celebrate something as important as her wedding. "Someplace beautiful like this, Quincy." She pointed out the window. "I would get married in the summer under the trees, near a lake."

Conversation in their little group stopped abruptly and all eyes fell on Quincy and Lindy. Grace broke the silence. "Sounds like you two are discussing getting married."

They locked eyes. Lindy could see Quincy was as panicked by the question as she was. "Not exactly. A wedding yes, but it was sort of a theoretical discussion and not based on anybody proposing or anything like that."

Quincy jumped in. "Yes, theoretical. You know, if you were getting married where would you want the wedding to be kind of thing."

Grace gazed at the two of them. "Uh-huh. And you agreed you would want to get married here on our property?"

Lindy fidgeted with her food. "I said it would be beautiful here in the summer and if I was getting married, I would like to do it someplace like here. Quincy didn't agree or disagree."

Quincy touched Lindy's hand. "But I do agree. And, yes, your house, your property would be perfect, Grace."

Grace responded with a mischievous glint in her eyes. "Well, it's all yours if you ever need it, either or both of you."

Lindy avoided looking at anyone. *Damn.* Every conversation was a minefield that led back to Quincy. Her eyes went to the windows again. But a wedding here would be beautiful.

CHAPTER TWENTY-THREE

Quincy picked up her phone Saturday morning, surprised to see Lindy's name on the screen so soon after spending time with her on Thanksgiving Day. Had she decided they should date? Or was she being harassed by Melanie again? "Quincy."

"Hi. Sorry to bother you so early on the weekend." Lindy spoke softly. "But since Sarah couldn't make it for Thanksgiving, she flew in yesterday and, um, she wants to meet you." She took a breath. "I thought maybe we could have lunch together. Of course, if you can't or don't want to meet her, that's okay."

Quincy hesitated, considering the request. This was a good thing, right? Sarah wouldn't even know about her if Lindy hadn't mentioned her, so it kind of confirmed that Lindy was interested. "I'd love to meet Sarah. But I have lunch plans with my grandmother."

"Okay, maybe some other time?"

Quincy couldn't tell whether Lindy was relieved or just feeling awkward at asking, but she didn't want to miss this opportunity to spend time with Lindy or to meet Sarah. "Why don't you and Sarah join Mama and me for lunch?"

"I like your grandmother. Do you think she'd mind sharing you with us?" Lindy sounded enthusiastic.

"I don't think so. She liked you a lot and hopefully she and Sarah will like each other. If you're up for it, I'll check with Mama and you can check with Sarah."

Lindy's car wasn't in the parking lot of the Chit Chat Diner so it looked like she and Mama had arrived first. Did introducing the most important women in their lives to each other mean anything about their future prospects or was she reading too much into the meeting? Why had Sarah asked to meet her?

Mama sensed her anxiety and took her hand as they walked from the car. "From what I observed Thanksgiving Day, you have nothing to worry about Quincy. Just be your beautiful self."

They were settled in a booth by the time Lindy and the motherly looking blond woman who must be Sarah appeared. Quincy waved, catching Lindy's eye, and the two women made their way to the booth. Quincy stood.

"Sarah," Lindy said, "I'd like you to meet Quincy Adams and Mrs. Summers, her grandmother. This is my mom, Sarah Wells." They all sat.

"Please call me Leigh. Mrs. Summers retired a while ago." Quincy's grandmother reached across the table to take Sarah's hand. "I'm so happy to meet you, Sarah. Lindy spoke highly of you at the Thanksgiving celebration in honor of Quincy."

While Lindy busied herself handing out the huge diner menus piled on the table in front of her, Quincy tried to figure out what to do or say. Happily, Mama sensed her unease and continued to carry the ball. "I presume Lindy has told you how these two met?"

"Yes, she has. I've heard about Quincy saving all those people and Lindy spending the weekend with her. And the strong connection they made. It all happened so quickly I wanted to meet Quincy to see if she's as wonderful as she sounds. I worry about Lindy, you know?"

Quincy hadn't expected Sarah's strong Southern drawl.

Lindy flushed. "Mom."

"Well, I do, honey. Except for Babs, you're all alone up here and—"

"I have lousy taste in women. Right?" Red-faced, Lindy eyed Leigh.

"Right." Sarah caressed Lindy's cheek. "You can hate me for loving you, but I don't want to see you hurt again." Sarah sighed. She looked at Leigh and Quincy. "I'm sorry to dump the family angst on you."

"We've been there, Sarah. Don't feel bad." Leigh smiled at Quincy.

"In any case, I wanted to meet so I could get to know you a little, Quincy, to find out who you are and whether you'll be a positive in Lindy's life. I'm probably being intrusive and meddling where I don't belong, but since I happen to be visiting in New Jersey this weekend, it seemed like a good time."

Lindy looked ready to burst into flames. "Oh, god, this is so embarrassing. We're just friends, Mom."

"But I'm definitely hoping for more, Sarah." Quincy understood where Sarah was coming from and respected her willingness to intervene to protect Lindy. She knew Mama would do the same. "The only other woman Lindy has been involved with that I've met is Melanie and I can state without reservation that I'm very different. For one I don't do drugs and I only drink socially. Even in the darkest time I've ever experienced, I've never been tempted to lose myself in either."

"So you weren't under the influence of either when you saved those people?"

"Absolutely not. In fact I had just gone off duty and was in my car on my way home when the call for assistance at a pileup came over the radio. I was tired, not high."

Sarah nodded. "You're a police officer?"

"Yes. I was a patrol officer but I've been promoted to detective."

"I gather you're a lesbian, so I assume you've been involved with other women. Why did your last relationship end?"

Quincy felt her stomach drop. Of all the things she thought about today, she didn't think she'd have to discuss Jen. She'd been talking about that day a little bit at a time in her group and individual sessions with Dr. Giles. "I—"

"Mom." Lindy cut off Quincy. "That's none of your business."

Leigh put an arm over her granddaughter's shoulder.

Quincy realized that given the circumstances of Lindy's last breakup it was a legitimate question. And Dr. Giles had been encouraging her to talk more about Jen. Besides, she just needed to answer the question, not tell the whole gruesome story. "Because Jen was killed when we were serving in Afghanistan together."

Sarah's face crumbled and tears filled her eyes. "I'm so sorry, Quincy. I didn't know. I didn't mean to be insensitive. I didn't know you'd served. Please forgive me."

"How could you know? Isn't this why you're asking questions?" Quincy took Sarah's hand. "I care about Lindy. I think we'd be really good together and I think she agrees, but we've also acknowledged that we each have things to work out before we can be in a relationship. Mine have to do with what happened in Afghanistan." Quincy smiled at Lindy.

Sarah wiped the tears from her face. "Lindy, from what you've told me and what I'm hearing from Quincy and sensing from Leigh, you might have hit the jackpot this time. Please accept my apologies for the interrogation, Quincy."

Having passed muster, Quincy relaxed. "No apology needed, Sarah. I assure you, if Lindy and I do get together, I will be as protective as you."

Lindy grunted. "You already are."

Leigh picked up her menu. "Now that we've got that out of the way, why don't we order and spend some time getting to know each other better."

"Thank you, Mrs., um, Leigh, I think that's a great idea." Lindy winked at Quincy, then opened her menu.

Quincy grinned and picked up her menu. Mama pinched her thigh. "Happy?"

"I am." Quincy looked over at her grandmother, then her gaze went to Sarah. Their eyes locked and Sarah smiled. Quincy was ecstatic. They had Sarah's and Leigh's approval and the rest was up to them.

CHAPTER TWENTY-FOUR

The text came in as Quincy and John were headed back to the station after questioning a witness to an assault. Quincy was driving so she handed her phone to John.

He read it to her.

Babs says Melanie is waiting outside. I'm afraid to leave work.

"Who is Melanie?"

"Lindy's ex. Lindy has an order of protection against her. She's an addict. I happened to be in Shop Rite's parking lot when she assaulted Lindy a while ago. I intervened. Ask if she's called the local police."

John texted.

Have you called the police?

Yes, all tied up at an accident. Will be a couple of hours.

"They can't get to her for hours," John said. "We should go."

Quincy pulled over and put the car in park. "So we follow her home today, but what about tomorrow? I'd love to arrest the bitch, get her out of circulation for a while."

John fingered the notebook in his lap. "What if we lured her to Hackensack?"

Quincy thought about it. "Then arrest her if she approaches Lindy? I like it." She grinned. "Okay, Captain Justice, let me text Lindy." He handed her the phone.

On the way. John will escort you to your car. Let her follow you to the Sears parking lot in Hackensack. When you see us, get out of the car. We'll take it from there. Oh, address of your job?

Quincy was tense as she drove to the trucking company on Route 46. She pulled into the lot and when John went into the building she scanned for Melanie. No surprise, she was in her car parked a few cars down from Lindy's Subaru. A few moments later, Lindy and John emerged. They seemed to be engaged in a lively conversation as they headed to her car. Lindy looked composed and Quincy didn't miss the quick flick of her eyes in the direction of the unmarked and the sweet smile that flickered on her lips.

Quincy relaxed and thanked her lucky stars that Connie had assigned her to work with John. She appreciated his willingness to stretch the rules a little to protect Lindy.

After Lindy started her car, John strolled back and slid into the unmarked.

"She's locked in and good to go," John said.

"Okay, let's do it then." Quincy drove out of the lot to give Melanie the impression they were leaving Lindy on her own but stopped at a nearby gas station. When Lindy, followed by Melanie, went by, Quincy fell in behind them.

As Quincy parked in the Sears lot, Lindy got out of her car. Seconds later Melanie grabbed her and pushed her against the car just as she had the last time. Lindy screamed. Quincy and John were out of the car in seconds. John called, "Stop, police," and pulled Melanie off Lindy. Before she knew what hit her Melanie was facedown on the ground in cuffs. Lindy clung to Quincy. A woman getting into her car turned to see what was happening. She had her phone in her hand. Quincy held out her ID and called out. "It's okay, we're police. We've got this." Holding on to Lindy, she walked over to take the witness's information. Lindy assured the woman she was okay now and thanked her for her attempt to help.

They'd agreed it would be better for Quincy to remain in the background and for John to make the arrest, so he pulled Melanie up. "You're under arrest for assault."

Lindy left Quincy and approached John and Melanie. "Not only that, she's violating an order of protection," Lindy said, as John had instructed her to do on the walk to her car.

"And for violating your order of protection." He dragged Melanie into the police car to take her in. Quincy stayed with Lindy.

They looked at each other in the dim light of the parking lot. "We've got to stop meeting like this." Lindy bent over. Quincy thought she was laughing, but when she straightened Quincy saw she was crying.

"Thank you for rescuing me again, Quincy. I'm so sorry to involve you in my messy life. This is exactly what I was trying to avoid."

"Everybody's life is messy sometimes, Lindy. I'm really glad you texted me. John and I are going to try to get Melanie sent someplace where she can get clean so she'll leave you alone, but whether it's her or someone else threatening you, I hope you'll always call me."

Lindy wrapped her arms around Quincy and rested her head on her chest. "My very own superhero. I like it."

Warmed by Lindy's actions, Quincy embraced her and gently pulled her closer. She brushed the hair off Lindy's face. "I like it too. A lot." Holding Lindy, being so close felt so right. Quincy breathed in the sweet fragrance of Lindy, her shampoo, her light perfume, and what was probably her sweat.

Lindy shivered and pulled back to look at her. "This is nice, but I'm getting cold. Would you have dinner with me, at our favorite diner? On me this time."

"I thought you'd never ask. But John took our car, so you'll have to drive, then drop me at the station later so I can pick up my car."

After the waitress disappeared with their orders, they were silent.

Lindy cleared her throat. "Will Melanie go to jail?"

Quincy eyed her. "Jail won't help her. John is going to see if he can get her fast-tracked into a rehab treatment facility. I hope you agree that's the right way to go."

"I do. This may be the only opportunity she'll have to pull herself out of this downward spiral."

"Since you'll probably have to testify when she appears before a judge, you can ask the judge to get her help."

"I will. I feel guilty I couldn't help her when we were together." Lindy's eyes glistened with tears. "It's painful to see her like this."

Quincy leaned forward as if getting closer would make her point. "I'm sure it is, but you shouldn't feel guilty. Addicts don't want help, they want money for drugs. Hopefully, once she detoxes she'll figure out whether or not she wants to live a different life. No one can do it for her. Melanie has to want to help herself."

"I'll try to remember that." Lindy dabbed at her eyes. "You made quite an impression on Sarah," she said, changing the subject.

Quincy straightened her silverware. "I'm glad. Especially if her approval encourages you to think about dating me officially."

"It wasn't just your answers to her questions, it was the discussion afterward, your close relationship with Leigh, your thoughtfulness, your caring for me, and your commitment to making the world a better place."

"Sarah got all that from our lunch?"

"Some from lunch and some from the discussions she and Leigh have had since. Who could have guessed they would become friends?" Lindy looked thoughtful. "And I guess she got some from me. I told her about your rescuing me from Melanie the last time. She'll probably put you in her superhero category after today."

"As long as I'm *your* superhero, I'm fine being in her run-of-the-mill hero category." Quincy grinned. "So what are you reading these days?"

Despite the stress of Melanie's stalking and the ongoing tension between them, the conversation flowed easily from books to music to both their jobs and the evening flew by. Lindy paid the check and they walked to her car in silence. Lindy opened her door but rather than getting in, she faced Quincy and kissed her cheek. "Thank you for being there for me again. I don't trust easily and up to now only Sarah and Babs have made the grade, but I do trust you, my superhero. I really enjoy being with you."

"I enjoy our time together too."

Though John had called to say Melanie was locked up, after Quincy retrieved her car from the police lot, she followed Lindy home and watched until she was safely inside.

Each time they were together they moved closer. And each time they were together she ended up yearning for more.

CHAPTER TWENTY-FIVE

When the phone rang, Quincy was in a rage at what Rachel Maddow was reporting. She grabbed her phone and answered angrily. "Yes." She heard an intake of breath, then silence. "Who's there?"

Throat clearing. "Hi, it's me. Lindy." She sounded so tentative Quincy was sure something was wrong. But it couldn't be Melanie. Had something happened to Babs or Sarah? "Oh, hi, Lindy. Is everything okay?"

"Yes." She laughed. "Since I only call you when I'm in trouble, I guess it's natural to assume something is wrong."

"It's just that you surprised me in a middle of a rant at the TV. These politicians make me nuts. You're sure everything is all right?"

"Yes. Fine actually."

Quincy tried to come up with something to say, but she seemed to have a sudden attack of brain freeze. Jeez, they hadn't been this awkward when they slept together as strangers. And certainly not in their recent encounters.

After a few seconds listening to each other breathe, Lindy laughed nervously. "This is harder than I thought it would be. Are you mad at me, Quincy?"

Quincy hesitated. "No, not mad, just awkward for some reason. I wasn't expecting you to call." *Very suave, Quincy, why not just tell her you've been counting the minutes, unable to think of anything but her?*

"Why would you, I've been kind of there and not there, haven't I?"

"You've been there whenever we're together, but then you disappear and I start to feel as if I imagined our connection. It throws me off balance." Since last week when they'd had dinner after the incident with Melanie, Quincy had felt sad, yearning to see Lindy, yet fearing they might never be more than casual friends.

"Sorry, I'll explain when I see you. That is if you still want to go on that date? With me, I mean."

Quincy's heart rejoiced. "I do, I mean yes. Is tomorrow night too soon?"

"It's perfect." Lindy's voice was stronger, and Quincy could almost hear her smile. And her relief.

"All right. Dinner. I'll pick you up at seven at your apartment." She couldn't stop grinning.

Lindy laughed softly. "So I'll see you at seven tomorrow?"

"You definitely will. Thanks for calling. And for asking."

"You're welcome. I'm sorry it took me so long to get here. Good night, Quincy."

"Good night, Lindy." Quincy turned off the TV, got online and researched vegetarian restaurants. She made a seven thirty p.m. reservation at The Veggie Place, a highly rated restaurant in River Edge, a nearby town. She did a little dance around the house, took a shower, and went to bed, anxious for tomorrow to arrive.

The Veggie Place was perfect. The blazing fire in a large stone fireplace, the peach walls lined with pastel paintings of fruits and vegetables, peach tablecloths and napkins, and glowing candles on each perfectly set table created the romantic and intimate atmosphere she'd hoped for. They were seated at a table facing the fireplace. Quincy ordered a glass of cabernet for herself and a Perrier and lime for Lindy.

Sitting across from Lindy in the beautiful candlelit restaurant, Quincy's mind filled with images of her dancing alone in Maggie's the Friday night she first saw her. Even at one of the lowest points in her life, she'd been attracted to the beauty and the joy she'd seen in this woman. And if the accident hadn't happened, they might never have met. Lost in thought, she placed her napkin on her lap and fiddled with her silverware. Was she happy that people were injured and died so they could meet?

"Why the frown?" Lindy reached across the table and took Quincy's hand. "You seem distant."

Quincy loved that Lindy was not shy about touching her. She entwined their fingers, then raised her eyes. In the flickering candlelight, Lindy looked ethereal, almost too perfect for this world. Could it be they were meant to meet?

Lindy squeezed Quincy's hand. "Are you willing to share your thoughts?"

It felt weird to say it out loud, but after that weekend of intense conversations and the way they'd connected recently, she felt sure Lindy would understand. "That good can come from the most horrendous things. If it wasn't for the accident, I wouldn't have come to Maggie's that Friday and we might never have met."

Lindy nodded. "So maybe that was the goddess's intention, to test you, have you experience something awful, then find something…somebody you feel compatible with."

Quincy grinned. "A little convoluted on her part, wouldn't you say?"

"I'm just a poor sinner so I can't speak for the goddess. But however it came about, I'm glad we met, Johna Quincy Adams."

"Yikes." Quincy pulled her hand back and covered her face in mock terror. "I shouldn't have told you my full name."

"You absolutely should have. Full disclosure is necessary if we're going to be friends." Lindy sipped her seltzer. "And I hope we will be friends." She smiled sweetly. "More than friends actually. But first I owe you an explanation." Before she could begin, the waitress arrived, took their orders, and left.

Lindy fiddled with the stirrer from her drink. "The instant I saw you sitting at the bar all curled into yourself, I wanted to wrap my arms around you to comfort you. Then, I saw on the TV that you'd saved all those people and risked your life to save a woman trapped in her car and I was awed by your bravery. It was clear that you were spiraling downward rather than celebrating and I wanted to do something to make you feel better.

"But, then, as we spent time together over the weekend it became less about compassion and more about attraction, a strong attraction. By that Monday morning I was having fantasies of us being together, being a couple, but not really acknowledging them to myself. When you asked me to go on a date, it scared the hell out of me. I'd convinced myself that I was a loner, that I didn't want or need a relationship but after the closeness of the weekend, after experiencing the joy of being with you, I couldn't deny what I was feeling, what I wanted. So I did what I always do when I'm scared. I ran."

She sipped her drink. "Running didn't help. I couldn't stop thinking about you. I thought distance would help so I decided to move to Florida. Babs convinced me to take a little time to think it through before packing up and leaving town."

"Was it something I did?"

"No, sugah, it wasn't something you did. It was all about me." She lifted her gaze and took in the restaurant, the restaurant Quincy had chosen specially for her. She loved that it was vegetarian. She was charmed by its warmth and sensuality and color. Quincy saw her. No other woman had ever taken the time to look.

She shifted her focus to Quincy, her gentleness, her kindness, her bravery, her generous nature, and so much more. She wanted Quincy to know everything.

"I told you I lived with Melanie when we came to New Jersey from Atlanta. But I didn't tell you that once we were here she became abusive, emotionally and physically. It started slowly so I didn't notice at first. She expected me to shop and cook and pay for everything while she kept her money. Then she stopped working. When she demanded I hand over my full salary, I objected. That was the first time she hit me. When I withdrew, she forced me to have sex. I was miserable. I thought of leaving, but I had no money. She'd meet me at work on payday, drive me to the bank so I could cash my check and give the money to her. At first she gave me money each day to shop for food, but after a while she only gave me money for gas so I could get to work.

"I was friendly with Babs at work, but we weren't close and there was no one else I could talk to. Babs noticed I never had lunch so she started bringing extra for me, saying it was leftovers so I had to help her get rid of it. When I fought back, Mel beat me with her belt. The night I refused to have sex with her drug dealer she used the belt buckle. That was it for me. I snuck out of the house in the middle of the night and called Sarah. I was hysterical. After she got the whole story out of me, she told me to check into a hotel and wait for her. The next morning I called in sick to work. Sarah was able to get on the first flight to Newark and was at the hotel by noon."

Lindy stared into the fire. "She held me until I had no tears left, then she called a friend in Florida who had a friend who knew a therapist in Maywood and arranged an emergency family session for us. The therapist got that I was in crisis and saw us at seven a.m. the next morning and then every day for a week until I pulled myself together.

"Sarah wanted to take me back to Florida with her, but I wasn't fourteen this time and I didn't want to run away again. I wanted to understand why I had allowed myself to be abused and to learn to make better choices. I needed to be independent, to build a life on my terms. My therapist agreed it would be better for me to stay, so Sarah relented. The next week, I went back to work and confided in Babs."

Lindy laughed. "Babs had suspected something was going on but didn't want to be intrusive. She offered to organize a group to go after Melanie with a baseball bat. But better than that, it turned out her roommate was moving out in a week and she offered me her room. Before saying yes, I invited Babs to dinner with Sarah and by the end of the night Sarah agreed that living with Babs would be good for me. In the meantime, I stayed at the hotel with Sarah."

Lindy finished her seltzer. "At the insistence of my therapist, I got a restraining order against Melanie. The day after Babs' roommate moved out, two police officers came with Babs, Sarah, and me to my apartment and waited while we packed my clothing and the few other things I owned. They also followed us to Babs' place to make sure Melanie didn't come after us. Sarah stayed with us for a month, then when she felt sure I was back on track, she went home. I saw that therapist for a year. And I've been seeing her again for the last five weeks."

Lindy met Quincy's eyes. "Babs is the only one I've let myself get close to since Melanie. I'm ashamed I stayed with Melanie so long after the abuse started. And I haven't trusted myself to date anyone, afraid that I'll choose another abuser. That's why I ran."

"Thank you for telling me." Quincy held Lindy's eyes. "I am so, so sorry you had to go through that. I'll do whatever it takes to show you that you're safe with me."

"If I didn't believe I'd be safe with you, we wouldn't be here tonight. I can't promise I won't get scared again, but I'm willing to try if you still want me."

Quincy retrieved Lindy's hands and looked into her eyes again. "Devastated as I was that night, I was drawn to you the moment I saw you at Maggie's." She kissed her knuckles. "Given what you said about being afraid to date, why did you agree to drive me home and then stay overnight with me, a total stranger?"

"That instant pull and curiosity, at first. It was unusual to see a cop in Maggie's and you looked bedraggled and out of it. But then when Maggie pointed out that you'd saved all those people, I was impressed and sympathetic. I felt bad that you seemed so alone, and I wanted to make you feel better. I almost didn't stay when you invited me, but I could see you needed the human contact, so I said yes."

She grinned. "What I didn't realize was how much *I* needed human contact. Touching you, holding you, talking to you, cooking for you, caring for you, and sharing with you opened me up, made me feel alive. By Saturday afternoon, I was feeling close to you and happier than I had been in a very long time. And, though I didn't admit it to myself, I felt the connection too. I wanted to be with you as much as you needed me to be there."

Lindy brought one of Quincy's hands to her lips. She grinned, then blew out her breath. "Why did you let a stranger drive you home? And why did you ask a stranger to stay with you?"

Quincy thought back to that night. "You seemed so happy, so full of life. I was drawn to your light or what I saw as your light. After we talked for a while, I could feel myself pulling back from the dark. So when you offered to drive me home I accepted. But as we approached my apartment, I could feel the despair moving in again, filling the light spaces, and I knew I would sink into the dark if I were alone. That's why I asked you to stay. It was the best decision I've made in a very long time." She smiled.

They eyed each other quietly for a few minutes. "Okay, sugah, now that we have that out of the way, let's discuss some limits. We met when you were quite stressed. We've already spent more time together than we would have if we'd dated intensely for a couple of weeks. And we've even spent three nights sleeping in each other's arms. We know that we both want a relationship. But I don't want to screw this up, so I'd like us to get to know each other before we make love. Is that okay with you?"

"It's perfect. I've been in a PTSD group with an army shrink dealing with the trauma of the accident and I'd rather regain my equilibrium before getting too emotionally involved. But I hope we don't have to wait too long between dates."

"Let's enjoy this date before we worry about the next." Lindy let go of Quincy's hands and looked up at the waitress who had arrived with their dinners. "That looks and smells fabulous." She sniffed her stuffed cabbage. "I love the spices." She took a bite. "Yum. It tastes as good as it smells." She held her fork out to Quincy. "I'm offering you a taste of my wonderful stuffed cabbage hoping you'll give me a taste of your lasagna." Quincy opened her mouth to take in the cabbage, then reciprocated with her lasagna. They smiled as their eyes met.

"I was so proud of you the night you got your medal. You looked like you'd adjusted to being a superhero. Is that true?"

Quincy laughed. "Dr. Giles finished what you started, helping me own the praise and recognition, helping me believe I'm a hero. I don't know if you noticed the group of women in military uniforms sitting in the audience, but Dr. Giles was there with the other women in the PTSD group to support me."

"How do you like being a detective?"

"I love it. I got to work on the Tiffany Maggio kidnapping case. And since I'm your superhero I'll share something I'm very proud of. It was my interview of a witness that elicited the information that led to finding her."

Lindy's fork stopped halfway to her mouth. "Why haven't I read anything about your part in it?"

"I wasn't really a detective yet, I was just shadowing John, so I wasn't officially on the task force. He tried to give me credit, but the powers that be felt it was his interview and he deserved the credit. As far as I was concerned, the last thing I wanted was more attention, so I was fine with it."

They were chatting over dessert of fruit and gelato when Quincy remembered the photos. "I almost forgot. The day I went back to work I received a package at work with a gift for each of us."

Lindy frowned. "You received a gift for me, at your job? Did Chief Trubeck get me something?"

"Nope. I'll be right back." She dashed out to the car and came back with the bag containing the photos. "Ta-da!" She handed the photos to Lindy.

Lindy's eyes widened. "Oh, my god, they're gorgeous. I framed the picture that appeared in the newspaper, but these are so much better. That photographer was right. We look beautiful together." She was glowing when she looked up. "We do, don't we?"

"We do. Here's the note she sent."

Lindy read and reread the note. "I guess I have to forgive her because I love these pictures. Which do you want?"

"Either one is fine with me. You choose."

Lindy deliberated for several minutes, then selected one. A few minutes later, the waitress brought the check and noticed the pictures with Quincy in uniform. "Now I know why you look familiar. You're the officer who saved those people, right?"

Quincy glanced at Lindy and was rewarded with a mischievous grin and a nod. "Yes."

"I'd love to buy you another glass of wine."

"Thanks, but I'm done for tonight."

"A rain check then. Next time." Her eyes went to the pictures again. "The photographer captured a lovely moment between you. How long have you been together?"

"Actually, we'd only known each other about fourteen hours when the photographer snapped that picture." Lindy studied the photos. "She saw something we didn't know was happening. This is our first date."

"That's amazing."

The roads were slick on the ride back to Lindy's apartment so Quincy focused on driving, but when she felt Lindy's hand on her thigh, she glanced at her.

Lindy flushed. "Is this okay?"

"More than okay. It feels wonderful."

Lindy cleared her throat. "I don't mean to rush things, sugah, but I'm feeling… Um, I'd love for you to spend Christmas with me, Babs and Dani, and some friends, mostly hers but to some degree, mine. We do a grab bag and a big Christmas Eve dinner, then a more relaxed Christmas Day."

"Christmas Eve with you and your friends sounds wonderful. I've agreed to have Christmas Day with Grace and Mike. I know they'd love for you to come too. How about it? And Amelia and Jackson always have a Day After Christmas open house that I help out with. Many of my friends will be there. Would you come with me?"

Lindy gently rubbed Quincy's thigh. "Yes. To both."

Quincy's body heated. "Better be careful how you touch me when I'm driving." She pulled up in front of Lindy's apartment and put the car in park. They locked eyes and grinned at each other for a few seconds before leaning in for their first kiss, which turned into several real kisses.

Finally, Lindy pulled away and fanned herself. "This is fun, but tomorrow is a work day so I'd better go in while I can still walk. Goodnight." Brushing Quincy's lips lightly, she got out of the car, slipped into her chocolate-colored faux sheepskin coat, zipped it, then waved.

Quincy enjoyed the easy swing of Lindy's hips as she walked up the path. At the door, she waved again and stepped into the house. Quincy put the car in gear and drove home, feeling happier than she'd been in years. Since Jen.

CHAPTER TWENTY-SIX

Quincy had never had such a full calendar of holiday events. And at many of them she was being honored and celebrated. And if Lindy hadn't been at her side for every event she probably would have freaked out. But Lindy being there made being celebrated tolerable and even enjoyable. She'd also received numerous gifts, flowers, candy, books, gift cards, CDs, scarves and gloves, and even a couple of sweaters from the people she'd rescued, from others who'd been there and witnessed her efforts to save everyone, and from people who'd read about her.

Christmas shopping, which Quincy had always found painful, became an entirely new and wondrous experience in the company of Lindy. Together they bought gifts for the grab bag at the Christmas Eve get-together with Lindy's friends. Lindy helped her pick out gifts for Mama, Amelia and Jackson, Gina and Heather and their two girls, and Grace and Mike and their four children. They also shopped for Maggie and Lane and Quincy's other friends, some of whom they'd see Christmas evening, others they'd see before or after the holiday.

Quincy arrived early on Christmas Eve. Lindy welcomed her with a sweet kiss, took her coat and the wine and beer she'd brought as her contribution to the dinner, then escorted her to her small, neat bedroom. Lindy's copy of the photo of the two of them had the place of honor on her dresser, but Quincy was surprised to see the newspaper photograph of the two of them framed and hung on the wall along with a collage of photographs of them at the park and some of the newspaper articles about her. She embraced Lindy. "It's nice to see your space and nice to see that you keep me here with you."

Lindy brushed her lips over Quincy's. "I thought I made it clear that I want you with me as much as possible." She looked up at the sound of voices from the living room. "We should join the others."

During the wonderful potluck Christmas Eve dinner Lindy's friends asked Quincy questions about the accident and how she felt while saving people. She hesitated, not wanting to be seen as bragging. Lindy touched her thigh lightly to get her attention and whispered in her ear. "It's okay to talk about it, sugah."

Encouraged to be forthcoming, Quincy described the horror of the scene and acting despite her fear, then contrasted it with the wonder of meeting Lindy and spending the weekend together. When Quincy stopped talking the group was silent. Everyone seemed absorbed in her own thoughts.

Quincy took a sip of water. "So, now you've learned something about me, would you each share something about yourself, what work you do or your hobby, something you're proud of or whatever you'd like to share."

They shuffled in their seats, glanced at each other, then Dani spoke. "By day, I work for the US post office, but by night and on weekends I'm a jock. Depending on the season, I play baseball, soccer, or basketball in a lesbian sports league. And, oh, I'm also in a relationship with Babs."

"And occasionally she fits me in." Babs laughed and elbowed Dani. "Lucky you remembered to mention me." She turned to Quincy. "As you know I'm Lindy's roommate and I work at DiMonte Trucking with her. I'm responsible for accounts receivable. And, oh, Dani is my girlfriend." She poked Dani again. "Right?"

Dani feigned injury. "Right."

"I'm a hairdresser and the owner of the Perfect Style hair salon." Judy, the strawberry blonde, fluffed her perfectly styled glossy hair. "I've been admiring your haircut. Who does it?"

Quincy laughed and ran a hand through her hair. "Actually, my friend Heather has cut it for years. She trimmed it over Thanksgiving, but she's living in Maryland now so I'll be looking for someone the next time."

"Try me." Judy handed her a business card.

Debbi, a petite redhead, had been bug-eyed hanging on Quincy's every word. "I'm just a secretary for a lawyer in town. But I'm a shortstop on the baseball team and a guard on the soccer team."

Quincy gripped her shoulder. "We don't do 'just,' Debbi. Everybody has different life challenges. I admire your bravery working for a lawyer. And it sure sounds like you have a little jock in you."

"Shayne Elliot, my boss, is a lesbian and she's great to work for." Debbi flushed. "I might have a tiny bit of jock."

"Don't listen to her, Quincy. She's a whiz on the field," Dani said.

"I thought so." Quincy smiled. "Shayne Elliot is well known for helping lesbians with legal issues and she's considered a hard-ass in police circles. A good hard-ass, so my guess is she doesn't hire wimps."

Pam raised her hand. "I'm a paraprofessional working with special needs elementary school children in Hackensack. My special talent is reading lesbian fiction."

"Ha, you and Quincy should get along. She loves lesbian romances." Lindy punched Quincy's arm lightly.

Pam brightened. "Maybe we can talk later. I love romance too."

"Sure." Quincy's attention went to the voice coming from behind her. "I'm Nora, a neonatal nurse at Hackensack Hospital." She was in front of the open refrigerator. "Anyone need another beer?"

Three hands went up. "My hobby is riding my Harley. And I'm pretty sure you almost gave me a ticket last year." Nora passed out the beers and sat. "Your turn, Teddi."

Quincy held up a hand. "Wait. Almost? Were you speeding, Nora?"

"Absolutely not. Do you think I'm nuts?" She grinned. "I might have been riding between the two lanes of traffic on Essex Street and weaving in and out because I was late for my shift. You stopped me, but you actually listened to my sob story and gave me a pass. No ticket." She tipped an imaginary hat. "Thanks, friend."

The butch sitting next to Nora put a proprietary arm around her shoulder. "I'm Teddi. I sell Harleys for a living. I taught Nora how to ride, but somehow she missed the lesson on not driving between lanes on a two-lane road. I'm honored to meet you. You must really be something to catch our little Lindy bird. She's always blown off anybody who asked her out. Until you. Welcome to our group."

Had she caught Lindy? She hoped it was mutual. "Thank you, I'm pleased to be here."

Teddi nodded to the woman sitting next to her. She'd been politely hostile to Quincy since she arrived, so Quincy assumed she was one of those Lindy had blown off. "I'm Lizbeth and if I'd realized Lindy wanted a superhero, I would have dashed into a burning school to save children or done something else noteworthy with my life instead of becoming a mere dance instructor with her own dance studio." She bared her teeth in what could pass for a smile, but it didn't reach her eyes and was contradicted by the tone of her voice.

"I'm flattered you consider me a superhero, Lizbeth, but you have a superpower I lack. I'm a terrible dancer. Perhaps you could show me a few steps at Maggie's sometime."

"Maybe." Lizbeth gazed at Lindy. "And maybe Lindy will finally grace me with a dance."

Lindy held Lizbeth's gaze. "I'm sorry if I hurt you, Lizbeth. I meant what I said. I thought I was a loner. I thought I couldn't be in a relationship so I kept everyone at arm's length. Ask Babs.

I tried to fight this thing with Quincy, but when something is right, it's right. And it's not because she's a hero, so don't go rushing into burning buildings or other dangerous situations on my behalf."

Everyone, including Lizbeth, laughed and the tension in the room eased.

Babs stood. "There's still plenty of food, so help yourself to seconds and fresh drinks." The group milled around the table for a few minutes, then settled down again with plates piled high and more drinks. The introductions continued.

By the time they got to the grab bag everyone was a little tipsy. There was much teasing and laughter and, as they each pulled gag gifts from the grab bag to which they'd contributed anonymously, the group became more raucous and raunchy.

Lindy slowly unwrapped a pretty package with a tiny Santa attached to it. "Oh, my god." Avoiding Quincy's eyes, she waved the strap-on dildo she'd selected. With much laughter and teasing the group discussed proper strap-on technique and the pleasures to be had, then debated whether Quincy or Lindy should wear it and whether you had to be a butch to use it. Quincy and Lindy were red-faced, and both refused to reveal whether they'd ever used one.

Quincy was next and she decided a small package might be a safe bet. Her gift contained nipple clamps and two anal plugs in different colors. She tried for blasé but couldn't keep the body flush from her neck and face. She glanced quickly at Lindy and was rewarded with a shy smile. After the requisite discussion of how to use them and the pleasures to be gotten, the group got back to the grab bag. The teasing and laughter continued while the remaining gifts were opened. The gifts they'd contributed, pink fur handcuffs and a pink whip, were a hit as were the vibrators, a double strap-on dildo, a single hand-held dildo, more nipple clamps, anal plugs, a riding crop, a paddle, and lesbian erotica and romance books.

"That was hot, ladies." Babs fanned herself. "Let's take a break and refresh our drinks and ourselves."

"Wait, there's one more gift. I forgot to put it in the grab bag." When Dani had their attention, she went down on one knee in front of Babs and took her hand. Babs looked like a deer caught in the headlights. "Babs, you are the love of my life and I want to spend the rest of our lives together. Will you marry me?"

Lindy gasped. Babs recovered from her shock and responded with a gorgeous smile. "Yes. Definitely. I will."

Dani slipped the engagement ring on Babs' finger and stood. They kissed while the group cheered. The evening ended with admiration of the ring by all, hugs, kisses, and heartfelt congratulations.

At the door, Quincy kissed Lindy goodnight. After all the sex talk and teasing, she was turned on. She wished they hadn't agreed to go slow. "I had a great time. It's been a long time since I laughed so much." She kissed Lindy again.

"I did too." Lindy responded to the kiss, laid her head on Quincy's chest, and wrapped her arms around Quincy.

After a moment, Quincy pulled away. "I'd better go before I throw you over my shoulder and take you home to my bed."

"Hmm." Lindy tightened her hold on Quincy. After a moment she looked up. "Speaking of bed, did you take your grab bag gift?"

"No, I left them. It seems like they belong with your dildo." Quincy kissed her again. "Goodnight. I'll see you in the morning."

CHAPTER TWENTY-SEVEN

Lindy arrived early Christmas morning to make a special breakfast for Quincy. She moved around the now-familiar kitchen singing and dancing while she prepared challah French toast with fresh fruit and maple syrup.

Quincy poured maple syrup on her toast and took a bite. "Yum, delicious as always, Lindy."

Lindy fixed her toast with butter and maple syrup, and piled strawberries on top. "Um, it is good."

Quincy took a second slice and some strawberries. "Are you close friends with any of the women from last night? I'm mean other than Babs?"

Lindy considered the question. "I sort of inherited them when I moved in with Babs. I like them and I'm friendly with all of them, but in reality they're not my friends in the way Amelia and Gina are your friends."

"You seem really relaxed with them."

Lindy thought for a minute. "I am. They're all really nice and they welcomed me into the group, and they tolerate my need for space and time alone. But Babs is the only one I share any feelings with. And she tells me I barely do that." Lindy shrugged.

"Hey, as long as you don't shut me out, I'm fine." Quincy kissed Lindy. "We'd better get ready or we won't have time to open our presents."

After they'd cleaned up, they turned on the Christmas tree lights and sat on the sofa to exchange gifts. They'd considered limiting the number of gifts they could get each other but decided on a dollar cap of two hundred dollars. Lindy put three gifts for Quincy on the coffee table and Quincy put two out for Lindy.

"I'll start." Lindy picked one and handed it to Quincy. It was a small, beautifully wrapped package with a splash of colorful ribbons.

Quincy rattled it, turned it around a few times. "Not an umbrella." She tore the paper and opened the box. Her eyes widened. She picked up the gorgeous silver and turquoise bracelet and read the card.

Quincy, this handmade solid sterling silver cuff with a unique oval turquoise stone surrounded by intricate details in silver reminded me of you, of your strength and beauty and uniqueness. Turquoise is a stone of protection and empowerment and healing, perfect for a superhero. Wear the bracelet and think of me. Merry Christmas, Lindy.

Quincy slipped it on and extended her wrist. "Wow. Bracelets are usually too girly, but this is perfect. I love it, thank you." She leaned in and kissed Lindy. "Now you get one of mine." She handed Lindy a box of about the same size as the one that had held her bracelet, neatly wrapped in gold foil and tied with a green ribbon.

Lindy methodically removed the wrapping paper and folded it for reuse. She hesitated, then removed the cover of the box. "Oh, Quincy." She removed the colorful silver cuff inlaid with a green, blue, yellow, and gold enamel design, silver studs, and orange stones. "This is so me. I love it." She undid the silver chain that locked the bracelet and slipped it on.

Quincy's grin split her face. "It's a handmade tribal Berber silver bracelet worn in traditional Afghani weddings and religious ceremonies. It's an antique. The stones are real coral. I knew it was you the minute I saw it. But um, I have to confess I went over the limit we set."

Lindy fingered the bracelet. "A lot?"

Quincy bit her lip. "Not much. Less than twenty percent. But I really, really want you to have it, so I didn't buy any other gifts."

"I love it and I'd love to keep it if you don't mind spending the extra money?"

Quincy pulled Lindy onto her lap and whispered in her ear. "You have to keep it." Their lips met and they got lost in kissing until they had to come up for air. Quincy glanced at the time. "Uh-oh, if we don't start moving, we'll be late for dinner."

They quickly opened the remaining presents. Quincy gave Lindy a CD she'd made of Lindy's favorite dance music. Lindy gave Quincy a black silk shirt and a new wallet.

Christmas dinner with Grace and her family was different than the lesbian potluck the night before, but it was fun and raucous in its own way, with the kids squealing and laughing as they tore the paper off the presents Quincy gave them. And best of all for Quincy, surrounded by Lindy's warmth and her strong connection with Grace and Mike and both sets of their parents, it felt like home, as if they were all family.

Quincy gave Grace a necklace and Mike a pocket watch, and since Lindy had reminded her both sets of parents would be there she had small presents for each of them as well. Grace stood and handed Quincy a small package. "This is for both of you. I hope you don't mind a joint gift."

Quincy and Lindy exchanged a glance. Quincy shrugged covering her surprise. "Well, unless it's in the vein of some of the grab bag gifts we got last night, I think it's safe to say we're okay with it. And please don't ask about those gifts." She extended the package to Lindy. "You open it."

Lindy pulled back. "I never expected—"

"We know." Appearing excited, Grace hovered nearby on her crutches. "One of you open the damned thing, please."

Lindy met Quincy's eyes and accepted the package. She picked at the ribbon, pulled the wrapping paper open, and stared at the several sheets of paper nestled inside. She read the note aloud.

> *Dear Quincy and Lindy,*
> *We thought a long time about what to get each of you and then decided on a joint gift of something that we have enjoyed in the past, time together in a beautiful place. We hope you will enjoy this five-day getaway in the Turks and Caicos as much as we have. It includes hotel with meals, airfare, and transportation to and from the airport on both ends.*
> *With love and eternal gratitude,*
> *Grace and Mike*

Lindy stood and hugged Grace. "Wow. Thank you. Thank you."

"We can't accept it." Quincy looked at Grace with regret. "It's too expensive, and it may not even be legal, given departmental regulations."

Grace put her hands on her hips. "I challenge anyone to say it's too much. Anyway, Mike checked with Chief Trubeck about this and the Thanksgiving celebration, and he was told there was no problem since we're friends and friends can give any presents they like. Besides, it's Lindy's gift too. So that's that. Go forth and enjoy."

Lindy burst out laughing. "Sorry, Quincy, it looks like you have no choice but to lie on the beach with me and sip frozen margaritas for five days. What do you say?"

Quincy looked at them and knew she'd lost that argument. "Thank you. It's an extravagant and wonderful gift."

"You're probably tired of hearing me say this, Quincy, but nothing could ever be as extravagant and wonderful as the gift you gave all of us." Grace swung herself over to Quincy on her crutches and threw her arms around her. "Be brave. We're just trying to show you how much we love you."

Quincy tightened her arms around Grace and kissed the top of her head. "It looks like I'll need forever to learn that I can't win when you make up your mind."

She and Grace had become good friends, not just because of the rescue but because they recognized something basic in each other. She wasn't sure what it was, but Lindy said it was because they were both exceptionally brave and caring women.

The cook announced dinner and they made their way to the table. The meal, roasted vegetables with a wine and mushroom gravy over polenta for Lindy and roast duck for everyone else, was delicious.

Grace and Mike were their first friends as a couple. She shouldn't have been surprised given the circumstances and the fact that she and Grace had bonded so quickly, but she hadn't expected the four of them to connect in such a deep way. They chatted comfortably during dinner, making an effort to include Grace's and Mike's parents.

Though she loved kids, she'd never seriously thought about having any. But she was captivated watching Lindy relate to Morgan, Tori, Felix, and little Annie at dinner, drawing the older kids out about school and other things in their lives, helping the younger ones eat, calming the baby when she was upset, and laughing with them.

Could they have children? One of each of theirs would be great, but she had no desire to carry a baby. Would Lindy want to carry both their babies? She'd read somewhere that in vitro fertilization cost thousands of dollars. Could they ever save enough to do it? Lots of women used the turkey baster method, but then both children would be Lindy's and she would be an outsider in her own family. She knew Grace and Mike would pay for the whole procedure if she asked. But she had her limits. Her family, her problem. It was better they didn't know she was even thinking about it.

Grace touched Quincy's arm. "Are you all right?"

Quincy blinked. "I just spaced out for a minute. Too much duck, I guess."

Of course, Grace didn't miss a trick. "Lindy is really good with the kids. Do you want children?"

"She is, isn't she?" She gazed at Lindy. "I've never given it a thought before, but I was just thinking it would be nice. I love children and, as you can see, so does Lindy."

Mike interrupted with a question, and the conversation changed to vacations and when Quincy and Lindy could arrange time off from their jobs to use their gift.

In the car on the way home, Lindy placed her hand on Quincy's thigh. "I had a good time. Are you okay with the gift?"

Quincy laughed. "I had a really good time and I'm looking forward to five days alone with you. I guess they assumed we're having sex, but we have experience sleeping in the same bed without it, so we'll be fine whether or not we've gotten that far by the time we go."

"Remind me why we're waiting." Lindy ran her hand along Quincy's thigh.

"Hey, not fair when I'm driving." Quincy lifted the hand off her leg and dropped it in Lindy's lap. "Something about going slow, I think." She cleared her throat. "Do you want children?"

"What?"

"I noticed how good you were with the kids today and I wondered whether you've ever thought about having a family."

"What about you?"

"I never gave it a lot of thought but watching you today I realized I'd love to have children. Ideally one of yours and one of mine. But here's the kicker. I don't want to carry a baby, not with my work."

Lindy was silent and Quincy felt queasy, as if she'd just ruined the good feeling between them. The seconds ticked by. "So you'd want me to carry your baby and mine?"

Quincy couldn't tell what Lindy was feeling. "Does that make you angry?"

More silence. Damn, she'd really screwed this up.

"I'm thrilled that you want each of us to have a child. And, I'd love to carry your baby. But that means we'd have to do in vitro fertilization and I don't know how we could do it financially. Unless you're thinking of asking—"

"No. I don't want to ask Grace and Mike. Despite what they think, I don't expect anything from them except what we had today, friendship and a sense of family. It's kind of early to think about the money aspect, but it's great to know we both want the same thing. We'll figure out how to make it happen."

CHAPTER TWENTY-EIGHT

Quincy and Lindy arrived at one to help Amelia and Jackson set up for their annual Day After Christmas Open House starting at six. Lindy and Amelia had cooked and frozen several briskets and some appetizers for the party the weekend before Christmas, so when they arrived Lindy immediately went into the kitchen to cook the remaining dishes with Amelia while Quincy assisted Jackson with the drinks, setting up the tables, and scattering chairs throughout the house.

"Would you do the bread stuffing? The recipe is on the counter." Amelia handed her an apron. "So how did dinner with Grace and Mike go?"

"It was fun. They're really interesting and their parents are nice. All four of us connect. Kind of like we do with you and Jackson. I really enjoyed the kids." She grinned. "They gave Quincy a five-day trip to the Turks and Caicos and I get to go along as her companion. How lucky am I?"

Amelia put a hand on Lindy's arm, stopping her movement. She stared into Lindy's eyes. "You're very lucky. And not just because you get to lie on a beach next to Quincy. Do I need to tell you that Quincy is special, that she—"

Lindy held up a hand. "Is this where you say 'hurt my friend and I'll kill you'?"

Amelia shook her head. "No, this is where I say 'thank you for bringing my dearest friend back from the war, for reviving the cheerful, fun-loving Quincy she left in Afghanistan.'" Her smile was gentle. "And, by the way, Lindy, I think Quincy is very lucky to have you." She turned back to the ham she was seasoning.

Lindy blinked back tears and moved behind Amelia to hug her. "That means a lot coming from you."

"Hey, what's going on here?" Quincy stood in the doorway, hands on hips, trying to look scandalized. "Do I have to worry about my girlfriend and my best friend?"

Lindy twirled and wrapped her arms around Quincy's waist. "We are well-suited to each other, but I haven't tired of you yet, so you don't have to worry."

"Well, that's a relief." She kissed Lindy's nose. "Amelia is giving me the evil eye so I'll get back to my duties."

Lindy and Amelia quickly slipped back into the easy-working rhythm they'd established. Lindy put on music and danced as she washed, chopped, sautéed, and completed the dishes assigned to her by Amelia, then switched to filling platters with the stuffing, pasta, vegetarian grains, vegetables, and salad items she'd prepared, while Amelia arranged the cold cuts, cheese, and olive platters. They sliced the briskets, turkeys, and hams together.

As Lindy shimmied to the music, Quincy wrapped her arms around her from behind, spun her around, and leaned in to kiss her.

Amelia put the knife down. "No time for smooching, ladies. Let's move the food out to the tables."

They'd timed it perfectly. The tables were set, the bartender and wait help Amelia had hired to serve drinks and clean up dirty glasses and plates had arrived, and the four of them had changed into their party clothes before the first guests arrived.

Lindy leaned into Quincy. "I'm nervous. I probably won't remember the names of all the people I met at Thanksgiving and they'll hate me. And there are tons of others I haven't even met yet."

"I followed you into that den of wild lesbians and endured their innuendos and being called a super sexual hero, so you'll just have to tolerate my staid and respectable friends."

"We'll see how staid they are after a few drinks."

Happily, Chief Trubeck, who Lindy knew, and her husband, who Lindy hadn't met, came first. Quincy introduced them. "Lindy, you've met the chief—we call her Connie in social settings—and this is her husband, Freddy." The four of them chatted a few minutes, then Quincy left to help some arrivals with their coats.

Connie leaned in. "Lindy, I'm so happy you're back in Quincy's life. It's a long time since I've seen her so happy, like her old self."

"Thank you. I'm pretty happy too."

"What did I miss?" Quincy put an arm over Lindy's shoulder.

A group of women arrived and made a beeline for Quincy. Maggie, Lane, and Gina Lindy knew and greeted. Then Quincy introduced her to Sandra, Monica, and Ellie, friends from various parts of her life. They were curious about Lindy and wanted to hear her version of how she and Quincy had gotten together. She had the distinct feeling that she had trampled a few hearts by taking Quincy out of circulation.

Gina appeared next to her. "How goes it? Got all the names memorized?"

Lindy laughed. "You bet. How are Heather and the girls?"

Gina grinned. "Great. I went down two days before Christmas Eve so we could do my shopping for the girls together and I was with them until this morning. I drove back for the party. Sounds like you both got some great Christmas gifts at the potluck." She winked. "And I hear you're headed for the islands."

"Ah, news travels fast. Yes, we are. I'm really looking forward to five days alone with Quincy."

"I'll bet." Gina wiggled her eyebrows.

Lindy blushed. Sandra pulled Gina over to meet someone who had just arrived and saved her from having to respond.

Between Thanksgiving and this party she'd met so many people who seemed to love Quincy, it was a little overwhelming. So from time to time she excused herself to check on the food and then headed into the kitchen to take a few deep breaths while refilling platters. From the doorway to the kitchen, she watched Quincy circulate through the party with ease, looking relaxed and beautiful as she greeted people. She was lucky that Quincy was in her life, lucky that Quincy wanted her to be in her life. It occurred to her that she was feeling like part of a couple and not only did she not want to run, she was head over heels in love with Quincy and wanted to be with her forever. Did Quincy feel the same?

CHAPTER TWENTY-NINE

Although Quincy's life was exponentially better since the accident or, to be more accurate, since Lindy, the happier and closer she felt to Lindy the more the sadness and guilt crept in when she least expected it. Right before Christmas Dr. Giles had pointed out that unless she resolved her feelings about Jen she could never fully commit to being happy, to commit fully to Lindy. Somehow that discussion had unlocked something in Quincy and she'd had a breakthrough in her PTSD group this past week.

The more she thought about it over the three days celebrating Christmas the more she realized that it was highly unlikely she would wake up one day thinking it would be a good day to talk about Jen's dying in Afghanistan. If it had been that easy, she would have talked to Connie. After all, she'd been there in Afghanistan. She knew. And she'd held Quincy when she freaked out.

But in order to survive, Quincy had had to compartmentalize, to cut off all conscious thoughts and feelings related to Jen's death, to learn to talk about Jen and her death without ever mentioning the fire and her guilt at not saving her. She couldn't control her subconscious, though, and the scene had replayed in her dreams nightly in the first few years, then only occasionally.

Since the accident the dreams were back. And since the accident Lindy was in her life and she wanted more than mere survival. She would always love Jen. But Jen was dead. She loved Lindy now, and she wanted to love her freely, without guilt and anxiety, like she'd loved Jen when she was alive.

She'd joined the PTSD group reluctantly, but it turned out to be an excellent decision. The shared military experience, the shared war zone experience, and the shared PTSD of the women made it easier to talk about her time in Afghanistan. If she were ever going to tell the story, work through the guilt and pain, it would be with these women who, like her, were damaged by the war. Others in the group had exposed their nightmares, and the group, including her, had been there for them, both in and outside of the group. She would trust these ten women with her life. And she trusted they would understand and help her heal.

Right after Christmas she had an intense individual session with Dr. Giles that was followed by an excruciating group in which she'd finally described the scene and allowed herself to re-experience the anguish of helplessly watching Jen burn in her vehicle. And then she'd dug deeper and exposed her shame, her fears, her guilt, and her pain.

When she collapsed the women took turns holding her, comforting her, and sharing their feelings about her story. The group had gone on until one in the morning, well beyond the regular time, to give her time to talk about it, to examine it. Her group mates knew the intense heat of a vehicle on fire made it impossible to get close. And each and every one reminded her that while Jen might have survived the gunshots, there was no way she could have survived the explosion when the car was hit by a rocket or the intense smoke of the fire. These women knew, they'd seen it happen over and over, and they helped her accept that Jen was dead before she burned.

Dr. Giles ended the group finally but stayed in the office with Quincy processing what had happened until six the next morning. Exhausted but at peace, Quincy was able to acknowledge that it wasn't cowardice that kept her from saving Jen, that no one could have penetrated the extreme heat of the burning vehicle to rescue her, and even if she had been able to pull her out, Jen was already dead.

Dr. Giles asked her to repeat those words several times and each time the pain and guilt she'd carried with her for five years eased a little. Dr. Giles ordered her to take the day off, get some sleep, and come in to see her later in the day for another private session.

By the time she'd left Dr. Giles this afternoon the weight she'd been carrying for years had eased, the wall she'd built between her and the world had crumbled, and the world without the wall, the world with Lindy in it, was a joyous place. All her senses seemed sharper, clearer.

She was tired, but it was a nice tired, like the feeling after a long run or an extended exercise session. After showering, she lay on the couch with the mystery novel she was reading and waited for Lindy. They'd planned to have dinner together tonight and Lindy was either going to cook or bring takeout, depending on how tired she was after an all-day training session at the office. Quincy couldn't wait to share her news.

Lindy arrived with Indian food. After a quick kiss she declared she was starving and herded Quincy into the kitchen. While Quincy set the table and put out their drinks, Lindy emptied the various containers into serving bowls. It wasn't until they sat to eat that Lindy took a good look at Quincy.

"You look different, more relaxed. Anything happen?"

Quincy took a slug of her beer. "Yeah. I talked about Jen in group last night and this afternoon."

Lindy frowned. "Last night? Didn't you go into the group because of the flashback about Jen?"

"Yes, but…do you remember our first night together I said I didn't know why I had risked my life to save a stranger?"

Lindy chewed in her mindful way before answering. "Yes, of course."

Quincy took a deep breath. "What I should have said was, I risked my life because I couldn't watch another brave woman burn to death."

"You mean—"

"Jen was shot, then the Humvee was hit by mortar. By the time I could get back to her, the car was in flames and my team held me back because it was too hot to get close. I watched her burn."

Lindy paled. "Oh, my god. I didn't know. Are you all right?" She jumped up and hugged Quincy from behind.

Quincy wrapped her arms around Lindy's. "I'm good, better than I've been in the five years since it happened. I was never able to face up to it to talk about what happened until last night. The group got me through it. I believed it was cowardice that kept me from saving Jen, but I see now that there was nothing I could have done. And understanding that eased the pain and guilt I've carried with me since standing by helplessly watching the car burn with Jen in it. I feel so close to Dr. Giles and the women in the group, I'm going to continue to go to the group and to see Dr. Giles once a week for a while."

Lindy pulled Quincy up and embraced her face-to-face. "And you're okay?"

"I'm more than okay. I feel as if I've just woken from a dream where I was alone in a dim, foggy place that was silent and depressing. Or something like that. I feel free and open."

Lindy stretched to kiss Quincy. "I'm so happy for you. And for me. I hope there's room for me in your heart."

Quincy lifted Lindy and spun her around. "Is it too cheesy to say my whole heart belongs to you?"

"It is, but I like it." She kissed Quincy. "Let's sit and eat before the food gets cold." They returned to their seats and passed the serving bowls. Lindy watched Quincy dig into the food. "Thank you for sharing that with me." She picked up her fork, ate a little, then put the fork down. "This might be a good time to talk to you about what I've been working on in therapy."

"Only if you're comfortable doing it." Quincy wanted to reassure Lindy. She was paler than usual and looked vulnerable and scared.

"I am." Seeming lost in thought, Lindy tucked her hair behind her ears. "I don't think I ever told you that my parents abused me physically and emotionally. They were harsh and loveless and religion-focused. My younger sister, older brother, and I were homeschooled. We had no friends other than the few children in our small church. Our only books were the Bible and a few children's religious books. Laughing, playing, running, skipping, dancing, and games were prohibited. Our parents beat us with a leather belt for the slightest infraction of their many rules. If we were really bad, we got the buckle."

She looked up at Quincy. "I asked too many questions, was too cheerful, and had a hard time sitting still so I was beaten often. But as I got older, they beat me for things I didn't understand." Her eyes filled with tears. "I was eleven, twelve, thirteen years old and I had no idea what they were talking about when they said I flaunted myself or flirted or made men want to do bad things. Later I figured out that my father and older brother wanted to fuck me and they blamed me for tempting them. So I got the buckle whenever one of them got a hard-on."

She swiped at her tears. "I was beaten almost every day and almost every day I got the buckle. I fantasized about killing myself, but I thought God would save me, so I prayed. In the end I saved myself. I ran away when I heard them negotiating with our pastor for money and increased status at the church in return for letting his sadistic son marry me when I turned fourteen."

Quincy was white with anger. "Those bastards."

"There's more. When I was first with Melanie, I told her this story and she reacted pretty much the same as you just did. But as she became more and more addicted and more and more abusive, she beat me with her belt and reminded me that I deserved it. As I told you, the final straw with her was the night she decided to beat me with the buckle."

Lindy stared over Quincy's shoulder, then seemed to come to a decision. "The Monday morning after our weekend I glimpsed the scars on my back in the bathroom mirror and images of the hate on my mother's face, the lust on the faces of my father and brother, and the glee on Melanie's face flashed in front of me. I freaked out. How could I deserve someone as wonderful as my superhero? I was sure you'd want to get away as fast as you could, so I did what I always do. I tried to make you go away."

She stood, turned her back to Quincy, and pulled her sweater up.

Quincy gasped at the welts covering her back. She traced them with gentle fingers and kissed them with soft lips. Lindy moaned at the gentleness, the caring, the love conveyed in that simple gesture.

"My parents abandoned me," Quincy said, "but they made sure I was born, and they left me with someone who would love me and give me a good life. Your parents chose to take their unhappiness and frustration out on an innocent child, in the name of God. I'm so sorry you had to endure that, sweetheart. I hope you know I'd never raise a hand to you. But if I ever do, I want you to leave immediately."

She continued to caress the welts. "I see *you*, Lindy. The scars are part of who you are, why you're you."

CHAPTER THIRTY

Even on New Year's Eve loads and trucks had to be scheduled, so Lindy worked a full day before arriving at Quincy's apartment to shower and change into her party clothes. They were getting together with Amelia and Jackson at their house for a quiet dinner before each couple went off to separate events.

Quincy and Lindy pulled into Maggie's parking lot around eleven. This was the first time Quincy had been back to Maggie's and it felt very different from the last time. It wasn't just that instead of coming from the scene of a devastating accident she'd come there from a fun afternoon of hiking with a couple of the women from her PTSD group and then had enjoyed a wonderful intimate dinner with Lindy, Amelia, and Jackson. Nor was it the Christmas lights outlining Maggie's building or the lack of snowdrifts on this cold but clear New Year's Eve. It was her. She was different.

"Hey, what's going on, sugah?" Lindy touched Quincy's cheek. "You parked, then drifted off somewhere. Are you remembering the last time you were here?"

Quincy blinked, bringing her thoughts back to the present. "Yeah. I was in a totally different state the last time. And I was alone. My life has changed radically." She leaned in and kissed Lindy. "Best of all, I'm no longer alone. Let me get your door."

The New Year's Eve party at Maggie's was in full swing—music blasting, dance floor crowded, happy women wearing masks and funny hats. Maggie had gone all out on decorations this year with a huge tree in one corner, wreaths dotting the walls, and streamers hanging from the ceiling. All in all it was festive, as New Year's Eve should be. Lane, Maggie's lover, was taking tickets at the door and jumped up to hug them both. She scanned the list of women who'd paid to come tonight.

Quincy leaned over the table. "Maggie insisted on giving us comps for tonight so we might not be on that list."

Lane slid a shorter list over. "Ah, yes, here you are." She looked up. "You haven't come to the New Year's Eve party for quite a few years, so you probably don't remember that Maggie never charges her close friends. I, on the other hand, should have known. No one is working coat check tonight so hang your coats in there and go have fun. See you later."

They stopped at the bar to say hello to Maggie, then circulated through the room, greeting friends with hugs and kisses and New Year wishes. When the DJ eased into "Bring It On," Lindy moved them to the edge of the dance floor. Quincy slid behind Lindy, enjoying the gentle sway of her hips moving to the music as they watched the dancing. Images of the first time she saw Lindy flashed in her mind.

Lindy turned to look at Quincy. "Damn, sugah, I just remembered your conversation with Lisbeth. Do you dance?"

Quincy spun her around and pulled her on to the dance floor. "I may have exaggerated my lack of ability a bit. Judge for yourself."

After twenty minutes gliding from slow, sensual to fast, frantic music as the DJ varied the tempo, Lindy dragged Quincy to the bar. She ordered a beer for Quincy and a seltzer for herself. "I should have known you would be a great dancer. So where did you learn?"

Quincy gazed at the dance floor, remembering. "Jen. She loved to dance as much as you do. She made sure we practiced, and we even took some lessons together." She smiled and met Lindy's eyes. "We danced all the time, even in the barracks in Afghanistan, though we had to be quiet because we were all jammed together."

Lindy studied Quincy. "This is the first time you've mentioned Jen that you didn't get upset or look like you wanted to vomit. Is it because of what happened in group?"

Quincy took a slug of her beer, leaned in, and kissed Lindy. "Yeah. Now I can think about her without shame and guilt."

"I'm glad." Lindy cupped Quincy's face and planted a quick kiss. "Let's dance."

They danced every dance, most of them with each other and some with friends, but even when separated their gazes were on each other. As they kissed with "Auld Lang Syne" playing in the background, Quincy knew she was the luckiest woman in the world to have found love again. And, yes, now she could say it. At least to herself.

They broke to breathe, then Lindy caressed Quincy's face and kissed her again, her lips soft. "I'd like to make love with you tonight if you're ready?"

Quincy pulled away, grinning. "Oh, yeah." She wrapped her arms around Lindy, fitting their bodies together as they moved to the music. "I'm definitely ready." The heat between them was incredible.

They danced for another hour, eyes locked, bodies fused, hands roving. Babs danced over to them. "Hey, guys, get a room. You're killing the rest of us."

"What?" They spoke simultaneously.

Babs put an arm around each of them. "Don't freak, everything's good, but you have an audience. I'm not sure whether it's Quincy's hero thing or because you look so sexy together."

They looked around at the group of women watching them, all smiles and thumbs-up, then looked at each other and burst out laughing. "Time to go," Lindy snorted.

After many hugs and kisses and Happy New Year wishes from their friends and others celebrating at the bar, they headed out into the freezing night. Quincy held Lindy close as they crunched over the frozen ground to her car. They kissed again. Quincy helped Lindy in, then ran around to the driver's side and started the car. The Subaru heated up quickly and Quincy drove out of the lot. Lindy pinned Quincy with her eyes. She took Quincy's hand, kissed the palm, and held it to her heart, and with her other hand she stroked Quincy's thigh.

It wasn't until they stopped that Lindy looked away from Quincy. "Why are we at the Hilton?"

"I reserved a room for us. For two nights. I wanted our first time to be special."

Lindy was puzzled. "How did you know tonight would be our first time?"

"I didn't. I hoped it would be, but if it wasn't, I figured we could still enjoy ourselves hanging out, getting room service, and just being together." Quincy looked away. She cleared her throat. "I hope you don't mind."

Lindy kissed her palm again. "I don't mind one bit, sugah. But I don't have anything—"

"You do." Quincy opened the trunk, got out of the car, and retrieved an overnight bag. "This is yours. I dropped my things off when I checked in earlier."

"Babs helped you?"

"Yeah. When we said we were going to the bathroom at Maggie's, we actually went out to the parking lot and transferred the suitcase from her car to mine. I wanted you to have clothing and options for sleeping, depending on how we felt."

Lindy kissed Quincy. "You're wonderful." Her lips met Quincy's again and her tongue sought entry to her mouth as she unbuttoned Quincy's jacket and caressed her breasts. Quincy struggled to get a grip on Lindy's zipper, but it was under her scarf.

The hoots, whistles, cheers, and comments like "get a room" and others not so polite from the people staggering to their cars from their New Year's Eve celebrations startled Quincy. She moaned and pulled back, surprised by the smiles and grins and thumbs-up of the passersby.

"We'd better take this inside, before we get arrested." She threw an arm over Lindy's shoulder and led her through the festive throng of happy people in the lobby. The crowd waiting for the elevator rushed the first one that arrived. Quincy pulled Lindy back to avoid being trampled. A happy group of fairly drunk seniors filled the next elevator but made room for them to squeeze in. They'd open their coats once they were inside, and now eye to eye, bodies smashed together, the heat between them was incredible. Could the others jammed in with them feel the sexual tension?

As they exited on the third floor, the group shouted "Happy New Year" then burst into "Auld Lange Syne." The hallway was empty. When the elevator door slid closed, they moved into each other's arms and kissed their way to the door of their room, the suitcase bumping along. Distracted by Lindy's hand rubbing her breast, Quincy struggled to get the key card into the slot. Frustrated, she held Lindy's arms in check with one hand and finally got the card in. The door beeped and they were inside, wildly pawing at each other. Quincy swung Lindy around so her back was to the door.

"Ouch. My head."

"Shit. I'm sorry. You got me all riled up out there."

"It's okay." Lindy clawed at Quincy's jacket, desperate to get it out of the way. She pushed one shoulder off and pulled the sleeve down. The weight of the coat pulled the other sleeve down and the coat fell between them. She tugged Quincy's shirt out of her pants, ran her hands over her muscular back, and unhooked her bra. She took a breast in each hand.

Quincy moaned at the contact. With Lindy's hands massaging her breasts, Quincy struggled to get Lindy's coat off. "Your coat." Lindy raised a hand to help.

"Ouch. Damn. That bracelet I gave you is a deadly weapon. Luckily you missed my eye." Quincy touched her forehead, expecting blood, but it was dry.

"Sorry, I was just trying to help." Lindy shifted out of her coat, stepped forward to grab Quincy, and tripped on Quincy's coat. Quincy caught her.

Panting, Lindy began to giggle. "We'd better cool down for a minute before we kill each other."

Quincy laughed. "You're right. Don't move. I'll put the light on."

Faces red, lips swollen, and breathing heavily, they grinned at each other. Quincy bent down to pick up their coats. Lindy gasped. "The room is beautiful, Quincy. It's so romantic with the candles and the flowers." She punched Quincy's shoulder. "You devil, you were going to try to seduce me tonight. No need, but I still love it. Thank you."

"We couldn't do open flames in the hotel so I found these battery-powered candles. They even mimic the flickering light of a real candle. There's a switch to turn them on. "

While Quincy hung their coats in the closet, Lindy readied the candles. Quincy turned off the lights. The soft glow of the candlelight created a warm and romantic atmosphere. She gazed at Lindy standing in front of the windows, eyes glinting, golden hair shimmering in the flickering light. She was so beautiful, so sensual. Quincy swallowed, suddenly nervous. It was not like she hadn't been with anyone since Jen. But her heart hadn't been in the room those few times, so it had only been sex. Now her heart was here and about to burst through her chest.

It wasn't sex she wanted tonight. Was she still capable of making love? With Lindy's eyes on her, she powered up the CD player she'd brought with her, loaded the CD she'd made Lindy for Christmas, and cued up one of Lindy's favorite Marvin Gaye songs. Hearing the first notes of "Sexual Healing," Lindy smiled. Her hips swayed gently, her fingers snapped, and she opened her arms. "Come dance with me, sugah." Her voice was huskier than usual.

Quincy stepped into her arms and pulled her close, fusing their bodies. As they danced, the sensual movement, the friction of clothing rubbing sensitive skin, the feel of Lindy's erect nipples pressing her own swollen breasts, and the scent of Lindy, of both their arousals, stoked her desire. Every nerve in her body called out to be touched. Lindy pulled Quincy's head down and explored her lips and her tongue and mouth. Quincy cupped Lindy's ass and pulled her tighter, edging her leg between Lindy's thighs.

Quincy was definitely ready to make love, but she needed to be sure. "There are pajamas and things in the suitcase if you want—"

"You." Lindy pinched Quincy's nipple. "I want you." She brushed Quincy's lips with her already swollen lips, then pressed into a kiss that deepened as her tongue found Quincy's.

Quincy lost herself in the sensuality of the kiss, the wanting to know, the wanting to merge, the wanting to touch, to smell, to taste. Lindy slipped her hands under Quincy's shirt and caressed her stomach, her back, her breasts. She spoke softly in Quincy's ear. "I love this shirt, but I want it off. Now."

Lindy's hot breath traveled through Quincy. She shivered and undid the top three buttons. But Lindy couldn't wait. She grabbed the hem, pulled the shirt over Quincy's head, and threw it on a chair.

Quincy's desire skyrocketed. She'd fantasized so many times in these past few months about making love to Lindy, and it always started with slowly undressing her.

"I'd like to undress you if that's okay?"

"Yes." Lindy's voice dropped into that lower register and her breath came in short gasps as Quincy ran her hands over her body, then lifted her sweater over her head. Quincy's eyes widened. Lindy's alabaster skin looked like silk in the glow of the candles, and her breasts, not quite contained by her red silk bra, seemed to undulate gently in the flickering light, beckoning her. She felt a rush of wetness.

She took a breast in each hand. While her thumbs rubbed the nipples, she licked the mounds peeking above the cups, then sucked in an erect nipple popping through the red silk. Lindy moaned softly. Quincy's body tightened and flooded with warmth. She unhooked Lindy's bra, slid the straps down her arms, and tossed it aside. She gazed at the fullness of Lindy's breasts, then sucked one into her mouth while her hand massaged the other. Lindy's very vocal arousal was making her crazy. She slipped her free hand into the waistband of Lindy's slacks, trying to tug them down. They were a tangle of arms and legs as Lindy held Quincy's head tight to her breast and Quincy tried to unzip Lindy's pants.

"Bed." Holding Lindy, Quincy walked them to the bed and unsuccessfully tried again to loosen Lindy's pants with one hand.

Panting, Lindy pushed Quincy's hands away, unzipped her pants, and pushed them and her panties down. Quincy knelt and pulled Lindy's boots, pants, underwear, and socks off, then quickly removed her own clothes, She touched the golden patch of hair, put her nose in Lindy's crotch, and sniffed. It had been a long time since she'd wanted to taste a lover.

Now she wanted to lick Lindy from head to toe, but before she could start, Lindy grabbed her hair and pulled her up. They were so close their nipples touched as they swayed. They'd been intimate from day one and they'd spent a lot of time kissing recently, but this was the first time seeing each other naked. And, the first time they'd be skin on skin. Quincy choked up. She cupped Lindy's face in her hands and kissed her. "You are even more beautiful than I imagined."

Lindy wrapped her arms around Quincy and pulled her so they were touching breast to breast, pelvis to pelvis, thigh to thigh. She ran a hand over Quincy's buttocks. "Thank you, sugah. I imagined you too, but it never occurred to me you would be so powerful and muscular. So sexy. I should have known."

Quincy tumbled Lindy onto the bed, then stretched out on top of her. She was on fire, but she wanted their first time to be slow. She kissed and licked Lindy's neck while her hands traveled down to squeeze Lindy's breasts, circled her stomach, and tugged gently on the triangle of silky blond hair.

She was moving her hand between Lindy's legs when Lindy flipped her, no longer happy to be on the bottom. Quincy knew she could overpower her, but there was no way she'd use force while they were making love so she held back and joined in

Lindy's playfulness. They wrestled for control and ended up laughing, on their sides facing each other.

Quincy leaned in for a soft kiss that lingered and then morphed into another deep exploration of Lindy's mouth and tongue. After a delicious interval, she moved her mouth to Lindy's breasts, switching from one to the other, licking and sucking. Her sex tightened and she could feel the wetness on her own thighs as Lindy writhed and moaned. She ran her hands over Lindy's hip and down her leg, then gently pushed her. Off balance, Lindy opened her legs and Quincy slipped a finger inside. Lindy was more than ready for her. Quincy groaned and slipped in another finger. While her mouth continued to lavish attention on one breast then another, she began to thrust in and out, using her thumb to create friction outside.

Lindy tried to put a hand between Quincy's legs, but Quincy didn't want to be distracted so she tightened her thigh muscles. She removed her mouth from the breast she was sucking. "Just enjoy, sweetheart." When she went back to the breast, Lindy relaxed and rewarded her with drawn-out moan. "Quuiinncy."

Quincy felt Lindy tense around her fingers. Her legs fell open as her body lifted off the bed. She cried "no" when Quincy abandoned her breast again but gasped when Quincy's tongue licked her juices and circled her center. She screamed Quincy's name over and over as the orgasm grew. Then she exploded, shaking and crying as she came down and then shaking again as the aftershocks hit.

Quincy crawled up and pulled Lindy to her, soothing her as she cried.

"I'm sorry for crying, Quincy. It was wonderful, but it was the—"

"Was that your first orgasm?"

Lindy laughed. "I thought I'd had orgasms before, but they were nothing like this, so I guess you could say it was my first real orgasm." She kissed Quincy. "I didn't know. Wow. I need to catch my breath." She rolled over until she was on top of Quincy. "I felt like you were totally focused on me, on giving me pleasure. It was wonderful."

Quincy knew it was because she was in love with Lindy and Lindy sensed it. "How else can you make love?"

Lindy stared at her for a long second. "I guess no one has ever made love to me before."

She'd known she was in love with Lindy for a while now but had hesitated to say it for fear of freaking her. This seemed like a good time. Why the hell not say it? "I love you, Lindy James, and I'm thrilled to be your first."

"Okaay. Since we're using the L word, I have to confess I've been feeling it for a while, but I wasn't sure I should say it. I love you too, Quincy Adams." Her eyes sparkled in the candlelight and the smirk was unmistakable. "Now let me see if I can make love to you."

She leaned over and captured Quincy's mouth. She caressed her face, her neck, and moved to the side to toy with the nipple of the breast she could reach. Quincy struggled to flip her, but she held tight.

"No, sugah, it's my turn. You've shown me how to make love, not just do sex. Now let me show you what a good student I am." She brushed Quincy's hair from her forehead and looked into her eyes. "Please don't fight me for control. Let me do this. I want to…make love to you."

Lindy loved her. For the first time she felt sure of it. She'd almost come while making love to Lindy. Now Quincy's heart raced, her temperature spiked, and her body felt as if it had been infused with molten lava. "I'd like that."

Lindy moved to the side and ran her hands over Quincy's body, nipped her ear lobe, her neck, her breasts, and then got down to the work of making love. It worked out so well that they reprised the action several times over. When they were both sated and sleepy Quincy turned off the candles and the music and crawled under the covers. Lindy rolled over into her arms.

No sooner had Quincy opened her eyes the next day, than Lindy kissed her, then kissed her again. "Good morning, lover."

Quincy grinned. "I could get used to being greeted like that every morning."

They made love and fell asleep, then woke and did it again. When they woke for the fourth time, it was two in the afternoon and they were quiet, holding each other, kissing, and touching.

CHAPTER THIRTY-ONE

Quincy whistled as she dressed for her Valentine's Day date with Lindy. They'd declared themselves an official couple New Year's Day, but in keeping with their decision to move slowly, they hadn't rushed into living together.

As she ran the comb through her newly trimmed hair, her eyes fell on the picture Patsy Mackenzie had taken of them in the ER months ago. Somehow Patsy had captured the glow and the electricity that was already there after less than twenty-four hours together. That glow seemed even brighter in the snapshots of them she'd framed after their trip to the Turks and Caicos in late January. Maybe it was the sun or maybe five days making love in such a gorgeous setting had intensified their feelings. Whatever. She smiled at the image of the beautiful woman she was in love with.

Things were great between them, but she intended to seal the deal with a more formal commitment tonight at their favorite restaurant, The Veggie Place. They planned to meet a group of their lesbian friends at Maggie's Bar after dinner, and though her friends and Lindy didn't know, it would be their engagement celebration.

As usual, thinking about Maggie's brought images of the accident that led to their meeting that night, but she blinked the memory away, reminding herself that saving twelve lives and meeting Lindy made it a great night. She'd come a long way in the four months since then. Actually, they'd both come a long way.

The doorbell rang. She pocketed the Valentine gift she'd bought for Lindy, grabbed her coat, locked up, and slid into Lindy's car for the drive to the restaurant. They chatted happily on the drive. Quincy wasn't sure whether she was projecting her own excitement onto her, but Lindy seemed even more upbeat than usual.

As usual, the Veggie Place had a roaring fire and candles, but tonight, for Valentine's Day, there were candies and roses on every table. They gazed at each other across the table. The electricity between them tonight felt physical. Once they'd ordered, Lindy was practically levitating. "I want to give you my Valentine's Day gift now."

Quincy had the whole thing planned. She couldn't wait to see Lindy's face. Maybe if she let Lindy get her gift out of the way it would be better, but then she would be distracted, and the food would arrive. She didn't think she could wait. "Let's exchange gifts at the same time."

Lindy nodded. Almost as it they'd choreographed it, they both slipped off their chairs onto a knee. Eyes huge, they stared at each other, realizing what was happening. Holy smokes, they were both proposing. Then, as if they'd rehearsed it, they spoke simultaneously.

"Lindy, will you marry me?"

"Quincy, will you marry me?"

They fell into each other's arms. "Yes, yes." They spoke in concert again, then kissed. The nearby tables broke out into applause as they exchanged rings.

Slightly embarrassed at the attention, they waved and mouthed "Thank you," then sat. And grinned at each other.

Lindy's eyes bounced between her ring and Quincy. "We never talked about marriage, Quincy. I was afraid you would say no."

"I felt the same. I didn't know what I would do if you rejected me, but I want you with me forever and I had to risk it."

"I love my ring." Lindy held out her hand to admire the diamond in a delicate, old-fashioned setting. "It's perfect." She kissed it.

"You managed to buy a ring that's me." Quincy displayed her ring, a diamond set in a wide sculpted band, tailored, modern, and strong looking. "I love it."

Edie, the waitress, appeared with their dinners. "Congratulations. Let me see your rings." They held their hands out. "They're so different, but both are beautiful. Did you plan this?"

Lindy was breathy with excitement. "We totally surprised each other."

Edie leaned in and spoke softly. "Tess is too busy to come out now, but she sends her best wishes and says dinner is on The Veggie Place tonight."

"Thank Tess for us please." Although Quincy wasn't a vegetarian, this had become their favorite restaurant after their first date. They ate here frequently and had become friends with Tess, the owner/chef, and the rest of the staff.

They stared into each other's eyes while they ate. Quincy groaned. "I want to take you home to bed and never leave."

"Our friends are expecting us. Babs helped me pick out your ring. She'll be dying to hear all about it."

Quincy laughed. "Babs helped me pick out your ring as well. Are you sure she didn't say anything?"

"What? She didn't breathe a word, that traitor. What kind of best friend sneaks behind your back like that." Lindy was indignant.

Quincy patted her cheek. "In this case, I would say, one who loves you."

Quincy couldn't stop looking at her ring as Lindy drove them to Maggie's Bar. "Have you given any thought to getting married? When? Where?"

Lindy shot her a gleeful look. "I sure have, sugah. I want it to be warm so May or June. I want it to be outside, in the afternoon, and if Grace and Mike are still willing to let us use their property, I'd love to do it there. I want Sarah to give me away and Babs to be my maid of honor. I want all of our friends to celebrate with us. We'll make it a potluck dinner, but we'll provide everything else. Oh, and let's ask Connie to officiate."

"I was so focused on proposing that I didn't give the wedding a thought. I'd like a little time and a little input if possible."

"Of course. We'll work it out together."

When they entered Maggie's the Valentine's Day party was in full swing. Maggie always bragged she had brought them together, so they stopped at the bar to give her the news and show her their rings. She kissed them both.

"Congratulations. I'm really happy for both of you. As you can see the place is a madhouse, so I opened the back room. Babs and your group are there. Go on, I'll send in champagne and some seltzer in a few minutes."

Hand in hand, they moved through the crowd to the back room. Quincy opened the door and the people inside screamed, "Surprise." The two of them stood there in shock as cameras flashed, Babs pulled them into a hug, and the crowd surrounded them.

It took a bewildered Quincy a few moments to focus on the individual faces, to realize that the crowd was not only their lesbian friends, that it included their straight friends and co-workers. Amelia and Jackson, Chief Trubeck and her husband, Grace and Mike, her partner John and his wife, Gina and her latest girlfriend, Patsy, and many more. Everyone wanted to see their rings. They told the story of their proposals about ten times. Patsy, now a close friend, took pictures, a lot of pictures.

It was all a little overwhelming. Quincy wasn't sure how it had happened. Actually, she was sure, on second thought. Babs had organized it. But how had she done it? And how had everyone kept the secret?

Maggie arrived with the promised champagne. She made the first toast, but it wasn't the last. So many friends lifted a glass and wished them well. When Babs uncovered the buffet and everyone focused on the food, Lindy and Quincy cornered her. Hands on her hips, Lindy confronted Babs. "How did you do this without me knowing?"

Babs flinched. "Oh, geez, you're angry? I figured since you both bought rings and both were intending to propose, it was a sure thing you would be engaged tonight. I made arrangements with Maggie in advance because I wanted her to cater the party and I also wanted to be sure it was okay to invite men. She reminded me that she welcomed gay men, but she asked that for the party we enter through the back door into the private room and stay out of the main room. I waited until yesterday to call people to limit the possibility of someone spilling the beans. Some people couldn't make it, but I told those who did if they wanted to get you a gift they could do it later. Tonight was just to celebrate. Please don't be angry." She had tears in her eyes. "I did it because I love you both."

Quincy and Lindy exchanged a look over the shorter woman's head, then pulled her into a three-way hug. Lindy kissed her cheek. "We're not angry, Babs. We're in shock." She grinned. "Let's dance." They celebrated late into the night.

CHAPTER THIRTY-TWO

Quincy blew on her hands and stomped her feet. Damn, it was cold and she'd left her gloves in the car. Her thumb went to her ring finger, a new habit to reassure herself she wasn't dreaming. After four eighty-degree days in Florida, New Jersey felt like a walk-in freezer this morning. They'd visited Sarah in St. Petersburg so they could announce their engagement in person, but Sarah had a surprise of her own. She'd invited Mama to come down too, making it a real family celebration. They'd had a good time. Smiling, she entered the station.

Her partner Detective John Fields was already at his desk facing hers. "What are you so cheerful about? Enjoying the freaking cold?" John complained about the cold constantly and had moaned when she told him she was taking a long weekend in Florida.

She dropped into her seat and flipped through the short stack of pink telephone message slips on her desk. *Grace—Dinner this week? Amelia—Dinner this week? Gina—Lunch today?* She smiled. It seemed her friends were food obsessed. She turned over the last slip. She didn't recognize the name or the number.

"John, do we have anything going with the Silver Foundation?"

"Silver?" He scratched his head. "Never heard of them."

"It's a New York City phone number, came in two days ago."

He shrugged. "I fielded all the calls on our cases so it must be personal."

Prioritizing as usual, she put the slips aside. Her friends could wait and since she didn't have the foggiest idea who would be calling from New York that could wait as well. "Want to brief me on what's been happening?"

He glanced at his wristwatch. "We're meeting with the chief in twenty minutes. I have some calls to make before we see her, so how about I update you and her at the same time?"

Quincy grinned. "Always happy to lighten your load, Johnny boy. And that'll give me a chance to return these calls."

She set up a time and place for lunch with Gina, put the other two invitations aside to discuss with Lindy, then punched in the New York number. It rang twice, then a woman with a husky voice answered. "Darcy Silver."

She took a breath. "This is Detective Quincy Adams. I've been out of town and I'm returning your call from last Friday."

"Ah, Detective Adams. Thank you for getting back to me. I have something I'd like to discuss with you. Are you available for dinner tonight or tomorrow? I'll come to New Jersey. You choose the restaurant and bring a date if you'd like."

Quincy rearranged the papers on her already neat desk. "I, uh, can you give me a hint what this is about?"

"I'd rather talk face-to-face. What do you have to lose, Detective? At the very least you'll have dinner in the restaurant of your choice and maybe some interesting conversation with a couple of scintillating lesbians. Give us a chance."

She burst out laughing. "Well, when you put it that way, I'd be stupid to say no. But my fiancée doesn't eat meat. Is a vegetarian restaurant a deal breaker?"

"To be honest it wouldn't be my first choice. Do they have pasta?"

"I often have the veggie lasagna and they serve several other pasta dishes."

"That sounds doable. It'll be me and a member of the foundation's board of directors."

"Great. I'll make a reservation for four at eight."

"Sounds like fun. Tell me where and when and we'll be there."

Quincy gave her directions to The Veggie Place, then called Lindy.

As Quincy and Lindy walked toward the restaurant a sporty BMW with New York plates parked and two women exited. One, with long black hair, was dressed in black slacks and a cream sweater that looked like cashmere; the other, who was taller and had collar-length dark hair, was wearing a suit and tie. *A striking couple.* When Quincy and Lindy reached the entrance, the long-haired one flashed a brilliant smile. "Quincy Adams, I presume?" She extended her hand. "I'm Darcy Silver and this Renee Rousseau, chief financial officer of the foundation."

"Nice to meet you." Quincy shook both their hands. "And this is my fiancée, Lindy James."

Darcy smiled again. "Shall we go in?"

Tess, the owner of the restaurant, greeted them with hugs. She smiled at the two women standing behind them. "I see your party of four is here."

"Yes." Quincy turned. "Ms. Silver, Ms. Rousseau, this is Tess, the owner and chef."

"Welcome." Tess picked up four menus and a wine list, then escorted them to the private table in the corner that Quincy had requested. Darcy spoke quietly to Tess before sitting. "By the way," she said, "it's Darcy and Renee."

Lindy spoke for the first time. "And we prefer Quincy and Lindy."

Edie, the waitress, appeared with a bottle of champagne in an ice bucket, four flutes, and a glass of seltzer and lime. "Lindy, I have a flute for you, but I presume you're not having champagne so I brought your usual." She placed the seltzer in front of Lindy.

"Leave the flute for me, Edie. Depending on what we're celebrating I might have a sip. And, uh, Darcy and Renee, this is Edie."

Edie turned to Darcy. "Shall I pour?"

"No, thanks. We have some things to discuss first." Darcy addressed the table as the waitress walked away. "I thought it would be best to get the business out of the way before dinner so we can all relax and enjoy ourselves." She focused on Quincy. "The Silver Foundation's Shehero Award honors and celebrates women who have performed above and beyond what's expected for women in our society. And based on our research and the recommendations we received, we'd like you to be this year's recipient of the Silver Award for Bravery."

"Recommendations?"

"Yes. We hire a firm to track news stories in the US to help us identify women who meet our definition of heroes, then we research to find out as much as we can about them personally and about the event. We look at media coverage and talk to friends, co-workers, family, and people involved in the event, if possible, and ask for letters recommending the individual. We had a huge number of letters recommending you from people you saved, people who witnessed it, and others who know you. Including Ms. James, here."

"You knew about this?" Quincy glared at Lindy.

Lindy moved her hands up into a defensive position. "No, sugah, I swear I never heard of the Silver Foundation before this afternoon. Grace told me she was organizing a campaign to get you some award and asked me to write a letter about your character. How could I resist?"

Darcy cleared her throat.

"Sorry, honey." Quincy switched her attention to Darcy and Renee. "I'm honored to be considered. What would I have to do?"

"Not much, really. We hope you'll attend our annual May fundraising dinner in New York City to accept the award. We usually have about four hundred guests and raise quite a bit of money to fund programs to bolster the self-confidence and skills of girls. We give scholarships, support sports-, arts-, and technology-focused after-school programs and summer camps, things like that."

"Sounds like a good cause." Quincy's eyes shifted to Lindy. "The dinner is formal, gowns and tuxes?"

Renee answered. "Yes, it's a formal affair, so we provide the honoree and their families with whatever formal clothing they need, plus transportation and accommodations for the weekend at the Waldorf."

Darcy lifted the bottle of champagne. "What do you say? Will you accept the award?"

Quincy turned to Lindy and seeing the pride and love in her eyes and the huge smile on her face, grinned. "You bet."

Darcy looked up from pouring the champagne. "Oh, did I mention it comes with a fifty-thousand-dollar prize?"

"Fifty. Thousand. Dollars?" Quincy's gaze went to Lindy. "That means we…"

Lindy lifted her flute. "Please pour me a tiny bit of that champagne. I need to toast to this."

Renee turned to Lindy. "Are you sure?"

Lindy laughed. "I don't have a drinking problem. I just don't like the taste or the way it makes me feel. But only champagne will do tonight."

Quincy was struggling to take in what Darcy said about the prize. "I…wow. That's a lot of money."

"The women we honor have made a huge difference in people's lives and we wanted to give them a large enough amount to make a difference in their own lives. I'll bet the people whose lives you saved won't think it's too much."

Quincy reached for Lindy's hand. "It will make a tremendous difference in our lives. We've been trying to figure out how to save enough for in vitro fertilization before we're both too old to have children. This award means we can afford to try a couple of times."

"I can't think of a better way to spend the money." Darcy poured three full glasses and a quarter of a glass for Lindy, then lifted her flute. "To Quincy and all the brave women who fight against the odds every day without being recognized. And to healthy babies." They drank. "We're thrilled that you've accepted, Quincy."

Lindy sipped the champagne, then switched to her seltzer.

Quincy kissed Lindy's hand and grinned. "Could I wear a tux?"

"No problem. Renee and some of our other friends like tuxedos, though I prefer a gown. What about you, Lindy?"

"I…a gown would be fun." She flushed. "But I've never worn one and I wouldn't even know how to pick one out."

"Don't worry. We have buyers who will help you select things you like and feel comfortable in." Darcy eyed her. "You'd look fantastic in a gown, something slinky."

Quincy kissed Lindy's flaming cheek. "You'll look amazing in whatever you wear. But I agree with Darcy about the slinky."

"All right, ladies, let's stop embarrassing Lindy." Renee smiled at Lindy. "The important takeaway is that we want our honorees and their loved ones to feel comfortable, so we have people to help you find clothing and accessories you love and the foundation picks up the cost."

Renee picked up her menu. "What's good here, Lindy?"

Lindy's color returned to normal and she picked up the menu. "I've never eaten anything here that wasn't delicious, so it's just a matter of what you like. We should ask Edie about tonight's specials, though." She waved the waitress over and asked about the specials.

They took a few minutes to make their selections, then ordered dinner and a bottle of wine to go with it. As Edie walked away to place their orders, another server dropped off a basket of warm crusty bread, a plate of raw vegetables, and three dips. She took a minute to describe each of the dips.

After a few seconds of silence, Darcy turned to Lindy. "Obviously the staff knows you. You must come here often."

"Quincy brought me here on our first real date and we liked it so much that we've come back a lot, so we know the owner and the staff pretty well by now."

"How long have you been together?" Renee dipped a carrot stick in the spicy spinach dip. "Yum."

Lindy looked at Quincy for permission to tell their story. Quincy nodded. "Actually, we met the night of the…when Quincy rescued all those people."

Darcy looked puzzled. "Were you there, in one of the cars?"

"No, no, it was later that night."

"Really?" Darcy buttered a slice of bread and considered. "As I recall, when I looked through Quincy's file earlier today, I saw a picture of the two of you in the newspaper that was taken the afternoon after the accident. You looked very involved."

"It's true." Lindy laughed. "But the photographer surprised us, and she captured the love in our hearts before either of us realized it was there."

Darcy nodded at Lindy's hand. "I assume by your rings that you both got in touch with it."

Quincy showed her ring. "We did. It's a funny part of our story."

Darcy opened her mouth to ask another question, but Renee put a hand on her arm. "Let them tell it, Darce."

Darcy looked chagrined. "Sorry, I always get ahead of myself. Please go on, I'm really interested."

Taking turns, Quincy and Lindy described the night of the accident, how they met, how they bonded, how they started falling in love without realizing it, and the story of their mutual proposals. Darcy and Renee listened without interrupting.

"That's quite a story, love rising from the ashes of disaster."

Quincy nodded. "I was such a mess, lost in the horror of the night and past memories, and even if she wasn't beautiful and smart and loving and gentle and…well, you get the picture, the fact that Lindy stayed with me and gave me hope would have been enough to cause me to fall in love."

Darcy nodded, then the waitress arrived with their appetizers and they turned their attention to the food. The silence was broken only by the noises of pleasure.

Quincy was the first to look up. "So you both work at the foundation?"

"I do." Darcy looked at Renee.

"I'm a volunteer. In real life I'm the senior partner in Millford, Cooper, and Anderson. We're a management consulting firm." Renee smiled. "We know what you do, Detective Adams. What about you, Lindy?"

Lindy finished chewing. "I'm the scheduler for a trucking company."

Renee nodded. "That's a pretty intense and responsible job. Do you use a computer?"

"It was totally manual when I started, but we recently installed software that does some of the work. It's still challenging, though, because it's not just a mechanical calculation. It requires understanding of the customers, the drivers, the trucks, the product and quantity being shipped, weather conditions, and priorities, so I and the other scheduler still make the decisions."

"Do you enjoy it?"

"I like the challenge of the work and the pay is good. But I don't enjoy working in an almost totally male environment. Some of the older men can be piggy and pushy. If my best friend didn't work in Accounts Receivable, I probably would have quit a long time ago. I'd like to teach elementary school, but I still have a couple of years of college to go."

Lindy moved her silverware around, then looked up. "If this is too personal just ignore me, but are you two a couple?"

Darcy and Renee locked eyes for a second, then Renee cleared her throat. "No. We were involved off and on during our freshman and sophomore years in college and, as many lesbians do, we've stayed close. We have a tight-knit group of friends and ex-lovers from college. You'll meet many of them at the gala."

Darcy sipped her wine. "So, Quincy, we hope you'll share your story with the people attending the fundraiser. All of it, as you did tonight, if you could."

"It was easy talking to the two of you, but I don't think I could talk in front of such a large crowd."

"I know it was presumptuous of me, but I recorded the whole thing for just that reason. You'll sound natural. I could have it typed up and you two can work on it. If you'd rather, we could have someone read it or you could have a friend or a couple of people do it instead."

Quincy turned to Lindy. "What do you think?"

Lindy didn't hesitate. "Grace should do it. She was there, she knows us really well, and she's used to speaking in front of large groups."

Darcy looked from one to the other. "Grace?"

"Grace Lee Walcott. The woman trapped in the burning car. And from what you've said, the one who organized the campaign to get me this award. She'd be perfect."

CHAPTER THIRTY-THREE

As Darcy and Renee promised, Quincy and Lindy had been guided through the selection of clothing for tonight's gala. Lindy's gown and Quincy's tux were fitted and accessorized by a designer assigned to them, and now a dresser and a makeup artist had helped them get ready.

Alone for the first time in their finery, Lindy stood in front of Quincy wearing the green gown she'd selected for the event and adjusted Quincy's black bowtie. She grinned. "You are devilishly handsome in that tuxedo, sugah. You should wear it more often."

Quincy adjusted the silk cummerbund and slipped into the jacket. "We both look beautiful. You're always gorgeous, but the gown brings out the green in your eyes and shows just enough cleavage to keep a woman interested. And I'm very, very interested."

Laughing, Lindy pushed her away. "The car is waiting. But if you don't stop looking at me like that, we may miss the party."

They settled into the limousine waiting to take them to the museum where the fundraiser was being held. Lindy took Quincy's hand. "Nervous, sugah?"

"Yes. So many fancy people in such a fancy environment is scary. What if I freeze when they introduce me?"

"Hey, darlin', you'll be great. Just thank the foundation and say whatever else you want, like you did when you got the medal in Hackensack. Grace will tell the story." Her lips lightly touched Quincy's. Quincy leaned in for more, but Lindy laughed and pulled away. "Sorry, can't screw up the makeup."

At the museum, the people she'd saved, plus her mama, Sarah, Gina, Amelia and Jackson, Babs and Dani, and Chief Trubeck and her husband were seated at tables near the one she and Lindy shared with Grace and Mike, Darcy, Renee, and some other impressive women. Mama, Sarah, and Babs had accepted the offer of gowns, and Dani, a tuxedo. The families of the people she saved were also outfitted. It was magical. Everyone looked beautiful.

After the cocktail hour, Darcy invited everyone to be seated. When the room had settled somewhat, she spoke about the foundation and its goals, then Renee spoke about some of the programs that would be funded by the money raised. Darcy, Renee, and the other board members Quincy had spent time with were all women in their thirties, attractive in different ways, fun to be with and caring. Despite the obvious wealth and responsible jobs of these women, neither Quincy nor Lindy felt intimidated by them. And tonight Quincy was struck by their intelligence, their competence, and their commitment to improving the lives of girls.

Grace was up next. She was healing but still unsteady on her crutches, so Renee helped her onto the stage. At the microphone, she stared out at the audience for a moment before beginning. And it hit Quincy. Grace fit right in with this group of women, not just because she was wealthy but because she was someone who worked to better the lives of others. Before she met Grace, before she knew this group of Silver Foundation women, Quincy would probably have written them all off as "rich bitches," but she now knew that despite their wealth, they worked hard to make the world a better place. That's more than could be said for most people. She hoped that in her small way, being a detective and coaching children on the weekends, she was doing her bit.

Grace was the right choice to speak for her, about her. She brought that night alive for the people in the room, allowed them to share her fear and hopelessness, then her joy at being alive. She had them in tears. She described Quincy as a true hero, someone who should have been home with her feet up and a warm drink in her hand, who had risked her life for a total stranger. Her. By the end of her speech, the crowd was on its feet, clapping for her and calling for Quincy.

Darcy escorted Quincy to the stage, and they stood side by side to thunderous applause. Finally, Darcy raised her hand to silence the crowd. "Now you understand why Quincy Adams is the recipient of this year's Silver Foundation SheHero Award. Would the twelve people Quincy saved please stand." She waited until they were on their feet. She'd insisted that the children were not only welcome but desired, so Bella was in Bonnie's arms and Annie in Mike's arms.

"Quincy, on behalf of these twelve people and the Silver Foundation, I'm pleased to present you this award for bravery." She held up an engraved glass slab. "And," she held a large facsimile of a check, "later you'll receive a real check like this mockup for fifty thousand dollars, something which we hope will make the kind of difference in your life that you made in the lives of these twelve people."

CHAPTER THIRTY-FOUR

The second Sunday in June was spectacular—sunny, in the low eighties, no humidity—a perfect day for an outdoor wedding. Always looking for ways to repay Quincy, Grace and Mike had offered to pay for the wedding. Quincy and Lindy didn't feel right accepting such a generous gift, but they happily agreed to use the Walcotts' beautiful, spacious house, large swimming pool, lake and well-tended grounds for the ceremony and the reception. They ultimately decided a potluck was more informal than they wanted, so they hired Grace's professional caterer to manage the reception and provide delicious food for the one hundred vegetarians and meat eaters invited. Quincy was pretty sure that going through Grace had ensured they'd received a reduced price.

Guests were encouraged to dress comfortably in shorts, slacks, sundresses; constricting dresses, high heels, starched shirts, suits, and neckties were specifically forbidden.

The caterer had set up the large tent with tables decorated in the lavender color scheme the brides selected, the string quartet was playing softly in the background, and the guests gathered on the lawn chatting in small groups while waiters circulated with drinks and hors d'oeuvres. Everyone seemed in high spirits as they waited to witness the marriage of these two wonderful women.

The brides were dressing in separate parts of the house. Lindy was with Sarah, who was giving her away, and Babs, her maid of honor. Quincy was with Mama, who was giving her away, and Amelia, her maid of honor. Patsy, the photographer, darted in and out of both rooms snapping pictures while they got ready, then circulated amongst the guests taking pictures of individuals and groups.

At the appointed time, Mike used the microphone and asked the guests to move to where the ceremony would take place, an area of the lawn set up with chairs, a red carpet, and an arch decorated with flowers. Once everyone was seated, Quincy moved toward the red carpet with her grandmother and Amelia. She stopped suddenly, ignoring the music cue, when she spotted her mom and dad stepping out of the crowd. "How did you—?"

Her mom and dad hugged her. "We know we've not been the best parents, Quincy, but we do love you and we wouldn't have wanted to miss your wedding."

Her mother tightened her arms around Quincy's waist. "You can thank your friends Grace and Mike for us being here. They tracked us down in the jungle through the Peace Corps headquarters and made arrangements to fly us out of the village to the airport where they'd booked a flight to JFK."

Quincy glanced at her grandmother, and the tears in her eyes and the look on her face indicated she was surprised too. She took her grandmother's hand and tugged her into their little circle, thrilled to have her family all together to share her happiness. Over their heads, she searched the crowd and when her eyes locked with Grace's, she mouthed, "Thank you." She was sure her parents didn't have the money to fly here and equally sure Mike and Grace had picked up the tab. She looked around at her friends standing watching them, many with tears in their eyes, and nodded to the musicians.

The music started again and the five of them moved down the red carpet to the arch where her escorts took their seats. She turned to wait for Lindy.

Lindy appeared on the red carpet with Sarah and Babs. She smiled at Quincy. The quartet struck up the wedding march and the three of them slowly made their way toward the arch. Quincy's heart leapt as she watched her beautiful Lindy with her gorgeous smile coming toward her. She stepped forward to meet her. They grinned at each other, then hand in hand, turned.

Lindy in her flowing white summer dress and Quincy in a white suit faced Chief Connie Trubeck, who had been thrilled when they'd asked her to conduct the ceremony they'd written. Connie grinned at the two radiant women before her, then looked at their friends and family.

"Before I begin the official ceremony I want to say how wonderful it is that in the aftermath of a horrendous accident that affected some of you here personally"—she sought out the eyes of Grace and Mike and the others in the audience—"Quincy found Lindy. And miraculously Lindy not only helped Quincy heal but brought love and happiness back into her life after too long without it. And how wonderful that in offering human kindness to a brave stranger struggling to avoid the blackness of depression Lindy not only saved her but miraculously found love, though she didn't know she was looking for it."

She focused on the couple before her. "I can speak for most of your guests and say we love and admire you both and we're thankful you found each other." She stepped forward and kissed each of their cheeks.

"Now. We the friends, family, and chosen family of you, Johna Quincy Adams, and you, Lindy James, are gathered here today by your invitation to celebrate your love and your commitment to each other and to witness you binding yourselves together in the eyes of the State of New Jersey. Please face each other and state your vows."

Quincy took Lindy's hands, locked onto her eyes, and began. "Lindy, you are my light and my joy. Seeing your smile and your radiant beauty, I fell in love with you before I even knew your name. You gave me back a part of myself that I didn't know I had lost and made life worth living again. I love you and I promise to take care of you in sickness and in health and I commit my life to making you happy as long as we both may live." She squeezed Lindy's hands.

Lindy smiled through her tears, and her voice when she spoke was huskier than usual. "Quincy, my love, my lover, my life. Astounded by your bravery and floored by your humility, your kindness, and gentleness, I fell in love with you almost immediately. You gave me what I've never had before. The love of a wonderful woman and a sense of security and trust. Every day I'm with you is better than the previous one. I commit to be with you in sickness and in health and I promise to strive to make you happy every single day as long as we shall live." She reached up and lightly kissed Quincy.

Connie stepped forward. She led them through the official ceremony and the exchanging of rings, then smiled. "You may each kiss the bride."

The crowd cheered and whistled as the brides kissed. "You've made me the happiest woman in the world," Quincy whispered.

Lindy smiled. "Fight you for that honor, sugah."

Quincy's parents hung back as the bridal party followed them back down the aisle. Quincy stopped and went back to pull them into line next to her grandmother. When they reached the spot where they would greet their guests, the wedding party surrounded them and showered them with hugs and kisses. Her eyes filled as she smiled at her parents.

"I'm so happy you're here, Mom and Dad." She hadn't let go of Lindy since the kiss, but she pulled her closer. "I'd like you to meet my wife, Lindy. Lindy, my mom Cory and my dad Ben."

Lindy hugged Cory, then Ben. "I'm so happy to meet you both and I'm thrilled you're here. Let me introduce my mom, Sarah, and my best friend, Babs." She took Quincy's hand. "We have to do the receiving line now and that includes you all in the wedding party."

It was a love fest with lots of hugs and kisses and happy wishes as their guests streamed by to congratulate them. When Grace and Mike appeared, Quincy took their hands. "I don't know how you managed it, but thank you for bringing my parents here. I didn't even know it was important to me until I saw them."

Grace, who was now walking with a cane, grinned. "Hey, I'm thrilled that Mike's friend who is a big deal in the Peace Corps was able to help so it wasn't necessary for me to traipse through the jungle looking for them. He got my message to them, then helped with arrangements to fly them out. And back, whenever they're ready."

"I'm sure you paid—"

"Pfft." Grace made a face and waved the comment away. "Just a tiny deposit toward the rest of our lives."

Before Quincy could comment Patsy appeared, cameras around her neck and in her hand, followed by her videographer, and the wedding party was swept away to a spot near the lake to take formal pictures. Patsy would take less formal photographs and video during the rest of the reception.

The large room in the house was the fallback in case of rain but given the gorgeous weather, they went, as planned, with the buffet and tables set up under the tent for people who wanted to be out of the sun, tables with umbrellas scattered around the lake for those who preferred to eat outdoors, several bars, and the low wooden platform used by Grace and Mike as a dance floor during many of their fundraising events.

Quincy insisted that Grace and Mike sit with the wedding party at a round table for twelve and was pleased to see her parents engage with them, her grandmother, and Sarah deep in conversation, and Amelia and Jackson chatting with Babs and Dani. She locked eyes with Lindy, feeling the love spark between them. In her wildest dreams she'd never conjured a scene like this.

Lindy squeezed her thigh. "I love you." She tilted her head to their loved ones talking and laughing. "And it looks like we're becoming a family."

Of course they soon became the focus of attention and questions, especially from Quincy's mom and dad, who had a lot of catching up to do. Grace had explained how they'd met Quincy, and they were both in awe as the others she'd saved dropped by the table to say hello and wish them the best.

"So," her mom said, "any plans for children?"

Quincy and Lindy had definitely made plans. Lindy smiled. "You go ahead, sugah."

Quincy cleared her throat. "We're planning on at least two, maybe three. Lindy has agreed to be the birth mother for my child so we'll do in vitro fertilization first and later Lindy will bear a child of her own."

"I'm sure you two will do a better job than we did," Quincy's dad said. "But how can Lindy carry your child?"

"A doctor will harvest my eggs and put them in a petri dish with the sperm of our donor. Hopefully, a couple of eggs will find a couple of sperm and the doctor will implant a couple of the fertilized eggs in Lindy."

"It sounds complicated. And expensive," he said.

"It's pretty routine now, but it is an expensive process and there's no guarantee that any of the implanted eggs will take, so it may take a couple of tries."

Her dad glanced at her mom. "We don't have much money, but we'd be happy to help as much as we can."

Quincy felt her heart open to her parents. They were good people, if not the best parents. "Thanks. We appreciate the offer, but we've got it covered. The award I received from the Silver Foundation for saving Grace and Mike and the others should cover the expenses. Besides, you've already paid for the wedding and that leaves us more money for the babies."

Her parents looked confused. "We didn't—"

"You did." Quincy walked around the table and put an arm over each of them. "Mama told me a number of times when I was growing up that you sent money to help support me, but she never told me she deposited every dollar you sent into a saving account for my college. Since I didn't go to college out of high school, she kept it for a time I would need a large amount.

And when we started planning the wedding she gave it to me. It made me happy to know you've always thought about me. Thank you."

Cory and Ben stood and shared a three-way hug with Quincy. "You've always been in our hearts and minds, Quincy," her mother said. "When I got pregnant, we were both eighteen, naïve and unformed in a way. We had so many dreams, so many things we wanted to do. We were torn. We wanted you, but we didn't think we'd be good parents since we could barely take care of ourselves. I knew your grandmother would be a wonderful mom for you as she had been for me. Our one regret is that we've not been part of your life. We're so proud of you. You're a strong, warm, loving, brave woman, and we can't tell you how much being here for your wedding means to us. Can you find it in your heart to forgive us for abandoning you?"

The three of them huddled together, crying. "I do forgive you. Mama is a great mom and I admire your willingness to admit your failings as parents. There are plenty who won't and whose children suffer for it." Lindy broke into their hug. "Hey, can I join you in this love fest?"

"Perfect timing, Lindy. Mom and Dad were just telling me how thrilled they are to share our day."

Lindy took in the tear-stained faces. "And I'm sure you've told them how thrilled we are to have them here." She kissed Quincy's lips lightly. "I know you traveled a couple of days to get here and we both appreciate it. But I don't think Quincy let herself know how important you both are to her until she saw you today. And, personally, I hope your grandchildren, when they come, will see more of you two."

Everyone was wiping tears as they moved apart.

Right on schedule the disc jockey started the music, then invited the brides up for their first dance together.

As the lead into Aretha's "You Make Me Feel Like a Natural Woman" played, Lindy led Quincy onto the dance floor. Accompanied by hoots and clapping, they faced each other. Lindy began to move. Quincy's heart felt ready to explode as Lindy's hips and arms and legs moved as gracefully and as sensually as the first time she watched her dance in the mirror at Maggie's Bar.

This time, though, Lindy was not dancing alone. Her eyes were locked onto Quincy's and as Aretha started, she stepped into Quincy's arms. Their bodies fit together perfectly, and Quincy could feel the rapid beat of Lindy's heart and Lindy's warm breath on her neck. Her heart filled with love and a surge of heat traveled through her. They kissed, only slightly aware of the roar of their family and friends cheering them on.

"I will love you forever, Lindy," Quincy whispered in her ear.

Lindy leaned back to meet her eyes. "You are my forever, sugah."